CLIFF HOUSE

An Evans Novel of Romance

CLIFF HOUSE

DEBORAH PERLBERG

M. EVANS & COMPANY, INC. NEW YORK

Library of Congress Cataloging-in-Publication Data

Perlberg, Deborah.

Cliff House / Deborah Perlberg.
p.   cm.—(An Evans novel of romance)
ISBN 0-87131-609-9 : 15.95
  I. Title.   II. Series.
PS3566.E691488C5 1990
813'.54—dc20   90-37156
                              CIP

M. Evans and Company, Inc.
216 East 49 Street
New York, New York 10017

Manufactured in the United States of America

2 4 6 8 9 7 5 3 1

With thanks to Nick and Slota, and to Rosalind Noonan, editor and friend, and to Jay Perlberg of Stratford Mortgage Corporation, Blue Bell, Pennsylvania, for his help in explaining property development and financing, and to Roman Niedzwiedz of Scarpon, Schneider and Niedzwiedz, in Marlton, New Jersey, for his help in explaining the intricacies of international banking.

Prologue

THE PROMONTORY OVERLOOKED the sea. Below its outcropping of cliff the dark rocks glistened under the steady slap of the waves. That was the way it was, the way it had been, and the way it always would be. There were the changing skies; the shifting, floating clouds, the slow-moving fogs, and the drifting vaporous mists. These things came and went, ever-changing, and their change was a part of the constant thing. The seals came and played upon the rocks and their barking echoed the sound of the waves. The seals came and went and then the ships came and went and then the buildings came upon the cliffs and the people who made them. The buildings and the ships and the seals upon the rocks came and went. Ebb and flow, slap and recede, advance and withdraw. These things were always changing. But the promontory stayed, overlooking the sea. That had been and was and would always be. That thing would not change.

One

THE WIND SHIFTED, kicking up a swirl of sand. It was not sunbathing weather. She had heard enough about San Francisco to know not to expect summer weather in summer; still, she'd expected the sun to cooperate with her plans. Instead a foghorn hooted mournfully and the ominous cloud bank that had been hovering offshore slid directly overhead, throwing her into shadow.

She shivered and pulled her shirt tightly across the top of her bathing suit. That was another mistake—the bathing suit. She blamed the guidebook. It was misleading, making it sound like the shore from the Golden Gate Bridge down to the Marina was one long stretch of wide, sandy beach, like the beaches she was used to back East. Instead there was a wide, green lawn dotted with benches. Stubbornly, she'd spread her beach towel over the sunniest bench. An occasional dog walker had gone by, and once a pair of hikers plodded past with grim determination. But the crowd she'd expected, a crush of sunbathers and happy tourists, had never shown up.

Her walking tour had already suffered. Even with a transit map and a tourist guide, she'd planned an impossible route. The trek from Chinatown to Telegraph Hill had left her winded and dismayed, but the view was spectacular and she had pushed on, up impossible streets of inhuman angles, promising herself a nice lunch when she made it to Russian Hill. Somewhere along the way she abandoned her schedule and her pretenses and scuttled with gratitude into the nearest coffee shop, ignoring the noise and the dinginess for the consolation of strong coffee and a fat, greasy hamburger. She should have abandoned her plan then, but she compromised instead, hopping a bus to the Marina, still hoping for a reward.

And there it was, beyond the boats dipping at their moorings, dim in the distance but majestic all the same—the Golden Gate Bridge. Powerfully and gracefully it rose, smoldering orange against the darkening sky. Its topmost arches pierced the fog. A separate cloud bank moved beneath the bridge, growing a gray underbottom as it lumbered across the bay. The water darkened as the cloud passed, turning choppy and murky.

She was thinking about leaving when a man approached from the moorings and dropped onto the next bench. He made himself comfortable, loosening his shirt collar and rolling up his sleeves. He took off his shoes and socks and rolled his pants almost to the knees, as if her example, her determination to sunbathe, was more persuasive than the chill in the air and the dark of the sky.

She dropped her eyes to the stack of index cards on the bench between her knees and leaned over, shading the side of her face with one hand as if to protect it from the wind. By now the last of the lunchtime stragglers had gone, and except for the two of them, the Marina green was deserted.

She imagined he was some kind of lowlife, a professional gigolo, winding down from an all-night tryst with a wealthy, pampered, overaged, and overweight matron, the type of woman who was desperate for the attentions of a sleekly handsome man in a too shiny suit.

She glanced his way and their eyes met and before she could pull hers away he had nodded with a kind of bemused curiosity. She flushed with embarrassment, suppressing a flash of terror; perhaps he had mistaken her for an easy mark, younger than most of his clients but just as confused and eager. She was afraid he'd taken her glance as an invitation, as if she were making the opening move. But of course, her imagination was running wild again.

She adjusted her face into an expressionless mask, shuffling her note cards. She should put her imagination to work on her article. The thought rankled; Dan always said she had too much imagination. Too much, when it was probably her strongest asset. If she had any hopes of becoming a journalist, it was her imagination that

3

would pull her through, put her above the rest.

It was annoying that Dan's criticism lingered when he was thousands of miles away. It was even more annoying that he hadn't gotten it right; it wasn't imagination that got in her way, it was something else.

She scribbled on a card: The Hidden Pleasures of San Francisco. That sounded like an exposé of opium dens and sex pits. She crossed it out and tried again: A Walker's Guide to San Francisco. Dry, but serviceable. "One's first sight of the Golden Gate Bridge is unforgettable, one that—" She crossed it out and tossed the card onto the bench. She wrote instead:

> Dear Dan,
>   I was right, SF *is* wonderful. I'm already into the piece, lots of research, which means lots of walking. But I'm pleased, there's opportunity for description, and that's my strong point, my greatest strength. I think.

She paused, staring moodily at what she'd written.

> Or maybe I don't have a greatest strength. Maybe my greatest strength is admiring other people's work. Maybe I have no strength at all.

She crossed that out, too. Enough was enough. Standing abruptly, she brushed sand off her heels before fumbling with her cotton pants, pulling them on self-consciously, aware of the stranger watching. She tugged up the zipper and fastened the snap at the top of the waistband. The cloud overhead slid away, leaving clear blue sky behind it. The warmth of sunshine streamed onto the bench. She made a noise of surprise and heard a similar grunt from him. She found herself smiling openly and he returned the smile, seeming not at all sinister or evil but somehow engaging and even innocently endearing.

"Beautiful, isn't it?" He nodded at the bridge in the distance.

She nodded back, unwilling to leave now that the weather was meeting her expectations. The wind picked up again, lifting a few index cards from the top of the pile. She stopped to catch them, but the wind shifted and the cards scattered, skittering across the grass. She gave chase, and he saw what was happening and jumped up to help her. They scuttled after the cards, zigzagging across the lawn. He made a startling leap after the last of them and brought them back to her, beaming.

"Got 'em," he said. "And no harm done."

His tone was mildly sarcastic, but his voice was warmly rounded with the low-pitched timbre she'd always admired.

"Thanks. They got away." She was waiting to hear his voice again. He startled her. His eyes were more intelligent than she'd expected, and more patient, with a wash of something like sadness or disillusion. Soft gray eyes that mirrored the color of the sea, offsetting the rough angles of his face. His features were irregular, not crisp or perfect in that magazine way—the way the models were in Dan's magazines—but handsome enough and somehow more accessible.

"Well, thanks again," she said. She tried to straighten the stack of cards in her hands, and to her consternation they slid through her fingers, dropping onto the grass. They both bent down at the same time.

"Wait—I'll get them." She reached out cautiously, but the wind sent them teasingly out of reach. She groaned out loud.

He grabbed her arms. "Don't move," he ordered with such ferocious authority that she felt a flicker of renewed fear. But he released her and ran alone after the cards. Then suddenly he was sprawling in the sand.

She thought first that he was playing the teenager, clowning to impress her. He seemed too graceful for such an awkward fall. But when he didn't get up immediately, she realized he was really hurt.

"Dammit, I'm always doing this." He sat up, and she saw a rusted metal bar protruding from the ground, next to his right leg. Gingerly he touched it, and blood coursed down his calf.

A wave of sickness shot through her, but she went quickly to his side. She prided herself on staying calm in a crisis.

"Okay, it's okay," she crooned mindlessly.

"Damned stupid goddamned thing." He kicked at the metal bar with his good leg. "Ow," he said, wincing. "Damn."

"Well, don't kick it again, for godssakes," she scolded. "Be calm. Here, let me take a look at it."

The hair on his calf was already matted with blood. The gash ran a good six inches.

"It's deep," she murmured. "Pretty nasty."

"I can feel that." He tried to stand but winced and hopped awkwardly. "Ow. Goddammit."

"It's okay. We can stop that bleeding—that's the first thing to do."

He glared at her, crouching over the hurt leg and pressing against the gash with both hands. "I hate blood."

"Be brave." Slipping off her shirt, she wrapped it tightly around his leg, tying the sleeves together as if they were a long bandage. She yanked them tight.

He protested, openmouthed. "What are you, the Red Cross?"

She hesitated. "Mara Brightfield." She held out a hand. It was sticky with blood.

"Brightfield? Funny name. Suits you." He paused. "Guy Levin, stranger in distress."

She gave the improvised tourniquet an extra twist. "Well, Guy"—she said his name fiercely, to conquer her shyness—"that should help, but you're going to need stitches. And you'd better clean it out pretty well. That pipe, or whatever it is, looks rusty. You could get a nasty infection."

"Sure, Doc, anything you say."

She turned away to hide a smile. His sarcastic impatience was like a small boy's petulance. Dan hated accidents. He would have been angry at the intrusion on his time and annoyed with her for making any fuss.

"Is there an emergency room nearby?"

He tested the leg again, setting it down and pulling it back quickly. "Not in hopping distance."

"Well, I guess I could get you to one. We'll grab a cab."

"Grab a cab? You're either an out-of-towner or an optimist."

"Just hold on." Mara ran back to her bench, stuffing the note cards and towel into her tote bag. She grabbed Guy's shoes and socks, tied the shoelaces together, and stuffed the socks inside, one to each shoe. She slung the shoes over one shoulder and offered the other shoulder to Guy, who was balancing awkwardly on one foot.

With him leaning against her, they hobbled to the street. He was a bulky and complaining patient, but his cursing was more comic than angry, and she was beginning to feel at ease. There were no cabs in the passing traffic.

"What's wrong with this town? Is New York the only place with real cabs?"

"Don't knock my town, Brightfield. We don't like ungrateful tourists." He pulled his arm away from her shoulder. "My car's over here."

A flashy white Cadillac was parked several feet away. Mara took his arm to help him toward it. "There we go."

"Not quite." He hopped past the Cadillac to the car behind, an old-model Jaguar, smoothly rounded and low to the ground.

"Yours?" she asked.

"No, I'm a car thief. I always steal when I'm bleeding." He reached into a pocket for his keys. "Thanks for the lift."

"I'll have to drive. You can't manage the clutch."

He looked at her closely. "No one drives that car but me."

"Sorry, today *I* give the orders." She held out her hand and he dropped the keys dutifully in her palm.

He eased himself into the passenger seat, and she slid behind the wheel, giving the door a forceful yank. He grimaced. Ignoring him, she fastened her seat belt and locked the door. "Better buckle up," she advised.

"Do you know how to drive a stick?" he asked uneasily. "Or do you only take cabs?"

With only a little trouble, Mara shifted into reverse and slowly backed away from the Cadillac. She found first gear and nosed the car toward the boulevard. A space appeared in the flow of cars. With squealing tires she pulled into traffic, moving almost at full speed, and crossed smoothly into the passing lane.

"I think I've got it now. Where to?"

"Take a left at the light," Guy said dryly, "if you don't mind being told what to do."

Mara brought the car to a halt at the emergency entrance. She slammed the car door behind her as she hurried to help Guy out of the low front seat.

"Lady," an attendant shouted, "you can't leave that car there. You're blocking the door."

"It's an emergency," she answered indignantly. "We're talking life or death here."

As the swinging glass doors closed behind them, Guy pulled back to look at her. "Life or death?"

"Well, almost," she said.

"You're a real take-charge type."

"Sometimes. Sometimes it's easy to get things done."

Mara stopped a passing nurse. "We need stitches. It's an emergency."

Guy's bandage had soaked through with blood. His good pant leg had partly unrolled and now hung disheveled around his ankle. He was barefoot. Mara's hands and pants were smeared with blood. The nurse glanced at her bathing-suit top disapprovingly.

"Sign in at the desk." The nurse turned away.

"Hold it," Guy said. "I want to page Dr. Evan Macy. Tell him it's Guy Levin, the architect."

"All right," the nurse said. "I think he's on emergency room duty. But you'll still have to wait." She crossed to the desk and spoke to the nurse behind the counter. The desk nurse spoke into a telephone.

Guy nodded at two empty seats. "Over there?"

Mara helped him over and he collapsed onto a chair. She sat beside him. "Architect?"

"You seem surprised. What did you think I was, a beachcomber?"

Mara smiled and changed the subject. "Is Dr. Macy your own physician?"

"I met him at a party," Guy told her. "He did ten minutes on why you can't trust an emergency room."

"Great."

They were both silent. Mara wondered if she was taking a risk, obligating herself to a stranger.

"What kind of architecture do you do?" she asked.

He paused. "Renovations."

"That's interesting. What kind of renovations? Making over old houses?"

"Brightfield, this may surprise you, but I'm not really in the mood

8

for small talk." He leaned back wearily. "This is a matter of life or death, remember?"

"I'm sorry," Mara said automatically. "I'm not very thoughtful."

Guy looked at her sharply. "Who told you that?"

"No one. I mean, I don't know," she said, startled.

"I would think it was very thoughtful for a total stranger to do what you've done for me."

"Oh, but I caused it. It was my fault."

"Don't apologize."

The desk nurse appeared in front of them. "Could you fill out these forms? In ink, please."

"We're not checking in, we just need to see Dr. Macy," Mara protested.

"It's required."

Guy took the papers from the nurse. "Sure, but check on Dr. Macy for me, would you?" He flashed a grin and the nurse grinned back. She waited while he filled out the forms. When she had gone, Guy leaned back again and closed his eyes. His good leg jiggled up and down impatiently.

"I guess I could leave now," Mara said doubtfully.

The elevator doors slid open, and an elderly man strode briskly toward them. His white coat flapped open as he walked. He leaned forward at a slight angle, as if he were impatient for his body to follow where his mind led. Although his white hair was thinning and a sprinkling of age spots covered his slightly yellowed skin, he gave an impression of meticulous vigor.

"Levin! What brings you here?" Reaching to pat Guy on the shoulder, he turned simultaneously toward Mara. "Evan Macy," he said, holding out a hand for her to grasp. He spoke with a caressing drawl as his pale eyes scanned Mara's face closely, as if checking for medical imperfections.

"Hello, Dr. Macy. I'm Mara Brightfield, and Guy—"

"Brightfield?" he interrupted. "Isn't that an interesting name?"

"Yes, isn't it? But Guy—"

Dr. Macy nodded. "So, Levin, is it money or a job?" To Mara he added, "I've got a little houseboat over in the Marina. I thought Levin here could make it more livable. Put in some finishing

9

touches." He squinted thoughtfully. "What'd we talk about, Guy? Partitions or no partitions?"

Guy answered tolerantly. "I believe it was minimal partitions."

Macy peered at Mara again. "And which side of the controversy are you on?"

"Controversy?"

Macy looked at Guy and back at Mara. "You're not aware of the scandal? Of course, it's a fairly minor scandal. No offense, Levin."

"None taken," Guy answered.

"Dr. Macy," Mara cut in impatiently, "what about his leg?"

"Oh, yes," he said with all the patience in the world. "What did you do to it, anyway?"

"Fell," Guy said.

"It's a deep gash, at least six inches long, from an extremely rusty piece of metal," Mara said. "It needs a good cleaning."

"Well, I don't see what I could do," Macy said jovially. "Though I suppose I could clean it out a bit, maybe do some fancy embroidery for you." He tilted his head back, focusing on Guy through the center of his glasses. "Make him a little prettier. Nothing to worry about," he assured Mara. "I'm the best, or at least as close to it as you're gonna get. C'mon, Levin." He hustled Guy to his feet. "Don't waste time. Brightfield," he demanded, "you sticking around to get this fellow home?"

"Oh, no, I don't think so."

Dr. Macy gave her an angelic smile. "He shouldn't be putting weight on it. No driving. I was thinking, Guy, maybe a pergola on the roof deck? Just a small thing, with a marine motif, nothing too fancy." With Guy hobbling, they headed down the corridor.

Sighing, Mara went to find the nearest ladies' room. Looking in the mirror, she gasped out loud. She hadn't realized what a mess she was, stained with blood and with no shirt on. She pulled at her bathing-suit top and earned a look of disgust from the woman at the next sink. Mara scrubbed her face and hands and wet a paper towel to swipe at the stains on her pants, asking herself why she was waiting for a stranger. It wasn't the sort of thing she would normally do.

She pushed at her hair. Thick and shiny, a deep auburn color, it had been newly cropped just below her chin. Dan had approved the stylish look. It went with his image of her, companion to a successful young man who was moving higher still. She'd had some trouble getting used to the stark lines of the cut at first. But as she looked in the mirror she appreciated the way it had fallen easily into place, the one undisturbed part of her appearance.

She swung her head vigorously, enjoying the way her hair splayed out around her head and settled back into place. The woman beside her gave her a startled look and fled the room. Mara grinned and finished cleaning up. In the hallway she spotted an empty telephone booth with a phone book inside. She flipped to the Yellow Pages and looked under Architects. There it was, Guy Levin, name, address, and phone number. She tried to imagine what kind of office it was, what kind of work Guy might do that was so controversial.

Impulsively she confronted the desk nurse. "Excuse me, but I've been hearing about a local scandal—about an architect? The man with me, the one who hurt his leg, Guy Levin. Have you ever heard of him by any chance? I know this sounds crazy, but I thought you might have heard something—on the news, maybe?"

"I don't know anything about it." The nurse turned her head away dismissively.

Dr. Macy tapped Mara's arm. "I heard," he said, looking amused. "Trying to gauge public opinion on that Cliff House thing? It's not the usual conversation around here. Personally, I think Guy has the right idea. To hell with the rest of them." He clapped her on the shoulder. "He's being seen to now. Be out in no time. Prescribed some painkillers, but he's a stubborn one, so I'm going to give them to you. Try to get these into him as soon as you can. When he starts moving around—and he *will* start moving, no matter what I tell him—it'll hurt like the blazes."

He held out a white paper packet. Mara hesitated. "I wasn't planning to stay with him, just see him home."

"Oh, come on," Dr. Macy said. "He's not as bad as all that. You can handle him. Keep him off the leg for the rest of today—you'll think of something. After that, these things heal quickly enough." He put the packet in her palm and squeezed her fingers closed around it.

Mara waited. In a while Guy appeared in a wheelchair, a thick white bandage showing below his rolled-up pant leg. The orderly pushing the chair had a grim, impatient expression. Guy's temper seemed to have worsened.

"C'mon, if you're coming." He glared at Mara and she followed them out to the parking lot. Guy pushed the orderly away as he eased himself into the passenger seat.

"Where to?" Mara asked as soon as she was settled behind the wheel.

He rattled off his office address. "What's the matter?" he asked when she didn't move.

"Dr. Macy said you should go home for the rest of the day. He warned me you wouldn't."

"Warned you how?"

"Said you were stubborn and difficult. So tell me how to get to your house. If you direct me to the office instead, believe me, I won't stop. You'll have to leap from a speeding car. And I might not return it." She patted the dashboard approvingly.

"How do you know that wasn't my home address?"

"I looked you up in the phone book."

"Ah, you're the Red Cross *and* a detective."

"And an aspiring journalist."

"Very interesting. Okay." He sighed. "I know when I'm licked. Out of the parking lot and take a left."

Two

"GRAY HOUSE," Guy said tersely. "Over there."

Mara eased the car to the curb and pointed it up a narrow driveway that was almost hidden by an overgrowth of shrubs. The house sat to the right of the drive, partially hidden behind a wooden fence. It was a squarish building and perfectly symmetrical, three stories high, with a low-slung, squat design that seemed to her vaguely Japanese. Silvery-gray, weathered wood siding softened the formality of the shape, so that its forthright symmetry seemed comfortably reassuring.

Yet there was something almost contradictory in its design. Mara realized what it was: the lower floor, with its fences and shrubs, and the second floor, with its windows veiled by soft curtains, gave a feeling of guarded privacy. But the uppermost floor was the complete opposite. It sat inside the roof like a glittering, modern bell tower—four walls of glass made of many tiny-paned, white-trimmed windows. A spectacular aerie, with what must be a spectacular view. The street itself crested a difficult hill, and the view from the drive swept through a checkerboard of residential streets to the business district in the distance, and finally down to the bay.

She nodded at the house and back at Guy. "One of your renovations?"

"Still the tourist. Yes." Guy pointed ahead, and Mara saw he wanted her to pull the car farther up the drive, where a small entry gate led into the front courtyard. She did, stopping the car, and Guy swung his injured leg clear of the car door and straightened up with some effort.

"Modified Arts and Crafts," he said.

13

"What?"

He gave her a slightly impatient look. "The house. Modified Arts and Crafts—that's the style, the period." Before she could help him, Guy had pushed through the gate and up a flagstone walk through a well-tended garden. Crimson flowers climbed a trellis to one side of the front door. Guy found his key and wearily pushed the door open. Mara hesitated, but Guy made no move to shut the door behind him, so she followed inside.

"I guess you'll be okay now. I'll get your pills and leave." She dug into her pants pocket, intending to drop them on the small hall table, but the painting centered over the table caught her eye. She peered at it closely.

"Is this . . . yes, it's an original." She examined the textured surface, tracing the exuberant splotches of wild colors with delight. It was an American expressionist work, instantly recognizable as a minor piece by a world-famous artist.

"You know about painting?" he asked dubiously.

"Enough to recognize that." Her glance at him glimmered with a new appreciation. "This house seems so bare-boned and pared-down, and then there are all these pleasant contradictions."

"And you were expecting a grimy little hut with a drawing board." Guy's face held a peculiar half-smile. "It's okay, I didn't think your type knew anything about painting."

"My type? What type is that?"

"Forget it."

"No, what type is that? What did you think of me?"

"I didn't think anything."

"I want to know what you thought."

"I thought you were a little addle-brained."

"Addle-brained?"

"I don't know, confused. Dithery. You were sunbathing, and we weren't at the beach."

"That was because of the guidebook. They made it sound like the whole shoreline was a beach. How was I to know? Anyway, it doesn't compare to what I thought of you."

Guy hobbled down the single step into the living room and eased himself onto a couch, stretching his leg across the length of it.

She glanced at the room casually, then gave it her full attention. Like the startling note of the wild painting in the otherwise stark

14

hallway, the main room had its own contradictions. It was basically a cool white box but so carefully proportioned that it conveyed a sense of perfect completeness. One wall was filled with a rough stone fireplace. The doors and windows and the wide, bare floors were of wood darkened to a deep, rich patina.

At first the furniture seemed an afterthought. But then she realized that furniture, so unassuming—unmatched couches and armchairs of distinctive shapes, upholstered in pale gray-blue—had to be carefully planned. The greenery in the courtyard beyond the windows filtered the light, giving the room an indirect glow. The room seemed to look in on itself, but the warmth of the woodwork, the soft light against the whitewashed walls, and the openness of the space dispelled any sense of confinement. It was peaceful and content.

She wandered the room as if on a treasure hunt, admiring the objects that perched on carefully placed, low-built pedestals. There was an ornate child's puppet theater, gilded in Victorian abandon, a collection of elaborate clocks, a set of ancient wood tools, and a half dozen worn and battered antique boxes.

She settled onto the couch across from Guy's, feeling welcomed, if not by him then by the room.

"It's so bare," she said, "yet it feels so furnished."

Though his face was strained, Guy smiled. "I guess that's a compliment."

Mara chuckled. "Now I believe you're an architect. At first I thought you were a gigolo."

"A what?" Guy lifted his head.

"A professional escort. I don't know. Your pants . . ." She snorted a laugh. "It seems kind of funny now."

He peered down at his pants.

"They were kind of shiny in the light." She gave an apologetic shrug. "And it was the way you walked over and sat down, as if you had nowhere to be and nothing to do. You looked like some fancy man getting in from a hot date." She settled against the couch. "And there was the way you looked at me."

"Uh-huh." His head dropped back wearily.

Mara was instantly remorseful. "Your pills, I almost forgot. You're supposed to get painkillers." She fished for them in her pocket.

"Don't want any," Guy murmured. "Hate pills."

"Dr. Macy said you'd say that. You're not doing yourself a favor by toughing it out. I'll get you some water."

She found the kitchen on the second floor, sharing the space with a bedroom just across the hall. If the living room was a model of restraint, the kitchen was where all discipline let go. Floor to ceiling, the room was jammed with bookshelves and plants and objects of every description. Remnants of architectural moldings and gingerbread trim were everywhere, across a doorway leading to a narrow deck and strewn haphazardly on top of the refrigerator and the double-doored hutch that substituted for kitchen cabinets.

Beneath the profusion, the working surfaces were neat and orderly and ready for use: a restaurant-style range top and gleaming stainless-steel sinks, a center island with a marble top, and an additional steel basin. Instead of the antique kitchen table she'd expected, a miniature office nestled into the far corner, with a computer centered on a sleek, efficient desk.

She liked the house. She liked the comfort and the peacefulness and the whimsy of it, the controlled chaos and the seriousness about work. She only wondered if the completeness of the place, the air of personal satisfaction, implied that it wasn't meant to be shared. She found a glass in the hutch where she'd expected to find it, filled it with water, and carried it to the hallway. A square of light on the landing drew her eye upward. A narrow spiral staircase reached to the top floor; the glass tower she had seen from outside. Without hesitation she climbed to the top of the staircase, pausing to blink at blinding sunlight through giddily bright windows. The view they commanded made her set down the water glass, instantly forgotten.

A drafting table and a longer, flat worktable ran down the center of the space. Wide, shallow filing drawers and bins for rolled-up drawings lined the circumference of the room, tucked low beneath the towering windows. Pale gray canvas shades were tied near the ceiling, leaving the glass unobstructed, except for the mullioned windowpanes. Houses and hills, towers, and the blue bay water spread below her in a dizzying array. She wondered how Guy must feel, owning this room, owning the view; did he feel that the city's singular, eccentric beauty somehow belonged to him?

From this vantage point the fog banks were nowhere to be seen. Instead a single wisp of a cloud moved overhead, straining past the hilltops.

She heard Guy on the stairs behind her. "Lose your way?" he asked.

"Sorry." She answered without turning around. "I had to see this view." She nodded toward the passing cloud. "That reminded me of the first time I realized clouds moved. I was a little girl, waiting on my back porch for my mother to come and open the door. She was taking a long time, and I laid down and stared up at the sky. And I saw the clouds move, kind of swooping behind the trees. I can't tell you how startled I was. I guess no one had ever told me they moved; they probably assumed I knew that. But I didn't. I don't know what I thought—that different clouds appeared each day and then went away, I guess. Anyway, I'm sorry, I didn't mean to be nosy by coming up here. It was too much to resist."

Guy leaned against the open doorway. "You apologize too much."

"Do I? I'm sor—" She caught herself and laughed. "Well, anyway, if this room is part of your renovation, I'd say you have awfully good taste."

His eyes scanned hers. "I know."

Mara turned toward the cabinets. A stack of photographs sat in a neat pile on top of them, and she lifted the top one. It was an old print of a storybook castle, steepled and peaked and gabled and towered. It clung to the side of a jagged cliff, hanging out over the ocean. A steamer ship puffed near it on the water below while a parade of horse-drawn buggies climbed the winding mountain road to the building's arched entry. The photo was inscribed: CLIFF HOUSE, 1896–1907.

"Cliff House," she murmured. "It's wonderful. What was it?"

"A palace for the people of San Francisco."

"And what happened to it in 1907?"

"It burned to the ground while the owner was doing renovations."

She laughed. "I hope your renovations fare better than that."

"That *is* my renovation. That's my baby," Guy said.

She stared from him to the picture. "I don't understand. That's a Victorian building, isn't it?"

"Or a gingerbread castle or a French château or an Austrian wedding cake, depending on who you talk to. That was the third Cliff House, the last one with any architectural distinction. There's a fourth one now, a modern one. Garbage. Nothing like it was, like

17

it should be. Nothing like what the site deserves. But I'm going to bring it back."

She smiled uncertainly. "As a wedding cake or a French château?"

"Neither. A new version of an old beauty. But better, I hope." Guy reached out, and she placed the photograph in his hands. "Right there, on the same spot. All new, all modern, but with a golden Victorian heart. That's the soul of San Francisco, you know, the Gold Rush and the Victorian era. Heartbreak and dreams and excess."

He pulled a leather work chair from under the long table and sat down, leaning the photo in front of him. His weariness had been replaced by a dreamy intensity.

She remembered the glass of water and set it on the table at Guy's elbow. She shook two pills onto the palm of her hand and held them out to him. He took them obediently.

"I'm glad you took those pills," she said, to cover her sudden self-consciousness. "I was afraid you wouldn't, after what Dr. Macy said." She was keenly aware that no one knew where she was, that she didn't really know where she was; that she was alone with a virtual stranger and had no idea what to expect from him. It was reassuring that he had a profession and seemed successful at it and that he was known by a legitimate doctor in a legitimate hospital, but those things hardly added up to a character reference or explained why she was lingering in a place she had no reason to be. Yet it seemed logical that she was there. It wasn't something she could easily understand. She wasn't used to working on impulse, and certainly not when it came to men.

Guy spoke suddenly. "One man's scandal is another man's dream," he muttered. His tone, both bitter and mocking, took her by surprise.

"You're tired," she said. "I'd better leave."

Guy set down the photograph. He picked up a pencil and started doodling on a drawing pad. She pushed back her chair, but his voice, little more than a murmur, stopped her.

"Did you ever have a dream, Brightfield? More than a dream? The man who built this Cliff House was named Adolph Sutro. Bavarian by birth, a self-made millionaire. Cliff House was a kind of gift he made to this city. It had dining rooms and bars, art galleries and food stands and open terraces, an observatory—all for the public, all open to the public. And the old Sutro baths—they were something special. Just burned in 1966. In our lifetime, Brightfield. Ever hear of them?"

He pulled a poster from a drawer and slid it toward her over the table.

"I've seen this," she said in surprise. "I've seen this poster. But I never knew what it was."

In greens and blues and antique gold, the poster illustrated a wonderland of a place. She had seen the poster somewhere before but had never stopped to think if it was real or someone's fantasy. It showed a building as cavernous as an airplane hangar, with a ceiling of exposed, arching steel beams, vast and wide, spread over what seemed to be a gigantic swimming pool. Light streamed in from all sides. Men in quaint, old-fashioned bathing costumes were lined up on piers that chopped the pool into separate swimming compartments. Rings and ropes and slides dangled over the pools. From a second-story balcony gents in bowlers and ladies in feathered hats peered at the pandemonium below.

Guy slid the photographs across the table. They showed close-ups of the place from different angles; the balcony and pools, the tiered grand staircase lined with potted palms, all as ornate and as majestic as any palace. There was one freshwater pool and five salt-water pools, each kept to a different temperature; a museumful of stuffed birds and exotic stones; flora and fauna from all over the world. Sutro's Cliff House, Guy told her, had changed a wild and brawling gambler's haven into a respectable family resort, and when the existing railroad line charged too high a fare in financially depressed times, Sutro built his own railway line to bring in the public at half the regular fare.

"What Sutro did, that's what I want to do," Guy told her. "Give this all back, with extraordinary design, design that enriches, makes people feel noble. A place to really use—not a museum, not some stuffy gallery, nothing holy, but something exhilarating and inspiring, a place to lift the spirits every day."

Mara found his enthusiasm catching. "It's thrilling, about the baths. I wish they still existed. And I understand wanting to give them back. But . . ." She hesitated. "Well, why rebuild Cliff House as something that already existed?"

"I'm improving on it, on what's there now."

"I understand, but why go back to a previous era and imitate an old design? Why renovate?"

He grinned. "I misled you; that was a joke. I am building something new. We're going to tear the whole place down. Some buildings don't deserve to exist. I can think of plenty of so-called landmark designs—monstrous buildings that mean no more to the average person than this pencil. Stupid, meaningless boxes at best. They influence us, don't you see? These buildings and public places make up the texture of our lives, they determine how we feel when we walk down a street. Would you rather feel insignificant and meaningless in a canyon of blank-faced monoliths, with nothing whatever of comfort, nothing recognizably human around you?"

"I didn't say that."

"Buildings should relate to the people who are going to use them; they should have some reference to human scale, at least on the street level, so when you walk by, you have a feeling for your surroundings, a feeling of fitting in, belonging. Because if you don't have that, where do you belong? Think what it does to you if your own surroundings are hostile. Do you know what kind of effect that has on you every day? Don't you think there's enough alienation in our lives, in our culture, without deliberately building more in?"

"I only said it seems foolish to imitate an old style, something that already existed. You should make a new building and make it human, but why copy from something old?"

"No, no," Guy said, rubbing his eyes, seeming to lose interest. "Forget it," he said warily. "I don't have the strength."

She bristled, feeling dismissed and diminished. "And I'm not interested in being bullied and browbeaten into someone else's point of view. I'm tired of people who think their opinion is the only one that matters. I suppose everything has to be done your way, or it doesn't matter at all. Is that the kind of power you're after? Maybe it is, and maybe you can get it, but all you'll find is that people resent you or fear you or loathe you. And that resentment won't go away. It never does, when you make someone feel small. And I'll tell you this, if that's your attitude, you'll never have any success worth having."

She realized her tirade was out of proportion. It shouldn't have been directed at him at all but at Dan, and the long history of resentment against him which she had never expressed.

"Well, now I know you have a temper," Guy said slowly. "What else should I know about you, Brightfield?"

She shrugged, embarrassed. "Nothing. Look, I've got to get going. I've got to get cleaned up and changed . . . I'm meeting a friend for dinner. And no one even knows I'm here."

She fled down the curved staircase and down the long front hall. Outside, the sun had disappeared completely. The wind had risen and the sky had taken on an uneasy shine. She hugged herself in dismay; she still had no shirt on, only the bathing-suit top. On the sidewalk an elderly woman was walking a tiny dog, craning her neck anxiously upward, as if expecting the weather to strike her down. She gave Mara an abrupt, startled look of disapproval.

Mara lacked the nerve to brazen her way back to Suzanne's place so skimpily dressed, and the chilly air and the threatening sky made her admit it. She retraced her steps and knocked with some insistence at Guy's front door. It took a while for him to answer; when he did, he looked pale and exhausted.

"I need a shirt," she said.

"Upstairs. Help yourself. I've had it." He limped into the living room and collapsed onto a couch.

Mara padded quickly to the second-floor bedroom, opening his closet reluctantly. A row of shirts hung neatly inside. Jackets and slacks hung in systematic order next to them. There was an uncomfortable intimacy to searching through his clothes, coupled with a pleasing but unfamiliar scent and the feeling of his lingering presence.

She pulled a pale blue shirt from a hanger. She would rather have found a messy cast-off, something not easily missed, but that would have meant searching through shelves or bureau drawers, and that idea was daunting. She threw the shirt on and hurried from the room, her eyes cast down in outlandish modesty. Guy was asleep on the couch in the living room. She was relieved that she wouldn't have to say good-bye. She could send the shirt back through the mail, and that way she wouldn't ever have to see him again.

Three

THE RESTAURANT HAD WINDOWS all around, showing other windows of the closely set buildings in the crowded financial district. At the dinner hour the tables were filled with men and women in suits, and it seemed to Mara they all had a certain hemmed-in, subdued look that defined them as lawyers and financiers. She was also wearing a suit, having felt a need to restore herself to some kind of order, some equilibrium. After leaving Guy Levin's house she'd lost her way, doubling back to Suzanne's on two buses. She still felt somewhat off-kilter, at once alarmed and amused and slightly out of breath.

Suzanne appeared in the restaurant doorway, straining her neck to scan the crowd. Wiry and tall, with dark curls that were always disheveled, Suzanne had a brisk, sardonic manner that Mara always found calming. Mara waved, catching Suzanne's eye.

"Sorry, Brightfield, I knew I'd be late. This brief is a nightmare. I'll never finish, even if I work all night, which I'll probably do. Why do I have an apartment? I should just move into my office. I live there already."

"It's okay. I just got here a minute ago."

Suzanne unfurled her cloth napkin and spread it over her lap. "I can't stay long. I'm only in the middle of this brief, and you know how hard it is for me to write anything. The food here is pretty good, but its true charm is that my office is right upstairs. And some interesting people come in here."

"Interesting how?"

"Interesting, I don't know. Accomplished people, people with different accomplishments."

"Anyone specific?"

"Oh, no," Suzanne said too quickly. "Just interesting people."

"Well, I don't care where we eat, as long as we can talk. I had a really strange day."

"We can go to a better place tomorrow night—your choice. Promise." Suzanne pushed her glasses up onto her head, mussing her hair even more. The waitress came by, and they ordered pasta dishes and salads.

Suzanne was on a perpetual diet, as if the adolescent fat she'd once carried might come back any minute, despite the fact that she'd been slim for the last twelve years. Meals to her were catch-as-you-can affairs, taken on the run or stabbed at perfunctorily at her desk. But she indulged Mara's penchant for styles and trends in food, or anything else. Though Mara thought herself the arbitrator of good taste, when she presented Suzanne with something of creative merit, Suzanne always took a gratifying interest in it.

"How were the walking tours?" Suzanne asked. "You probably saw more of this city than I have in the two years I've been here."

"Not quite. It's a long story."

"Oh, planned too much, did you? Bit off more than you could chew, as usual. I warned you—you can't walk the whole of San Francisco in one afternoon. It's bigger than you think, you jaded New Yorker. Plus, it's only your first day here."

Mara's tone was mild. "It's taken me two years to get out here, and I thought I should see everything I could." She leaned forward. "Suzanne, this article is important to me. It's something I have to do before I marry Dan."

"Listen, I don't blame you. If you're still not sure about Dan, why give in now?"

"This has nothing to do with being sure or not."

"Oh, right," Suzanne scoffed. "You finally agree to marry Dan, and the first thing you do is fly three thousand miles in the opposite direction. You should be home, making wedding arrangements for all those important guests you're going to have."

"This is important."

"To you, maybe. I bet those guests are important to Dan."

23

"They're his friends, not mine."

The waitress set their food on the table and Suzanne gestured with her fork as she began to eat. "Listen, I don't care one way or the other. I couldn't stop you from marrying Dan, even if I wanted to." She tore the foil cover from a tiny plastic bucket of cream and added it to her coffee, mixing it to a dull brown color. "You're supposed to be happy, all on your own."

"You're deliberately misinterpreting. I came out here to write an article, and that's all. Just once, before I'm married, I'd like to do something I'm proud of."

"I know I'm the wrong person to talk to. I don't like Dan. Not that I don't recognize his so-called good points. He's loyal to his friends and he's successful and hardworking and all that." She gulped a mouthful of coffee. "But he's a nasty bastard."

"He's the nicest guy in the world."

"Nicest guys don't have publishing empires at thirty-five. Don't interrupt," she ordered. "I know most successful men are bastards. They have to be, I suppose, to have gotten where they are. But who wants a bastard? I'm sick of that trade-off. I want one man who's not a wimp and isn't ruthless to the core. Is that so much to ask? Is that so unrealistic?"

"Dan is always nice to me."

"Why not? He doesn't have to manipulate you. You already do everything he wants."

"Dan likes being successful, and I like it, too."

"You like what his success can buy. Face it, you're shallow. I don't know how you do it, accept all those conditions. I couldn't."

"Give him credit, Suzanne. You or I could never be what Dan is. We don't have the drive."

"I still say I'll wait for a man with some soul left. And if he exists, with my luck, he won't be the least bit interested in me." Suzanne laid down her fork, looking suddenly less flippant.

"I haven't visited in two years. You could be a little easier on me. I know you don't mean half of it."

"You need me not to be easy on you; you're already too easy on yourself. You—" Suzanne broke off abruptly, half rose out of her seat, sat down again, pushed her glasses off her forehead and onto her nose, snatched them off her face completely, then replaced them.

Mara was aware of someone approaching their table. Glancing up sideways, she saw a hand lifted toward Suzanne in greeting. She had a hasty impression of a rather distinguished face, deeply creased, but enlivened by a winning smile. At the same time she noticed the man standing behind him, younger and slightly smaller. The younger man did a double take, then peered at her in genuine surprise. It was Guy Levin. He broke into a grin of recognition and leaned toward Mara as Suzanne was holding out her hand to the other man.

A round of greetings overlapped in a spurt of confusion:

"Mr. Musselman, hello, I didn't know you were—"

"Suzanne, what a nice surprise—"

"Brightfield, I didn't think I'd ever see you again."

Guy's words, spoken last, seemed to hang in the air. His grin opened into a nearly incendiary smile. As Mara blinked uncertainly, Suzanne looked at her in surprise. "You two know each other?"

"A little bit," Mara said.

"Slightly," Guy said.

He had changed into slacks and a sport coat and looked trim and rested and composed. He glanced at Suzanne, who seemed bewildered. Abruptly, he bent over and pulled up his pant leg. The white bandage gleamed.

"Look, it's better already." He let the pant leg drop. "Sorry I fell asleep on you. I never conk out like that. Macy must've given me a horse's dose. I was hoping you might come back with the shirt. Not that I'm worried about the shirt, it's just that I didn't know how I'd ever see you again."

Suzanne was wearing an expression of avid, horrified curiosity. The other man had an air of cautious amusement.

Mara flushed. "We met on the beach," she explained. "That's the long story I was going to tell you about. It's silly. He hurt his leg, and well, I helped him to a doctor."

"Naturally," Suzanne murmured.

The older man held his hand out to Mara. "Quite a story. You'll have to tell us more sometime. I'm Lowell Musselman. My office is upstairs, and I'm a client of Suzanne's firm."

"Mara Brightfield. I'm an old friend of Suzanne's." Mara gave his hand a forthright squeeze, as if to reassert her dignity. "It's nice to meet you, Mr. Musselman."

"Please, call me Lowell."

The gray that peppered Lowell's hair gave him a weathered, athletic look, as if the sun and not age had tempered his appearance. Mara noticed that his hands were finely made, shapely and almost feminine. His nails were lightly buffed. Tall and slenderly built but with wide shoulders, Lowell made Guy, standing next to him, appear suddenly bulky, where Mara had thought Guy slim and compact. But next to Lowell, Mara realized, thin men would seem pinched while stout men would seem brutish.

"I take it, Miss Brightfield," Lowell said, "that you're not with the firm?"

"Call me Mara, and no, not even a lawyer. I'm just visiting."

"I didn't think we'd met," Lowell responded. "I wouldn't have forgotten you."

There was no sign of affectation in Lowell's eyes. His voice mixed quiet assurance with the pleasing tones of the seducer. He had the kind of easygoing, yet slightly formal charm that seemed genuine and spontaneous; the kind both men and women responded to, drawn in whether they liked it or not. It was a formidable gift.

"Thank you." Mara was aware of Guy staring at her, and she felt the uncomfortable breathlessness return. She frowned.

"Mara is here on a last fling," Suzanne announced. "To celebrate her engagement. You might know her fiancée—Dan Wallace, the publisher? The New York publisher?"

Guy started imperceptibly. "Then there is more to know about you, Brightfield."

Mara pretended not to hear him, and Lowell took his cue from her, ignoring Guy's comment and nodding at her courteously. "Not personally," Lowell said, "but his name is becoming well-known."

Suzanne held her hand out to Guy. "Suzanne Shafer," she said, "since no one ever formally introduced us."

He took her hand. "Guy Levin."

"Oh, I know that." Suzanne waved a finger between Guy and Lowell. "You're Lowell's partner. I've seen you in the office—and in the newspapers."

Suzanne gestured to the empty chairs at their table. "Please, won't you both sit down?"

"It's been a long day," Guy said. "We're just leaving."

"We can make time to drink to this young lady's engagement," Lowell said, contradicting him. He patted the breast pocket of his jacket. "These papers are signed, and they're not going anywhere."

Lowell took the seat facing the room. Guy hesitated, then sat facing the window. Mara shifted slightly away from him. Lowell signaled the waitress, ordering wine for the table.

"Are you partners in the Cliff House renovation?" Mara directed the question to Lowell.

"Renovation?" Lowell raised his eyebrows. "Hardly that. It's a new design. A radical design."

"I'm sorry," Mara said, then caught herself, darting a glance at Guy to see if he had noticed her apologizing again. "But someone else called it a renovation."

"Brightfield hates the idea," Guy said matter-of-factly.

"*Hate* is a strong word," she retorted. She turned back to Lowell. "I only doubted the logic of copying the old Victorian style."

Lowell appealed to Suzanne. "Are you against us, too?"

"I just read about it," Suzanne protested. "I'm not against anyone."

"She's a lawyer," Guy said ironically. "She knows there are three or four sides to every story."

Suzanne shot him a poisoned look.

Lowell nodded to Mara. "Maybe you shouldn't read the papers. You'll end up not knowing what to think."

"The news would only ruin my vacation. And I won't be here long enough to get involved in local squabbles. Though, to be honest, I'm curious that people care so much. Why is there a controversy?"

Lowell smiled slowly. "I'll put it plainly. Some people think the design should be completely modern, whatever that means. They think Guy's design is retrograde."

"They think I'm stealing from the past," Guy said flatly.

Mara looked at him in surprise. "But you are."

The wine arrived and Lowell poured, passing a glass to each of them. "To Mara," he toasted. "That's something we can all agree on, I'm sure."

As Suzanne and Guy repeated the toast, Lowell's eyes took on the look of a storyteller with a captive audience. "But it is a fascinating dilemma, isn't it? Whether we should honor the past by repeating it—paying homage, as Guy would say—or simply ignore it."

"I wouldn't put it in exactly those words," Guy said.

"Maybe not. But for my part, whether the past is sacred or not, I believe in what Guy wants to do. And I don't mean that from the developer's point of view. It's a noble effort, a way to reconstruct local history. It's a way to give people back something they've lost."

"Now that makes sense to me." Mara nodded approvingly at Lowell, aware that she was ignoring Guy but unable to stop herself. "But why do you say it's what Guy wants to do? As partners, don't you both agree?"

"You caught me. I don't meddle with the design—that's Guy's business. I only handle the financial end. As far as design goes, I'm just along for the ride. And you know, Mara, it isn't a rehash of an old design. It's quite Guy's own. Unique. The best of the old combined with the best of the new, using modern technology to express things that couldn't be expressed in the past. Many people are quite excited about it."

"They'd better be," Guy said dryly, "or we'd go broke."

"Lowell is a successful developer," Suzanne explained. "A very successful one."

Mara looked at Lowell curiously. "And you think this new Cliff House will be a financial success?"

"No doubt about it," Lowell answered easily. "Those opposed to the project, the ones who say it's a misuse of time and resources, well, they're a small, misguided minority."

"A lunatic fringe?" Suzanne suggested.

Lowell half smiled. "No, those are the ones who believe in the curse."

"I beg your pardon?" Mara sat up, startled. She noticed that Guy suddenly looked uncomfortable.

"The curse of Cliff House—that the site is somehow damned." Lowell laughed. "It's a headline grabber, something to sell newspapers. Oh, there have been disasters. A schooner ran aground there in 1887, carrying forty-five tons of dynamite. It blew up, taking part of Cliff House with it. A few years later the whole place burned down. The third Cliff House made it through the big earthquake of 1906 and burned to the ground the next year."

"You know a lot about it."

"Guy's a good teacher. He's an expert on the place."

"But you can't believe there's really a curse," Suzanne said. "Those things were just circumstance, or slack fire regulations."

"Do you believe in curses?" Mara asked Lowell.

"Only if envy is a curse."

"I see." Mara was thinking of the way Guy had talked about Cliff House, of the photographs she'd seen. The idea of a curse appealed to her. It seemed fitting; dramatic and otherworldly. Involuntarily she glanced at Guy but glanced quickly away as their eyes met. "Well, curse or not, it's fascinating."

Lowell pushed back his chair. Across the table, Guy stood also. "We really should go," Lowell said. He paused. "Mara, have you seen Cliff House yet? The current one?"

"Well, no."

Lowell smiled. "Then I have the perfect opportunity. Guy and I are hosting a dinner dance there—nothing too formal. A chance to woo potential investors and thank the ones we've already got. People like to get a little something for their money, even people ready to drop hundreds of thousands of dollars into a project. If you sweeten the pot by giving them something back, they're happy. Rich or poor, we're all the same, we all like presents—something for nothing. Isn't that right, Guy?"

"I guess so."

Lowell nodded to Mara and then to Suzanne. "Why don't you both come? It would give Guy and myself something to look forward to. A little present."

Suzanne said "We'd love to" at the same moment that Mara answered, "No, we couldn't possibly." Suzanne's foot pressed meaningfully onto Mara's.

"I won't take no for an answer," Lowell insisted.

"We'd love to come," Suzanne said. Mara nodded her agreement.

"Wonderful," Lowell said heartily. "That's settled, then. Cliff House, tomorrow night—about eight?"

"Fine."

As they left the restaurant Guy looked back once and caught Mara watching him. Hastily she dropped her eyes and faced Suzanne. "You must be happy," she said. "Lowell is the man you meant, isn't he? The successful one with the pure heart?"

29

"I'm not happy. He asked you, not me."

"He asked us both."

"C'mon, Brightfield, he was only being polite to me. He's seen me enough around the office. If he was interested in me, he'd have asked then. No," she said gloomily, "it's just like with dogs. They get the scent. Like goes to like. You're used to rich, powerful men, and Lowell caught that scent right away. Power to power and money to money. I sure haven't got it. And it's not something you can fake."

"Suzanne, if there is any such thing, it's Dan's, not mine. And don't forget, I'm not available. You are."

"Whatever you say. I've got to get back to work upstairs. But don't think you're off the hook. I want to hear every gruesome detail of how you met Guy Levin the instant I get home—assuming I ever do get home."

The doorbell rang in two short, punchy squawks. Through the tiny viewer in the front door Mara could just make out Suzanne's dark curls. She pulled the door open and Suzanne burst in, flinging her briefcase onto the kitchen counter.

"Hi, kid. Sorry it's so late."

"That's okay." Mara closed and locked the front door as Suzanne went into the bedroom. By the time Mara followed her in, Suzanne had already stripped off her jacket, shoes, and skirt.

"What are you doing up?" Suzanne asked. "I thought you'd be asleep by now."

"Oh—no, I've been working." Mara felt vaguely disappointed. She had taken Suzanne literally, fully expecting a barrage of questions about Guy Levin the minute Suzanne came in. Mara was always taking the things people said too literally. "I'm typing up my notes for the walking-tour article."

Suzanne grunted.

"I took your portable typewriter out of the closet," Mara continued. "You don't mind, do you?"

"No, I don't mind."

Mara went back into the living room and began tidying up. She put her note cards and papers in a pile on a shelf and lifted the heavy typewriter into a corner. "I remember this clunker from college," she called. "It hasn't improved with age. Why don't you get yourself a new one, or a computer?"

"Don't need one." Suzanne appeared in a long T-shirt and a terry-cloth robe. "I'm beat. I'll make fresh coffee. Want some?"

"No, I'll be up all night."

"That's okay, I only have decaf."

"Then sure," Mara said gratefully.

Suzanne bustled around the kitchen area, setting out mugs and milk and measuring coffee into the automatic pot. "I'm impressed you're working so hard. I thought it'd take days for you to get started."

"I wasn't sleepy, so I kept working. Overtired, I guess."

"You should watch that. Jet lag will catch up with you. You'll be a wreck."

Suzanne measured a teaspoon of sugar into the bottom of her mug, poured two inches of skim milk in after it, and mixed them together.

Mara laughed. "I love your little systems. They're great. You must take comfort in rituals."

"Me? Maybe. Maybe that's what you need, Brightfield—systems and rituals."

"I'm okay."

"You're the least systematic person I know. I don't think I ever saw you do anything the same way twice. You don't even care which side of the bed you sleep on."

"No one really cares about that," Mara said.

"They shouldn't, but they do. If people didn't care which side of the bed they slept on, they'd never get up on the wrong side. It would save everyone a lot of trouble."

Suzanne handed a mug to Mara. "I'm not wrong, by the way. Lowell is interested in you, I'm sure." Suzanne paused. "You look disappointed. I think you're interested in Guy Levin."

"Don't be ridiculous. I couldn't care less about him."

Suzanne eyed her thoughtfully. "Well, if you're going to act so embarrassed, why'd you pick him up in the first place?"

"It wasn't a pickup, Suzanne. It was an accident." Quickly she described what had happened at the beach. When she had finished, Suzanne gave her a dumbfounded look.

"That's quite a story. But you're wrong about one thing—Levin doesn't look like a gigolo. He looks like what he is—an arty professional with a raw, unfinished look. That's my observation."

"I'm glad you're into raw, unfinished men."

"Oh, not me. Lowell's more my type. No unfinished edges there. No edges at all."

"Then you'll be glad to know I'm not going to that dinner thing tomorrow night. You can have Lowell all to yourself."

Suzanne froze. "Brightfield, you've *got* to go with me."

"You have more reason to be there than I do. You can talk business, and Lowell already knows you."

"That's not the point. You're my excuse; he only asked me to get *you* to come."

"My God, Suzanne, you're a real pain." Mara carried her coffee across the apartment to the couch under the window.

"You shouldn't go around picking up men if you won't respect them in the morning."

"Please shut up."

"I don't see what the big deal is," Suzanne protested. "I'm the one with something to complain about. In one day you've got two men interested in you. Two handsome, eligible, straight men—and in San Francisco, that's no small feat."

"But I'm not interested in them or anyone. I'm engaged, remember?"

"Oh, that. Face it, Brightie, you're going to leave Dan, whether you know it or not. His hold is pretty powerful if it takes two men to get you away from him. But this could be one hell of a transitional period."

Mara laughed wryly. "I don't doubt that you know more about me than I do."

"Either way it's only one night, and it would mean a lot to me if you came. You'll enjoy it. Levin's your type."

"My type? He's the type that doesn't ask your opinion because he already knows your answers aren't worth listening to. I call that opinionated and obsessive."

"Exactly. Your type."

Mara drew herself up. "I know I can be opinionated, but I'm not as bad as that."

"Not you—your beloved Dan. Next to him you're a pussycat."

"Dan?"

"Everything you just said is true about Dan Wallace. He's the one who disdains people. He's the one who won't let anyone disagree with him. You've said so. You said everyone he knows is part of an in group or an out group, depending on whether or not they agree with Dan Wallace. The ones he doesn't agree with are dismissed—or crushed."

"I've never said that."

"Then you don't listen to yourself. At least not between the lines."

"Whatever I say or don't say, I'm sure you're twisting it."

"Well, it doesn't matter, anyway."

Mara began to make up the sofa bed, hoisting the big, square cushions onto the floor. "This is a stupid conversation."

"Agreed." Suzanne paused at the bedroom door. "But I kept my promise. I said I'd take you someplace nice for dinner tomorrow, and I am—to Cliff House."

Four

THE ROAD CURVED CLOSELY alongside the embankment. Down below, where the cliffs dropped to the Pacific, the surf rolled in on white-frothed breakers. It was still light enough to make out the rocks offshore. The water rushed up wildly against them, slapped their sides, and ebbed away. New waves came back to lash at them again, shattering and reforming over their glistening, dark forms.

Suzanne swerved the car, crossing against traffic to pull into a parking area near the wide swoop of beach leading down to the ocean.

"Cliff House," she announced.

Across the sweep of sand was nothing but ocean and the low-lying mountains across the bay. To their right, up the road, was a promontory of land, a chewed-off bit of cliff jutting into the open sea, at once majestic and ethereal. Cliff House number four sat on that bit of land, every window blazing with light as if to fight off the dusk, in a valiant attempt to proclaim its own importance. It was a sad try. This Cliff House, centered securely on the flat cliff top, safely inland, square and flat and mundane, was nothing compared to Sutro's Cliff House, which had balanced daringly on the very edge of the cliff itself, hovering over the sea, as fanciful and somber as the landscape.

"Pitiful," Mara murmured. "Just pitiful."

Suzanne looked at her in surprise. "I thought you'd like it. The view is incredible."

"The view is spectacular. But that building . . . no wonder Guy wants to tear it down." The lights in the windows seemed to glow brighter as the sky around them dimmed. "Well, I owe him an apology. Anything would be an improvement over that."

"Arbiter of public taste, are we?" Suzanne started the engine again. "I'll pull closer to the entrance so we won't have to walk to the monstrosity."

Suzanne squeezed the car into a narrow space at the far end of the parking area. To their left a straggly row of concession stands led to the entrance of Cliff House. Groups of people hurried past them, their voices ringing with a festive air. Suzanne gazed after them moodily. "Oh, boy, a big noisy crowd of strangers. My favorite kind of party."

"Don't worry," Mara assured her. "We're civilians here, we don't have to work the room. All we have to do is eat and drink and have our own good time. And you look great, so relax."

Suzanne hesitated. "This suit is all wrong, isn't it?"

"Don't be a dope."

Suzanne chose clothes with one eye for how they fit and the other for how they would look to clients. The soft red silk of her fitted suit answered both requirements; it flattered her and had no potential to offend.

"That's just the kind of suit Lowell would admire," Mara told her.

"It's too plain. Not that he's going to notice me, so it doesn't even matter."

"Suzanne, you look wonderful."

"Even if I do, a hundred other women will look better. You were right, we shouldn't have come. I should have listened to you."

"I hate when you do this. You drag me somewhere and then decide you don't want to go. You've got to stop acting like you're a gawky kid. You're not, and plenty of men have told you so."

"Not the right ones."

"Suzanne, you are very attractive and you know it."

"Maybe sometimes I know it, but sometimes I'm not so sure. Anyway, you look great." She gave Mara's dress an admiring glance.

It was a simple white-linen sheath with a matching jacket, shaped to skim lightly over the body. It had exactly the kind of demure sexiness that Suzanne thought of as Mara's trademark.

"Thanks. I did a speed trip through the department stores in Union Square today. A walking tour of the shopping district," Mara quipped. She paused at Suzanne's startled expression. "What's wrong?"

"I thought you worked on your article today."

"You're the one who told me not to pack anything dressy. I had nothing to wear tonight."

"You're terrible. You always procrastinate. You never finished one paper in school without an incomplete, and you're still doing the same thing. I don't believe it. You already started the article. Don't lose steam now."

"I took one day off. I was having trouble, anyway."

"You're your own worst enemy."

Mara laughed. "We all are. C'mon. If you're going to captivate Lowell, we'd better find him."

As they neared the entrance the voices that had seemed gaily festive sounded quarrelsome and angry. A handful of people spilled onto the sidewalk near the concession stands. They were dressed in jeans and windbreakers. Placards and signs dropped from their hands, momentarily forgotten. People passing into the building stopped to crane their necks, then hurried on. The group in jeans surged and fell back into a loose circle, and Mara saw two men in the center of the circle. One of them was Guy.

"What is that? A demonstration?" Mara asked.

"Everyone said it was controversial."

They hurried closer. Guy would have looked handsome and dignified in his tuxedo, except that his face was contorted with impatience as he shouted. His antagonist had one arm raised to his face in a gesture that was both protective and taunting. The smaller man's face was framed by a flaming red beard, and thick red hair stood up wildly on his head, glowing like a demonic halo under the bright lights. He wore a pullover sweater and glasses. His face was also distorted as he answered Guy's threats with threats of his own.

"Who is that, do you know?" Mara asked.

Suzanne shrugged. "A professor or a lobster fisherman, from the looks of him."

Up close, Mara could read the protestors' signs:

LIVING ROOMS—NOT BALLROOMS!

HOUSING—NOT CLIFF HOUSE!

THE HOMELESS DON'T NEED ANOTHER TOURIST TRAP!

Deep into their argument, Guy and his opponent seemed evenly matched. They shouted in bursts, gestured heatedly, poked and jabbed at each other like bullies picking a fight.

The redhead thrust a fist under Guy's chin. "Do you deny that this city has a housing crisis?"

Guy slapped the fist away and made a threatening fist of his own. "That's why I object to you! This site is some of the most valuable real estate in the country. It was never used for housing, and it never will be. Fight where the fight makes sense—not here."

"Not as long as speculation and profit take priority over the needs of the people."

The redhead's supporters cheered, and Guy grimaced in disgust. Mara couldn't help thinking that their fight had the flavor of a high-school debate; each side seemed convinced of its own argument and pleased with the cleverness of each verbal thrust and parry, yet at the same time relishing its opponent's skill.

"This seems kind of silly," Mara said to Suzanne, keeping her voice low. "What does Cliff House have to do with the homeless problem?"

A heavyset blond man standing next to them poked a finger at Mara's chest. "That's exactly the kind of thinking that's ruining this country!" he shouted.

Mara jumped back in alarm. Guy saw her and deserted his opponent, leaping after the big blond. "Hey, you have a problem, buddy? Bring it to me." He pushed the man in the chest and he stumbled backward. Two or three demonstrators caught the big man and set him upright. He glared at Guy.

Mara felt relief and a silly satisfaction that Guy had come to her rescue. Their eyes met briefly before the redhead appeared behind them, grabbing at Guy's arm. Guy spun around violently.

"Back off, Manelli," he barked. "Enough. Unless you want a real fight." He raised his fists threateningly.

With one finger Manelli adjusted his glasses against the bridge of his nose. He shrugged in careless disdain, turning his back to Guy and clapping the big blond man on the back. The group reformed itself, lining up along the sidewalk and raising their signs.

Guy took Mara's arm, nodding to Suzanne to follow, and led them away.

"You know him? The redhead?" Mara asked.

"Always know your enemies. Paddy's a crank, always has been. He's harmless enough. A leftover Socialist from the old school.

Spent too much time in left-wing bookshops as a child."

"Paddy Manelli? What kind of name is that?"

"The kind you get when a North Beach Italian marries a hot-headed Irishwoman."

"Well, I don't get it. Your Cliff House is for the people, for everyone to use. Paddy should be happy. It's not like you're tearing down housing to make room for luxury condos."

"Doesn't matter. He's a smart old publicity hound. He's hoping for media coverage out of this, that's all he wants. A little notice, a little attention for the cause. Hell, it's always worth a try."

"But this couldn't make the news. It's a sorry excuse for a demonstration."

"If it's a slow news night, he could get lucky."

Suzanne hurried to keep pace with them. "You could have him arrested, you know. Creating a public nuisance. Or criminal trespass, if he does any damage. This is private property."

"Not worth it," Guy told her. "He's not going to scare off investors, and at this point that's all I care about. Paddy's okay. His heart's in the right place, he just goes about things the wrong way."

Mara gave him a knowing glance. "You like him, don't you?"

Guy squeezed her arm lightly. "Someday I'll tell you about me and Paddy Manelli."

He ushered them to the main entrance and they pressed through a crowded vestibule, climbing the stairs to the second floor.

Suzanne gawked in disbelief. "This is great. They've completely redone the place."

"Just for the night. Like it?"

"It's fabulous. If it always looked this good, you wouldn't have to tear it down."

They stepped aside to let several people down the stairs. "What do you mean?" Mara asked her. "Is this all new decoration?"

"Completely. The place was a dump."

The interior was decorated in the white, pale gold, and deep green that Mara had seen in the old poster of the Sutro Baths. And, as in the photos of the bathhouse, palm trees in giant pots lined the walls and climbed the stairway to a large, open room on the upper floor. Vaporous swags of a white, diaphanous material were discretely draped over every window, holding off the night, and more of the same swags billowed like ghostly sails from the ceiling overhead. Extravagant sprays of white orchids and exotic fronds dotted the tabletops.

"If this is how you're going to do the new place," Suzanne told Guy, "then Lowell is right; it'll be a tremendous success."

"Well, Lowell knows what he's doing," Guy said lightly. He nodded a greeting to a group of people. "Will you excuse me? I have to play host for a while."

Reluctantly he moved into the crowd. Mara watched him go.

"This is a real power crowd," Suzanne told her. "Half the city government is here. I expected the country club set, but Lowell's pulled in the heavyweight politicos."

"Or Guy did," Mara suggested.

"Not Guy. Lowell's the one with the real connections." Suzanne scrutinized the faces she recognized. "I think he got every big bank account in the city."

"Well, they would have to. And the patrons of the arts and society, and all the hangers-on who need to be part of every scene. It's just like one of Dan's extravaganzas."

"I guess," Suzanne said distractedly. "This is ripe ground. I should do some serious networking. I might walk out with a new job." She caught Mara's scandalized look and laughed. "Don't worry, I'm teasing. I'm not leaving when I'm one inch away from a partnership. But I swear, you can taste possibilities in the air."

Around them, noisy, happy talk rose and fell. Banquet tables overflowed with extravagant platters of food; cold meats and salmon and lobster were arranged like miniature sculptures. There were mountains of fresh fruit and a champagne fountain flanked by cliffs carved from blocks of ice. Live music played in the background, and Mara spied the small orchestra set up at one end of the room. A broad dance floor was ringed by tables. Waiters whisked through the crowd, handing out glasses of champagne from silver trays. Suzanne tugged Mara's arm, nodding to a table holding orderly rows of place cards. "Let's see if we're really invited," she said.

The band swung into a medley of smooth old standards, interspersed with Beatles songs and a smattering of show tunes. Here and there, couples began to dance. Suzanne pulled out two place cards, hand-printed with her name and Mara's. "We're legit. Now I can try some of that salmon. I'm going to eat myself silly."

Suzanne headed for the hors d'oeuvres. As Mara followed, she spotted Lowell in the crowd. He made a move toward her but was pulled away by a woman in pale blue satin. He eyed Mara regretfully. Nearby, Guy intercepted the look. He disentangled himself from a robustly overweight man and hurried toward her.

"How're you doing? All right?"

"Fine. It's an impressive turnout."

"It's a good crowd," Guy agreed. "Lowell's talented at this sort of thing. I never could have pulled it off. I'd probably have them all to the office for egg-salad sandwiches."

Mara laughed. "I doubt that. Anyway, I think the spirit of Sutro would approve. You've managed the kind of grand effect he understood."

"As long as we please the paying customers." Guy smiled automatically, and Mara realized he was uncomfortable with their party chatter and was waiting to get it over with.

"Don't worry. I've been to plenty of these shindigs," she assured him. "This is definitely a power party. It rates with the best."

"I guess you know about those things. Because of your husband, I mean. He must throw a mean power party."

"He's not my husband yet."

"That's why you forgot to mention him, I guess."

Mara drew back in surprise. "When? That day on the beach? First of all, it was hardly the circumstances . . . and you were a total stranger. I wasn't about to tell you my life story."

"You know mine." Guy shrugged. "Born, became architect, married and divorced. No surprises."

"You're wrong. I didn't know about the divorce."

"I have better stories to tell you."

"Perhaps you should tell them to my future husband instead."

Lowell approached, shepherding a man who turned out to be a magazine publisher with nothing but praise for Dan Wallace. Lowell left the man with Mara, and they exchanged several minutes of polite conversation, ending with Mara graciously accepting his congratulations on her engagement.

"Very smooth," Guy commented as the man moved away. "Very glib, facile with the social graces. I should take lessons."

"Maybe you should. You are a little blunt."

"Why do you think Lowell's running this thing? I'm the type who tells people what I really think of them."

Guy's steady scrutiny was unnerving. She turned her head to break his gaze and found herself looking at the overweight man she had seen Guy talking with earlier. She nodded in his direction. "What would you have told him?"

Guy followed her gaze. "That I don't trust him as far as I could throw him, which wouldn't be very far. Single-handedly, that man took so much in payoffs last year that he personally cut the city budget in half."

"Is that true?"

"I don't tell lies."

"No, I bet you don't," she said. It sounded too much like flattery, and she regretted it instantly. "Lowell is very smart," she said. "Introducing me to that publisher to make him feel connected. That man will feel safer parting with his money if he thinks Dan Wallace did first. Especially since he seems to admire Dan."

Guy looked uninterested. "Very manipulative."

"Not manipulative—just smart. Know who can be useful and learn how to use them. Isn't that the first rule of business?"

"That's where we disagree. I'm not looking to use anyone. That's Lowell's department."

"I think you're getting your definitions mixed up. You shouldn't leave everything to Lowell."

"Where appropriate, I bow to his superior knowledge." Guy made a slight bow himself and backed away into the crowd, leaving Mara standing alone.

Suzanne appeared with her arm linked through Lowell's. "Look who found me," she called triumphantly. Mara gave her a smile of encouragement.

"They're about to serve dinner," Lowell said.

"As if I have room for more food," Suzanne answered gaily. "The hors d'oeuvres were a meal in themselves."

"Well, I haven't had a thing yet," Mara said. "I'm starved."

Lowell withdrew his arm from Suzanne's. "I'll help you find your table."

Suzanne gave him a forlorn look. "I guess we're not sitting with you?"

"No, but I think you'll be comfortable where you are." Lowell scanned the room. "There." He nodded. Suzanne followed his gaze.

"Lawyers! We're at a table full of lawyers." Her voice filled with dismay.

"Well, yes," Lowell said. "I put you with Carter Berenson and several others you may know. I thought you'd be most comfortable there."

Mara could see the effort Suzanne made to be gracious. "I guess there are worse things than a social evening with the boss."

Suzanne started toward the table with such an air of martyred defeat that both Mara and Lowell laughed.

"Looks like I made a tactical error," Lowell said.

"She'll get over it. Really, the evening will be a tremendous success."

"I hope so. I'm hoping to pick up some important investors tonight."

Mara lowered her voice. "Do you need much more backing?"

"I wouldn't say we're in trouble, but it's all a gamble, isn't it? You understand these things from a publishing angle, and most business ventures are the same. It's a matter of shifting money from one pot to another. Guy and I threw the first funds into the pot to get others interested. Money attracts money, you know. Some of that was borrowed, some not. We used it to take our first loans, and we have to pay off those loans even as we cover our construction costs—labor and equipment and materials. It's all a juggling act. Hopefully we keep one step ahead of our creditors, and so do our investors, who may have borrowed the money they put in. In the end, the shareholders sell their shares and take their write-offs, and there's a big pot of gold for everyone." Humorously he shook his head. "Sounds ridiculous, doesn't it?" He shrugged. "Well, everything's a gamble."

Mara gave him a look of frank admiration. "You'll do well. I don't doubt that for a minute. I'd invest myself, if I had the money."

"Not only beautiful but smart," Lowell said teasingly. He touched her arm lightly. "It's true. You're the most attractive woman here." His face wore a wistful expression.

Impulsively Mara covered his hand with hers. She was used to such compliments but not so much that another wasn't welcome.

The waiters sprang suddenly to life around them, wheeling carts laden with platters of food. Lowell pulled her out of their path. "You'll stay for the presentation, won't you? I don't think you've seen the model of the building yet."

"I haven't, and I'll definitely stay."

"Good. I'll speak to you again later?"

"Of course."

As Lowell wound his way through the tables Mara saw Suzanne watching. She hurried to take the empty seat next to Suzanne's, shrugging out of her short jacket and hanging it over the back of her chair. She gave Suzanne's hand a squeeze of sympathy.

"Let me introduce you." With an attempt at her customary good humor, Suzanne named their tablemates. There were two couples whose names Mara promptly forgot and Carter Berenson.

Suzanne had privately described Carter as a condescending despot who treated everyone like mindless children. Everything about him, from his fanatically neat handwriting to the way he lacquered the thinning strands of hair across his gleaming forehead, was seen by Suzanne as part of a plot to frustrate her ambitions. Meeting him now, Mara thought Carter's smile was indeed condescending, but apart from that, he seemed harmless. Their meal proceeded pleasantly enough, and Carter made innocuous small talk.

"Everything was delicious," she said as they finished the last course.

Carter lifted his fork in an airy gesture. "Eat up, Suzanne. You need your strength to finish that Munson brief."

Suzanne smiled acidly. "Carter, we were together all day. Don't supervise my dinner, too."

Unfazed, Carter continued speaking to the woman on his left.

"Suzanne," Mara hissed, "behave. He's not so bad. Give him a break."

"I have no patience left."

"Well, he's not the ogre you described. In fact, he's fairly nice."

"Don't get ideas. I'd sooner date a barracuda."

Suzanne pushed her plate aside, and it was whisked away as the waiter set down coffee and dessert. The band struck up a dance tune, and the couples departed for the dance floor. Carter leaned forward, and Suzanne, afraid he was going to ask her to dance, deliberately bent over her cake, taking a huge bite and washing it down with coffee that must have been too hot to drink.

"Mara, would you care to dance?" Carter asked.

"Of course."

He was a passable dancer. Mara racked her brain for anecdotes, choosing old stories that showed Suzanne in the most favorable light. Carter laughed in all the right places but was more eager to tell his own interminable sailing stories than to listen. She was relieved when the song finally ended. As the band picked up another tune Lowell cut in, taking Carter's place.

"I thought you might need rescuing." Effortlessly Lowell swung her deeper into the crowded dance floor. "Carter tends to go on."

"How do you know him?"

"He handles the contracts on Cliff House for us. In fact, I was half afraid he was boring you with legal details about the project."

"No, he was just boring me in general."

With only a slight pressure at her waist Lowell guided her through dance steps she had never attempted before. Several couples stopped dancing and stood back to watch them.

Mara was delighted. "I always wanted to dance like this."

"You're a natural—all the right instincts."

"I guess I just needed the right partner."

Lowell laughed and spun her with a final flourish. There was a spattering of applause, and Lowell was pulled away to share his expertise with the other women. Guy stepped through the crowd to put his arms around Mara's waist.

"It's customary to ask first," she snapped.

"I'm no good at small talk, remember?" He stepped closer and reached behind her back. She felt his fingers paw at her skin and glared at him indignantly, pushing him away.

"Your strap is turned," he murmured.

Mara reached behind her, fumbling at the wide shoulder straps that crisscrossed the back of her dress. "Oh. Can you fix it?"

He worked at it for a moment while she stood patiently, like a small child.

"All done." He patted her awkwardly.

"Thanks."

He held his arms open. "Now, would you like to dance?" He held her closely and they began to move in a circle across the floor. Guy had none of Lowell's skill, but he moved naturally with the music, and Mara found herself settling comfortably into his arms. His dancing made her think of slow songs in high school, where the music and the dancing were a thin excuse for a long, slow caress. The thought disturbed her, and she leaned away from him. It gave her a chance to steal a quick but thorough look at his face, at the distinctive shape of his eyes and the curiously indented space at the arch of his nose. His features might not be as finely chiseled as Lowell's, but neither were they as clumsy as she'd first thought. There was a tilted crease at either side of his lips that gave some relief to the intensity of his expression, as if he didn't always take himself too seriously. They were a saving grace, those creases.

Guy glanced at her, feeling her gaze. "What are you looking at?"

"The funny space between your eyes."

"Thanks. You're full of compliments." He paused. "If you lean back any farther, you'll fall on the floor. How will that make me look? Especially compared to Lowell." He held her against him again.

"You're very competitive," she murmured.

The chorus of the song repeated, and Guy's hand moved rhythmically on her back, stroking in time to the music, his thumb pulling lightly against her bare skin. Lulled, her eyelids fluttered and closed. When the music stopped, she clung to him a second longer than she should have. Guy reached naturally for her hand, to lead her back to her table. It seemed rude to pull it away.

Instead of leaving her at her seat, Guy pulled out the empty chair next to Suzanne's. Mara had an impulse to leave the table, to ask someone—anyone—to dance, but instead she sipped at a cup of lukewarm coffee. Guy lifted a glass of champagne.

"Wouldn't you rather have this?"

"I've had my share already," she said. "I don't like to drink too much. It can be dangerous."

"You don't seem the type to worry about your liver."

"Dangerous in other ways. For instance, men who don't interest me can look very attractive after a few drinks. You could make a mistake that way. Haven't you ever done that?"

Guy lowered the glass slowly. "I can't believe you'd let yourself make those kind of mistakes."

Suzanne looked uneasily from Mara to Guy. She lifted her own champagne. "I'll have more. I've got nothing to lose."

Guy poked at the silverware in front of him, idly lining up forks and spoons in a precise arc conforming to the curve of the round table.

"It's impolite to play with utensils," Suzanne said, teasing.

45

"It's a habit," Guy apologized. "I like things precise. When I was a kid, I used to draw a little black dot on my forehead right here"—he demonstrated—"to mark the place where I parted my hair. I wanted to make sure it was in the same spot every day."

Suzanne snorted. "Now, I like that."

"You two are a pair," Mara said. "Suzanne has systems for everything, too—the way she drinks coffee and even the clothes she buys."

Suzanne protested. "Well, the coffee, I admit that, but that's taste, not habit. And I don't have any systems for my clothes."

"Then why do all your suits match all your blouses, which match your briefcase and all your shoes? I've seen you get dressed, Suzanne. You could pull things out with your eyes closed. They all match."

"Don't everyone's?"

"Only yours and Guy's," Mara said. "I've seen his closet, remember?"

Guy shrugged amiably. "Nothing wrong with systems."

"Exactly," Suzanne said. "Why waste time thinking if you don't have to? Brightfield's just jealous. She has no systems for anything. She doesn't have a repetitive personality. She couldn't do the same thing the same way twice if it killed her. She doesn't even sleep on the same side of the bed every night."

"Now that's quirky," Guy said.

Suzanne laughed. Mara would have retorted, but the room suddenly grew quiet. Lowell was standing near the bandstand with his arms upraised. He nodded toward the band, and they obliged with a dramatic fanfare, ending in a slightly comic drumroll and a clash of cymbals.

"What's that for?" Suzanne turned to Guy.

"The presentation. Watch carefully—Lowell is a master showman. This ought to be good."

Five

THE BAND PLAYED another fanfare, accompanying Lowell as he crossed to the green velvet curtain covering the windowless side of the room. The crowd surged instinctively in that direction. Guy hustled Mara and Suzanne away from the table, into the thick of things, as Lowell began his speech.

"This won't take long—there's dessert and dancing to get back to. But give me just a few minutes. You've all seen the proposed Cliff House in different forms, in sketches and rough models. But even though none of you have seen this final model, many of you have already invested your hopes, your dreams, and your hard-earned cash"—Lowell paused for titters of appreciative laughter—"into the latest, and, I feel safe to predict, the most successful Cliff House ever."

As Lowell continued speaking, mixing information with innuendo in a seemingly spontaneous flow, Mara studied Guy. He scowled, he grimaced, he rocked on his shoes, looking down, looking up, his hands clasping and flexing behind him. She felt a burst of sympathetic excitement, realizing for the first time what a big moment it was for him.

"Lowell is fantastic at this," Suzanne whispered. "He has this crowd in the palm of his hand."

The band played yet another fanfare, and there was a spurt of nervous laughter as Lowell built to a peak of anticipation. His pace slowed to a meditative air, as of someone finding his thoughts as he went along, speaking them afresh, seemingly as affected by his own words as anyone in the crowd hearing his thoughts for the first time.

"For those of you who haven't invested in our Cliff House but might be on the verge of doing so, I'll tell you that a funny thing happens. You start out, if you're like me, with a cold, hard plan. You want something for your money. You buy a share or two, strictly as an investment. Then, suddenly, it becomes more than cold, hard cash. It becomes an investment in tomorrow, in a particular goal for the future. Suddenly you become part of Cliff House, this grand vision, this piece of the future that in some strange, even magical, way, is also a piece of the past. An investment, yes, in a practical, necessary, much-needed building—but also something more. Something unique to San Francisco and to all the inhabitants of the world who might find their way here. A new Cliff House that embodies this magnificent city's past and proclaims its future. A single, unified vision. Your investment becomes part of a dream. This dream."

With an eloquent, swooping gesture Lowell drew back the curtain. Mara gasped along with the crowd. The curtain had concealed a narrow strip of room that was almost completely filled with an ambitiously realized architectural model of the most astonishing building Mara had ever seen. A building that commanded the site and yet did not diminish the rugged beauty of the landscape.

The cliffs seemed to be soaring while the waters of the ocean seemed magically frozen into a constant, eddying swirl. Above it, part of the site and yet completely distinct, the building itself, Guy's Cliff House, was an artist's vision made real; at once a model and a prophecy. It hugged the shore and flew above it. It soared over the water. Its intricate scaffolding, sheathed in clear glass, daringly exposed small, intimate passages and exhilarating plazas. In the openness there was a clean, sleek, thrilling feeling of limitless space, and yet, here and there, perfectly at home, were turrets and gables and a grandiose central dome; details and flourishes that even Sutro would have applauded.

In one body the crowd surged forward, hungry for a closer view.

Mara let them swirl around her. She felt cowed. "I didn't expect— it's incredible," she murmured.

Next to her, Suzanne seemed as affected. "Nothing I saw was like this—not the sketches in the papers. I never realized what it was going to look like. If everyone had seen this model, there never would have been criticism. I can't believe anyone would fight this design. Guy should have published working sketches or something. I guess he wasn't ready."

"That's Guy," Mara said, as if she had all the knowledge in the world of him. As the crowd fell back slowly, she made her way toward the model, approaching in an ever-tightening circle, as if she were stalking some prey, relishing the changing angles and shapes that appeared and disappeared as she encroached upon it. This Cliff House far surpassed Sutro's, she decided. Guy's Cliff House was a wondrous spectacle, a marvel of balance and airiness and contradictory solidity. It was his own contradictions, epitomized in a building that was a celebration.

Coming closer, she saw restaurants and ballrooms, pavilions and courtyards, snack shops and bookshops, a library and an observation deck that snaked through several levels. On the site of the old Sutro baths were new baths with sparkling pools and fountains, a health spa, and gym facilities, and places to eat and read and rest; spaces both expansive and intimate. It was a stunning gift to the public.

She saturated herself with every detail. When she'd finally had enough, she pressed toward Guy, pulling him insistently from a group of admirers.

"Why didn't you tell me how extraordinary it was?" she demanded. "You let me go on and on about copying from the past, and this isn't a copy of anything. It's like nothing I've ever seen before."

"There are some Victorian-style flourishes."

"All right, you made reference to the past, but you don't repeat it."

Guy's eyes twinkled. "I never said I did."

"It's a triumph. A total triumph, beyond beautiful. It's thrilling."

Guy chortled, enjoying her praise. "Well, let's just say I'm the best client I ever had. But thanks for the enthusiasm. It's a nice change."

Mara had the grace to look abashed. "Nothing I said ever mattered. You created this beautiful building, and luckily for all of us, you're the one who got the commission."

He took a moment too long to answer. "Let's say I bought it."

"I didn't mean that. Of course, you're not working on commission, you're a partner."

49

"I didn't become a partner out of the goodness of my heart. I need Lowell as much as he needs me. All I'm after is control. I couldn't let anyone else decide what Cliff House was going to be."

"I'm glad you were so insistent. Anyway, I owe you an apology."

"Is that what was wrong? You thought you wouldn't like my design, so you were hostile to me?"

"I haven't been hostile. It's just that I'm not looking for complications."

Lightly, almost absentmindedly, he touched her shoulder. "It's already complicated."

The woman in blue satin grabbed Guy's arm and the crowd swarmed around him again, offering compliments and praise. They pulled him toward the model to inspect it with the extra honor of having the architect at their sides. A path cleared before him, as if he were royalty. He reached the model, and a look of blank incomprehension filled his face, then grudging realization, then shock and anger. His posture went rigid and filled with tension, and the woman in blue satin dropped his arm, backing quickly away. Mara pushed up behind him, straining to see what he was looking at.

Guy reached down and wrenched at a corner of the model, snapping it off. There were gasps and stares of open disapproval. With the square piece in his hand Guy turned slowly, seeking Lowell in the crowd. Lowell was busy making the rounds, clasping hands, beaming, nodding and smiling, fending off compliments and excited praise. Unceremoniously Guy elbowed his way toward him. Mara fully expected him to grab Lowell by the collar and lift him, snarling, in a comic-book scene of furious anger. She ran to intervene.

"Guy, stop. Whatever it is, don't."

She could feel the readiness to fight in his shoulders and arms. Somehow she managed to pull him through a heavy glass door and onto an outside terrace. Thick mist from the ocean enveloped them.

"The bastard," Guy cursed, his tone disbelieving.

"What's going on? What's happened?"

Distractedly Guy ran a hand through his hair. "Sold me down the river, the dirty bastard."

"Who did, Lowell? What did he do?"

"I'll kill him."

She shook him. "Guy, whatever he's done, you can't do anything about it right now. You can't march in there in front of all those people and punch him in the nose."

"I will if I have to, the dirty bastard." He paced the narrow terrace.

"Tell me what you tore off the model."

Guy took a deep breath. "Early on, when we first began, Lowell wanted to put in condo units for time-share vacations. I wanted a public recreational facility, with nobody living on premises." Guy lifted the torn section of the model. "Lowell had this module made along the lines of my first design. I was completely against it. He pressed and we compromised. I said, maybe someday we could propose the units, for a phase three of building or something." His voice rose. "As a contingency—in case we got strapped. But not now, never now, and hopefully never at all. So you tell me who put this module there."

"Okay, so you feel betrayed," Mara said. "I see that. It was a skunky thing to do. Except you don't really know that Lowell did it. Maybe someone misunderstood your directions, maybe the model shop made a mistake."

"I've been in touch with that shop every day for months. There was no misunderstanding."

"Then say it was deliberate. Suppose Lowell had it added on. I see why you're offended, but it doesn't necessarily mean it would be built right away. It might still be for phase three, as you said."

"It's not his goddamned right." Guy's voice rose angrily.

The door opened as Lowell came onto the terrace. A look passed between him and Mara, as if he were counting on her to be his ally. Lowell raised his hands in a gesture that was at once submissive and challenging.

"Things can change," Lowell said in a controlled voice. "This model is still a proposal. Nobody's saying we'll build the units."

"Goddamned time shares were never part of our agreement," Guy countered.

"Until the final stone is laid and paid for, this project is still speculative. Investors need something to believe in, something they think will bring a good return on their money."

"I've heard that speech. Just keep your hands off. Don't redesign my building. Don't play games with Cliff House."

Lowell spoke in a conciliatory tone. "But, Guy, we're not building any units now. They're only a possibility. I dangled a carrot, that's all I did."

"Guy, he's right," Mara added. "Listen to him."

"We haven't met our target investment," Lowell said. "I did what I thought was necessary."

"You had no right."

"Legally or artistically?"

"Don't mock me," Guy said angrily. "I'll check our goddamned agreement and tell you what's legal or not. I don't remember you signing on as architect."

"Check the agreement. I have every right to bring in the backing we need. Otherwise Cliff House will never be built. What good will your design be then?"

"I'm checking my contract." Guy thrust the model unit at Lowell, scraping it against his dress shirt and letting it fall to the ground. He flung open the terrace door and disappeared inside, fighting his way through the crowd of well-wishers.

"He's unreasonable," Lowell said. "It was in his best interests. Both of ours."

"I see that."

Lowell smoothed the front of his shirt. "He'll cool off. He always blows up like this, but in ten minutes it's usually forgotten. Mara"—he gave her an intent look—"do me a favor, go after him, smooth over the rough spots for me, before he embarrasses himself."

"If I can."

"I think he'll listen to you."

She hesitated. "I understand why you put the units in, but shouldn't you have asked Guy first?"

"Would he have agreed if I'd asked?"

"No," she said. "He wouldn't have agreed. I'll try to stop him."

Mara caught up with him outside the main entrance. "Wait, Guy—let me come with you."

"If Lowell sent you, forget it."

"I'm coming with you."

The night air was so thick with moisture, it seemed to cling to her bare skin. She rubbed her arms to warm them as Guy stepped off the curb, moving toward the parking lot. She hesitated and then followed. To her surprise Paddy Manelli was still loitering at the concession stands, although only two of his demonstrators were left, and they looked cold and miserable.

As Guy strode past, Paddy lunged off the sidewalk at him, as if to block his way. Guy raised one arm and swept it in a backward arc, catching Paddy in the chest. Paddy staggered, his arms slicing the air. Before he could regain his balance, Guy thrust a threatening fist at Paddy's face.

"You want to make it personal, Manelli? Huh? Think about it."

There was a tense pause. Paddy shrank back, and Guy turned his back dismissively, walking away, leaving Paddy absently rubbing his chest. With a little skip Mara swerved to go around him, but Paddy grabbed her arm, pulling her to a halt. "If you think that people want—"

"Go home!" she shouted, and the words echoed ridiculously. She held a hand to her mouth, embarrassed. "Well, what are you complaining about, anyway? Cliff House is for everyone— even you."

She ran for the safety of Guy's car, suppressing a nervous bubble of laughter. She slid into the front seat beside Guy and pressed down the door lock.

"Go home?" Guy mimicked. "Harsh words, Brightfield."

She shrugged, and he slammed the car into gear. It bucked and stalled. He cursed and restarted the engine. It caught this time, and they burst out of the lot, heading for the far lane. They had gotten halfway across the road when a car appeared on their left, approaching at high speed and straddling the thick white line down the center of the road. It was too late to retreat. They were sure to be rammed broadside. Guy slammed on the gas, and the Jaguar lurched powerfully, leaping ahead, clearing the other car by several inches. There was a sound like a long scream, and Mara realized the other driver was leaning on his horn as he sped out of sight.

Her heart tripped; directly ahead was the mountainous embankment on the other side of the road. Guy swung the wheel, and the nose of the car swung out. Their rear wheels scraped and skidded briefly against the rock embankment. Guy straightened the car and exhaled an unconscious sigh of relief.

Mara pressed a hand against her eyes. "Could we possibly slow down before we kill ourselves?"

"I don't need your advice," Guy snapped back.

"You do when you're being an unreasonable hothead."

"Hothead—who said that, you or Lowell?"

"You're the one causing a problem, not Lowell. He's only trying to help."

"Oh, I see—another brave rescue of poor Guy Levin."

They stopped for a red light, and when they moved again, Guy slowed his speed.

"You're being childish," she said more quietly. "Lowell's offering the units as an enticement, a lure. He hasn't said he'll build them. You obviously need the cash to finance your construction now. You can back out later, maybe for some kind of surrender fee. That's legitimate business. You're being self-defeating. In business you can't be above a little dirty poker."

"You know that, do you?"

"Everyone knows that. Dan does. He plays favorites with advertisers, he gives favors, and asks for them back. It works. I don't see anything wrong with it. Everyone washes everyone else's back."

"And greases everyone else's palm. What do you care, anyway?"

"I just know it's necessary," Mara answered. "And what's so wrong? It's not illegal. No one's hiding anything."

"I see. You can't call it corrupt if you brag about it?"

"This isn't about corruption. It's mostly about your own ego."

Guy glanced at her, then looked away, shaking his head. They drove the rest of the way in silence. In the driveway of his house, Guy shut the motor and turned to her.

"Look, Brightfield, whatever I want, it's for a reason. I'm not blowing hot air. I know better than that. I know being a renegade won't get me anything but lonely. You don't understand me. I can accept it all, from underbidding to political favors. I see that it works, I see that it can work for me. How do you think I got to do this project in the first place? Was I born with that power?"

She frowned. "Then I don't get it. Why the big fuss over a few condos?"

"Because this is something else. Cliff House is something else. I don't want it tainted, that's all."

54

"Even if you lose it—and all your money?"

"I should never have told you I had personal money involved."

She smiled. "It seems like there's personal *everything* involved."

"If I could have financed it on my own, I would have. Sure, I need help. But I'm not going to be shut out."

"Lowell isn't trying to shut you out. You're the one who forced him to be sneaky about it."

"Me?"

"If he had asked, would you ever have considered proposing the units?"

"No."

"At least you're honest."

Wearily Guy rubbed a hand over his face. "Do you also think I'm a fool?"

"No."

He stretched his arm along the seat behind her. "I'm not trying to remake the world. I know all the so-called reasons why the best design, the best, most efficient, safest building methods will never be the norm. I know that excellence will never come first in this industry or any other. But I've come close, and this is my dream. It's always been my dream. That site, and Cliff House, it's been special to me all my life. I'm about to make a dream into steel and glass and concrete. Can you imagine how that feels? This is what I've got to do. This is the project that chose me."

He pulled his arm away abruptly, pushing his door open. "Let's go check the contract."

"I was hoping you'd forgotten that."

He turned, half out of the car. "You know me better than that."

"I don't know you at all. And you don't know me," she added.

"Oh, Brightfield, I know more than you think."

She followed him to the door. He unlocked it and they entered the dark house. Guy tossed his key onto the hall table and flipped on the light switch. He shrugged off his jacket and draped it over the banister.

"I'll be up in the kitchen, checking my files. Do what you want."

Guy went directly to his filing cabinets. Mara paused uncertainly on the stairs, then climbed up to the studio. The lights were out in the glass room, and the shades were up. A patch of fog swept past the walls. The city lights glowed dully, muted by the damp mist. The studio felt like a floating tree house, as if it were detached from the lower floors, resting on dense banks of fog.

From downstairs came a swell of music. It seemed to rise and fill the glass room. She stood, transfixed, at the window, watching the fog and the night. Guy climbed the metal stairs. He came into the room and stood behind her, putting one arm and then the other around her waist. He turned her to face him. There was a pleasing weight to his arms, a muscular weight. He reached around her and placed each of her arms at his waist. There was a springiness to his flesh, a yielding softness under the taut skin. He bent her head onto his shoulder and she leaned into him, testing the solidity of his presence. She felt his lips brush across her hair.

"I'm not much of a dancer," he murmured. He reached up, touching her cheek. "Where did you come from, Mara Brightfield, walking into my life and changing everything?"

She dropped her eyes and pulled away. She was too vulnerable to his searching gaze, to his caressing speech. "It doesn't work this way with me, Guy. It's not this easy."

"Does it have to be difficult? You're here and I'm here, and he's not."

"You forget—I'm not the one looking for complications. I'm not trying to be around you, it's not what I want, it's just circumstance."

"We make our own circumstances."

She turned away, tapping her fingers nervously on the table's edge. He reached for her hands, but she pulled them back.

"This isn't right for me. I'm not the least like you. I'm not patient or methodical. You're like Dan—you're intense, you get lost in your work. It's important work, but I need someone with me, someone to be with me."

"I'd be with you."

She edged around the table, clinging to it with her fingertips, pacing its long edge as he followed her around the room.

"I'm difficult," she said. "I exaggerate, I dramatize—oh, ask Suzanne about that—I can make a big deal out of nothing. I have too much imagination. You wouldn't understand that. You need to go along slow and steady, one thing at a time."

"Am I really that boring?"

"And I'm high-strung," she said. "Oversensitive. I'm not proud of these things, understand. I'm telling you what I've been told. I'm a perfectionist, but only about things that will drive you crazy."

"I don't care."

"You would."

"Try me."

By this time they had circled the table completely. He made an impatient move, as if to capture her again, but she stepped away.

"I only came with you tonight to help Lowell. I'm on his side. I see how you feel, and your work is beautiful. But I also see that Lowell makes more sense." She slid a chair out from under the table and sat on it ungracefully. Her voice was harsh. "He's right and you're not. Did you find that in your contract?"

"What are you so frightened of?"

"Lowell is very smart," Mara said, ignoring him. "And what's more, if you go against Lowell now, you'll be the one who loses. He has the backers. He can pull the strings."

Guy eyed her grudgingly. "All right," he said abruptly. "Okay, Brightfield, we'll play it your way. You tell me, what do we do now?"

"You go back to Cliff House and tell Lowell to proceed, module and all."

Guy glanced through the windows at the lights masked by the dull fog. "Okay," he said. "We'll play this one for you."

"Play it for Cliff House."

Six

MARA SCRUTINIZED her handwritten directions. Could this be the right place? She stopped a passerby, who assured her that the restaurant where Lowell had arranged to meet her for lunch was actually housed inside a warehouse on the deserted-looking wharf ahead. To her relief she found it easily, and inside the unlikely building, the restaurant was lush and comfortable, with bare wooden beams hung densely with hanging plants and accented by gleaming brass fixtures. Broad sheaths of sunlight streamed against rich velvet banquettes, and mauve tableskirts glowed under crisp white linen cloths. But the spectacular view was clearly Lowell's reason for bringing her there.

She spotted him immediately, bent over a table in the main dining room, squeezing in a few moments of work. She hurried over. "Am I too early?"

Lowell looked up, smiling easily. "Right on time." He folded the papers and tucked them away in his jacket pocket. "Sorry about that, there's always some work to catch up on."

As Mara took her seat Lowell gestured at the view; outside the wall of windows, boats were bobbing in blue water under white clouds and a sparkling sky, and the bright orange of the Golden Gate Bridge gleamed beyond.

"Picture perfect," he said.

"Now this is what I always expected San Francisco to look like."

"Oh, it always does," he joked, "under the fog." He nodded toward the view. "There are real beaches out there. Why would we have beaches if there wasn't enough sun to sunbathe?"

She felt a moment's trepidation. Was Lowell teasing, reminding her of her abortive effort on the beach the day she'd met Guy? But Lowell's expression was innocent, lacking malice. That was Suzanne's influence, making her suspicious; the result of Suzanne's non-stop ribbing and covert winks. Lowell would never sink to such adolescent thinking.

"Yes, I've heard of your beaches," she answered in a neutral tone.

To her relief Lowell let the remark pass innocently. "I hope you're doing a lot of sight-seeing. It is a beautiful city."

"Very. Are you from here originally?"

"Oh, from Cupertino, but that's no place for the kind of business I'm in."

A busboy filled Mara's water glass, and their waiter arrived. Lowell ordered a carafe of wine. "All right with you?" he asked.

"Yes, fine. I have no office to go back to."

She leaned back. The forest of hanging plants overhead gave off a warm, earthy odor in the strong sun. After a few glasses of wine she'd be too drowsy for any work that afternoon. Her conscience pricked; articles didn't write themselves.

"I was surprised when you called this morning," she said.

"I wanted a chance to clear my name. Last night, well, that whole condo business, it came off as a dirty trick against Guy. I didn't want to leave it that way."

"But we cleared that up. You did what was necessary."

"I want you to know why it was necessary."

"That was obvious, we said so last night. You thought the units would bring in investors and give you more clout in the marketplace."

Lowell shook his head. "It's more than that." He paused, and his eyes crinkled with good-humored patience.

She'd noticed that mannerism before; it was as if Lowell's thoughts leapt with a special agility, in quick and fluid phrases, and he was always waiting for others to catch up with him. Yet his look of merry resignation flattered her somehow, as if he felt her responses were worth waiting for.

The wine appeared, and he tasted and accepted it. When Mara's glass had been filled, he offered a toast.

"What shall we drink to?" she asked.

"To Cliff House, of course." He sipped and paused. "No, to understanding." He leaned closer. "You see, I like to think there's an unwritten clause in my partnership with Guy, that it's my job to protect Guy from himself. He's not always a practical man. It's easy to underestimate the costs of this kind of project. There's always something more, something unexpected. It can add up."

"I understand—for weather delays or labor troubles, things like that."

"That's part of it. And in this case some things were prepaid that might have been better left unpaid, given a choice. But there's no need to bore you with a lot of numbers."

"Are you saying Guy is somehow overextended, or that you're beginning the project in debt or underinvested?"

Lowell's glance held appreciation. "You're used to talks like this. I guess Mr. Wallace is to blame for that."

Mara smiled politely. The waiter returned for their orders. When he had left, Lowell continued. "Guy is talented and persistent, but he's put himself in the spotlight, and if he fails, he'll find it hard to pick up his career. It's more than a financial gamble."

"You're beginning to lose me. Are you saying he's in danger of failing?"

"Not at all. Guy truly believes architecture should be humanized, that people's needs and their likes and dislikes can help create the form of a building. Yet he doesn't like anyone else telling him how to do that. It's a contradiction, but contradiction is the flip side of genius."

"Then you think he's a genius?"

"You saw the model. It's brilliant. But it can be hard to reconcile genius with what the client wants."

"Guy said *he* was the client for Cliff House."

"That's Guy's opinion. He may be right in theory, but in reality our investors are the clients. If the building doesn't get built, it won't matter who's right or who's wrong."

"I said that myself."

He smiled. "You may not know we bought the land from the park service. If they'd been willing to sink our kind of money into the place, they would have. Any Cliff House will see enormous profits, as long as it's run correctly. It's a big chunk of money to come up with, and it hasn't been easy. That's all I'm saying. It's not easy, and we've got a long way to go before we're done."

"But it will get done—I mean, you're not implying that the project is just a fantasy?"

For the first time Lowell seemed hesitant. As his eyes scanned her face she sensed a decision being weighed; how much should he say?

"I should be more plain. I'm not saying what I mean at all. I was worried that Guy might have asked Dan Wallace to invest, through you. As a way to bring in enough money to eliminate the condos."

She was scandalized. "No, that's never even been suggested. Guy knows that isn't a possibility." Her mind raced; could it be true? Could Guy be angling for money? But Guy was so fiercely independent, she couldn't imagine him asking her for that kind of help.

"He hasn't suggested anything about Dan investing."

"And you?" Lowell asked.

"I don't have any money," she scoffed, "and I don't tell Dan which investments to make. So . . . that's the end of that."

"I'm sorry," Lowell apologized. "I thought you might be considering it as a kind of joint investment, since you'll be consolidating assets, so to speak."

"I don't believe in that kind of consolidation."

"You're uncomfortable. I'm way out of line here. It's the way I'm used to thinking, seeing people as connections—or possible connections. Everyone's an investor to me. It's my fault. I read more into this than there was, and I'm relieved that I was wrong."

"I appreciate your concern, but it wasn't like that at all."

"I'm glad." Lowell made a disparaging face. "I don't know nowadays—relationships, marriage, they all seem a little foreign to me."

"They can be strange."

"Strange," he repeated. They were both silent, and then suddenly grinned at the same time; and when they saw they were both grinning, they laughed.

Mara relaxed.

"I am sorry," Lowell apologized again. "I can be offensive."

"You? You're hardly offensive, Lowell."

"It's just that you seem so taken with the project. I was afraid Guy might have taken advantage."

"He's not interested in my money, or lack of it."

"I suppose, then, that it's a more personal interest."

Mara colored. "I'm not here to be around Guy. I'm here to do some work."

He leaned back. "You mentioned that. What kind of work is it?"

"An article. I'm here to research an article."

"Of course, you're a writer. I should have guessed. Yes, I can see you as a writer, expressive and perceptive. It's too bad, in a way. You seem to have a good effect on Guy." He toyed with the remains of his meal. "It's certainly a dramatic story, though, the history of Cliff House. The curse of Cliff House," he added facetiously. "Now *there's* something for you to write about."

She stared at him. "I wasn't writing about that."

"Oh, I just assumed . . . It's such a natural for a story, isn't it? A new Cliff House, rising from the ashes of the past." He laughed. "Now I sound like Guy."

"You're right. 'The Curse of Cliff House.' A story about the way it used to be and the way it will be again. A phoenix rising from the ashes." She felt a mounting excitement. She could forget the walking tours; she'd be glad, relieved, *thrilled* to scrap that story; no one cared about walking tours. But the story of Cliff House, of a young architect overthrowing a lingering curse; that was dynamic, that was alive and fascinating.

Lowell seemed to sense her enthusiasm. "You like the idea. Well, Guy could help with the research. He's got a library of books. No one knows more about Cliff House than Guy."

Lowell's eyes crinkled. He dropped his napkin onto the table and pushed back his chair. "Let's get you started."

"What do you mean?"

"I mean, if you're going to write about the new Cliff House, you should be there every step of the way. But I warn you, you won't believe your eyes."

Mara was astonished at the change. Cliff House was stripped bare. Gone were the neon signs and billboards, the curtains showing in the windows, the festive and extravagant decorations of the night before. Instead there was a slapdash plywood wall thrown up around the entire site, enclosing the buildings and shielding them from view of the road. It had the look of an abandoned construction site, a sense of desolation. No trace was left of the tourist attraction it had been only the day before. Lowell explained that the interiors were being demolished first and anything salvageable moved out. Then the real demolition would begin, with as little damage to the site as possible, using carefully placed explosives.

As he led her through the site Mara told herself she wasn't looking for Guy, but her glance slid to him instantly, picking him out in the bustling crowd as if he were the only man there. He was wearing a work shirt and jeans, close-fitting and becoming to him. With his hard hat and clipboard, he looked like an actor portraying the part of the architect-builder, a literate he-man. He moved through the crowd like the principal dancer in a well-choreographed ballet, gliding among the men in a whirl of quips and smiles and ready handshakes and hearty claps on the back, with an easy authority and a confident, quiet grace that was new to her. And the whole time she was aware that he knew she was there watching, as if she were the sole audience for his performance.

Guy separated from the crowd, and a red-faced man hurried after him. She realized he had been following Guy around the site, and part of Guy's blatant preoccupation was an effort to shake him off.

"Who's that?" she asked Lowell, pointing the man out.

"Ned Deets. Building inspector." Lowell frowned. "What's he doing here?"

Deets was a bulky man with thick hands, a thicker neck, and a heavy, fleshy face. As he and Guy neared the spot where Mara and Lowell were standing, Deets angrily waved a fist, brandishing a rolled-up piece of paper. Guy checked his watch and scribbled down a few notes while Deets blustered and raved. They were too far away to be overheard, but it was clear that they were in the midst of an argument. At one point Guy tried to wave Deets off. When that didn't work, Guy gave an exaggerated shrug, turned his back on Deets, and stalked away. For a moment Deets stared after Guy, his eyes widening in insulted disbelief. Deets tore at the paper in his fist, savagely ripping it to bits. Tiny pieces of paper wafted around him in a comic snowdrift. Deets stormed into the crowd of men, waving his arms and yelling. Some of the men looked at him bemusedly, but others immediately stopped their work. When Guy realized what was going on, he ran toward Deets, his face distorted with rage.

Lowell took off running, and Mara hurried after him. Deets was ordering the men to stop their work, and to Mara's astonishment the men were obeying. Slowly the noise and clamor eased and came to a complete stop as trucks ground to a halt and the men stood by uncertainly.

Guy and Lowell converged upon Deets. Guy shouted a mixture of threats and angry curses while Lowell struggled to get in a reasonable word. Deets made an elaborately disparaging gesture toward Guy, then strode off the lot, brushing deliberately into Lowell.

"Before you get another permit, every detail of this job better be exactly up to code," Deets warned. "Every detail!"

Lowell tried to slow the man down, but Deets flung him easily aside and strode past, muttering angrily. There was a moment of silence. Lowell tentatively reached for Guy, and Guy whirled, flinging an arm at Lowell. "What do you want? What are you going to do about it?"

"What have you done?" Lowell asked, his face grim.

Guy made an effort to calm himself. He took several deep breaths and glanced at the men, holding up a hand as if asking them to wait a moment while he took care of the situation. The men began to talk quietly among themselves. Guy turned back to Lowell with a chagrined look and his characteristic shrug, as if he were a naughty boy doing his best to evade a scolding. "Oh, you know Deets," he said with forced casualness. "He wanted a little something on the side."

"And?"

"And he's not the only inspector in town."

Lowell glanced at Mara and lowered his voice. He swung Guy by the elbow, so their backs were turned to her. "Are you crazy? What was that, what did he tear up—was that a permit?"

"I suppose, I haven't checked the pieces yet," Guy answered laconically.

"Dammit, Guy," Lowell burst out, "we can't afford Deets as an enemy."

"Okay, I'll find us a cheaper enemy," he joked. Lowell glowered.

"What are you talking about," Mara interrupted. "Bribes?"

Lowell gestured toward the trailer. "Come inside," he ordered.

Sweeping Mara and Guy ahead of him, Lowell strode into the cluttered office, pushing papers aside to perch on a corner of a desk.

"We don't call it a bribe," he told Mara. "Builders need permits, permits cost money, and there's always something lost under the table. It's money well spent," he said to Guy.

"It's the same piece of paper, no matter who's selling," Guy retorted. "And I'm not buying from Deets."

"You think someone else will be different?"

"Cheaper," Guy said coolly. "I'll have a permit in less than an hour," he added before Lowell could object. "I'm calling Arnold Ling. I'll have it in an hour, I'm telling you."

Guy leaned past Lowell and picked up a phone, punching in the numbers. They waited while he spoke to a secretary, then hung up. "Ling'll call back," he muttered.

"My God," Lowell said. "What a waste. My God, Guy, it was all in place. Now what?"

"What does this mean?" Mara asked anxiously.

"It means we don't have a demolition permit," Lowell spat, eyeing Guy in disgust.

"Correction," Guy said smugly. "It means we don't have a building permit. Deets didn't touch the demo permit."

Lowell sighed. "You amaze me," he said to Guy.

"What does it mean?" Mara asked. "You can do the demolition but not start to build yet?"

"Something like that," Lowell said heavily. "If this character is right"—he pointed to Guy—"we still have our demo permit. I wouldn't flaunt it, not if Deets decides to come back and check, which he will." Lowell's voice was thick with disgust. "This clown"—he jabbed a finger at Guy—"thinks he can out-bluster everyone. Oh, we'll get another permit, but you heard Deets. All he needs is one code violation anywhere down the line, and he'll shut us down."

"Can he do that?"

"He can do anything he wants. Find our work substandard and make us tear it out if he wants to. Revoke our permits or not renew them or make our lives so goddamned miserable, we'll wish we'd paid him fifteen bribes."

"We don't call them bribes, remember?" Guy said satirically.

Lowell threw up his hands helplessly. Mara stared at Guy in disbelief.

"What are you looking at?" he demanded.

"An idiot, I think. Why did you do it? Why are you like that?"

"I suppose you know everything about this business now?"

"Enough to know when you're being ridiculous."

"Thank you," Lowell said quietly.

Guy turned to Lowell. "I don't like Deets, I never have. Yeah, I enjoyed pulling his strings. But it's no big deal. I'll get a new permit from Ling. Don't worry, okay?"

Lowell stood, placing a hand on Guy's arm in a firm, almost fatherly, gesture. "Let me take care of it. You have enough to do."

"We're not making Deets any offers," Guy warned. "This is not negotiable. I won't deal with Deets."

Lowell made a gesture of surrender. "I'll call Ling, not Deets. Forget Deets, I wouldn't want to insult the man twice."

There was a tapping at the window—a tall, dark-haired man beckoned Guy outside. "There's Epstein. I'll see what he wants." Guy left the trailer.

When he was gone, Lowell pulled out a chair and sank into it wearily. "What you must think of all this . . ." he said wearily.

"Is Guy right or wrong? I'm not sure what it all means."

Lowell made a wry face. "It would have meant a few thousand above the cost of the permit. Is that unethical? I don't know. Is it standard procedure?" He paused. "Well, I'll say this much, I'm not going to start bucking the system now, not at this stage, if that's what you're suggesting."

"No, please, I'm not saying any such thing. If that's how it's done, that's how it's done. I accept that, I don't know why Guy doesn't. But tell me, is it as simple as Guy says? Is a new permit just a phone call away?"

Lowell raised his eyebrows. "Is anything that simple?" He sighed. "I don't know. It's out of Guy's hands now, and I'll do what I can. The important thing is not to lose more time than we can afford." Lowell glanced through the trailer window at the lot outside, where activity was beginning again as Guy assured the men their demolition permit was intact. Lowell rubbed a hand over his face and reached for the phone. "I'll try Ling again."

Sensing that Lowell would appreciate privacy, Mara stepped outside the trailer. Guy was finishing his conversation with Epstein.

"The carters should finish up tomorrow morning," Epstein was saying. He interrupted himself to smile at Mara.

"Danny Epstein, Mara Brightfield," Guy said, introducing them. "Danny's my second in command."

Epstein winked at Mara. "Let him kid himself—I run the place." He flicked a finger against his hard hat and sauntered off.

Guy nodded toward the trailer. "Are you hanging out with Lowell now? You two got together pretty fast."

"Lowell and I had lunch," Mara said stiffly. "And it's a good thing we came back here. Are you trying to destroy this whole project?"

Guy looked amused. "Don't let Lowell throw you. This Deets thing isn't a big deal. I told the truth, there are other inspectors. Not everyone's on the take. It's just a matter of style. Lowell's more the old, crooked school."

"And you aren't?"

"I'm as honest as the day is long." Guy grinned disarmingly. Mara found herself wondering if Lowell hadn't overreacted, if things weren't as simple as Guy said.

"Why'd he bring you here, anyway?" Guy asked curiously.

"To see the demolition. Lowell had an interesting idea. He thinks I should do an article about Cliff House, a kind of moody magazine piece about curses and bucking the odds and restoring something special to San Francisco."

"Nice publicity," Guy said mildly.

"Great publicity," Mara answered. "I'm on your side, after all."

Guy glanced at her sharply. "Last night it was Lowell's side."

"The side of the project, then. Not against you or for Lowell. I'm for whatever helps Cliff House. I admire the project. You know that's true."

"Well, all is not lost," Guy drawled. "I've made one real convert."

"Do you want my help or not?"

He grinned slowly. "Who's helping who?"

"Okay. It could be a good thing for me," she admitted. "I'd love to sell the article. But published locally, it could do some good for

Cliff House. There's no such thing as bad publicity, right? But I can't do it at all without your help."

"I'd be glad to help."

"Okay, then. Great."

Lowell emerged from the trailer. "No luck yet with Ling. I'll try from my office. Mara, where can I drop you?"

"At the library, I suppose. I'd better start my research."

"Guy has the best books for that," Lowell said. "Why don't you two arrange something? I'll meet you at the car."

"My books?" Guy looked doubtful.

"Lowell says you have a library full," Mara said.

"I guess I do. Well, okay." Guy pulled a key ring from his pocket and slipped one off. "My house key," he said, holding it out to Mara. "But you'd better be there to let me back in tonight."

"Oh." Mara hesitated. She hadn't planned on spending time at Guy's house, but he was obviously protective of his books, and it seemed a sensible plan. "I suppose it will take me all afternoon, if there's a lot to read. I guess I'll be there." She reached for the key and Guy grasped her fingers, holding on to them a moment too long. She pulled her hand away.

"The books you want are in the kitchen," Guy said. "There's a whole section on Cliff House and Sutro and San Francisco history. You'll find them."

She thanked him perfunctorily and hurried away, crossing the lot quickly to catch up with Lowell.

Mara stretched and rubbed her eyes. She'd been reading for hours. She dumped a cup of cold tea into the sink and put on a fresh pot of water. While she waited for it to boil, she wandered into the hall and climbed up to the studio. It was dark out now, a clear night. The shades were up and the city lights spread out around her in a glittering panorama. She stood for a while, watching nothing, enjoying the quiet and the darkness. She hadn't expected Guy to work so late, and now she wondered if she could leave the key for him in a safe place and call herself a cab. It would be good to get home, to Suzanne's, to gather her thoughts and get something more to eat than the odds and ends she'd been scavenging from Guy's refrigerator. Turning her back to the view, she switched on the desk light, blinking in the sudden brightness. As she reached for the phone book the room exploded behind her. A series of sharp, sudden explosions sent glass flying out of the windows, broken shards scattering over the floor. She threw an arm over her face and instinctively ducked and rolled for cover under the table.

Earthquake, she thought first, fearful and intrigued at the same time. She braced herself for the tremors to follow, but there were none. The earth stayed put; nothing moved or swayed or trembled, and the floor was firm beneath her. She raised her head cautiously. Something small and dark, more than one thing, many dark things, lay on the floor around her, mixed with the shattered glass. They were rocks, she realized. Ordinary rocks.

She rushed at the ruined windows, straining her eyes into the darkness. Dimly, she saw someone running—a bulky dark form, with a wild halo of hair. He disappeared into a neighbor's shrubs. Mara pressed a hand to her chest, suddenly afraid. There was another sharp noise, and she screamed and ducked, realizing instantly that it was only a knock at the downstairs door. Guy's voice called her name.

She flicked off the studio light and ran down the stairs. The knocking repeated. She threw on the stair light and then the light in the hall, flinging the front door open. "You won't believe what just happened."

Guy stared at her. "That's a nice welcome."

She took a deep breath, shaking her head. "Just come up to the studio, and be prepared."

She led the way, pausing at the top of the metal staircase before turning on the overhead light in the studio. "At least it's only glass," she said.

In the blaze of light Guy surveyed the damage calmly. "Are you hurt?" he asked.

"No."

He stooped and picked up a stone out of the glass on the floor, turning it in his fingers. "No threatening notes wrapped around this with a rubber band?"

"Be serious, Guy. Someone is serious. I think it was Paddy Manelli. I'm not sure, he was running away when I saw him."

"Amateur terrorist," he murmured. "When did it happen?"

"Just now. Right before you got in. I came in and turned on the light and . . ." She swallowed. "He was waiting for you. He must have been hiding out there and when he saw the light, he thought it was you, coming home from work. He couldn't see the light in the kitchen where I was. He was aiming at you. How hateful. Why would he do such a thing?"

Guy shrugged. "Maybe it wasn't Paddy. Maybe it was Deets."

"It seems a little juvenile for Deets."

"Okay." He thought for a moment. "An unhappy investor?"

"Great. You're gonna stand there making jokes?"

He grinned. "When you get upset, you talk very New York."

"Guy, seriously, it could have been very dangerous. He could have really hurt someone."

Hands on hips, Guy surveyed the damage. "I'll have to get this taken care of tonight."

"Guy, answer me. Do you have any enemies?"

"Oh, hundreds. Damn," He sighed. "It'll be a long, cold night." He turned to her and held out his hand.

Automatically she gave him her own hand in return.

"My key," he said. "You won't be able to work here tomorrow."

"Oh." She pulled her hand away, flushing. "It's downstairs. I'll go get it."

Guy followed her down to the kitchen. "You can take the books home, if you promise to bring them back. Some of them are one-of-a-kind." He pulled a canvas bag from a cupboard. "Here, take this. Be gentle with those books. I don't want any broken spines or food stains."

"I don't believe you! You're more worried about your precious books than about someone out there trying to hurt you."

"Try to scare me, I think" he corrected. "I can be scared again, but I can't get these out-of-print books again."

"Guy, I'm worried. If you're not, I am."

"It's nothing to worry about. Somebody went a little crazy. I'll be fine. I'll get someone to help board up the windows. No one's going to bother me again, at least not tonight. But you should get out of here, just in case."

"If you think he might come back, you should do something. Call the police."

"I'm not worried."

He held out the bag for her. She chose a few books to take home and slipped them inside. "Is that all?" he asked. "Maybe you should take the biographies."

His face was unguarded and eager, more interested in helping her choose books than in the possibility that someone meant him harm. He was just as Lowell had described, a genius and a dreamer, stubborn and impractical.

"You're crazy," she said. "You can't treat people like enemies without having them react like enemies. You could at least protect yourself."

"How?"

"How? By being less aggressive. I saw the way you handled Deets today, and even Lowell. You deliberately goad and push, and you're arrogant."

"I like to keep things under control."

"You can't control people that way."

"How about biographies?" He held out the canvas bag. "I think you might need to read them too."

"Not tonight." She dropped her notes into the bag and took it from him.

"I'd better call a cab for you. I'd drive you home, but that might not be such a hot idea."

"No thanks. I don't want to be followed by a local thug. I'll feel safer without you."

As Mara slammed the cab door something leapt from the shadows of the garbage cans near the street. It was only a cat, but its startled squeal made her heart jump unreasonably. She fumbled for Suzanne's spare keys and let herself into the tiny lobby. Clattering down the stairs toward her was a chubby woman wrapped in a bath towel. Her wooden clogs made a racket on the steps.

"It's a good night for a sauna," the woman said as she pranced past.

"Perfect." Mara smiled to cover her surprise.

The woman smiled back gladly. "Want to join me? I have a spare towel." She held out a towel invitingly.

"No thanks. Uh, I'm busy." Mara backed up the stairs, running the rest of the way to Suzanne's apartment, flinging the door shut behind her and twisting the lock. Crossing the room, she made herself sit quietly the couch, folding her hands in her lap. She closed her eyes and breathed deeply, feeling absurd. Nothing had happened to her. There was no real reason for her agitation, for feeling threatened and breathless. She was annoyed at herself and tried to pretend she felt perfectly calm. She bent and picked up a magazine from the coffee table. It was a law journal, dry and incomprehensible. She flung it across the room, then felt immediate remorse and ran to pick it up, placing it back gently on the table.

Leaning against the couch, she twisted her neck and pushed the drapes open, peering idly out the window. Still restless, she got up and pulled the drapes wide open, staring at the already familiar view of Noe Valley backyards, a vista of rambling wooden terraces draped with hanging plants and laundry, stacked upon each other in diminishing perspective. She imagined the inhabitants of every house on the street, purposeful behind their drawn curtains, busy with lives that placed great demands on their time and energy, whereas the only focus of her life was some half-started research and an unwritten article.

In the kitchen, she poured water into the automatic coffee maker. Suzanne was out of decaffeinated coffee. Irritated, she slammed the cabinet door and liked the noise it made and slammed it again. There was a bottle of sherry on top of the refrigerator and she fetched a glass, filled it, and took it to the kitchen table, fussing distractedly at the odd pieces of mail strewn there. Suzanne's bookcase caught her eye, as did the pottery bowls Suzanne collected. The bowls seemed all the wrong sizes and shapes for the spaces they were in. She shoved some books aside and stacked others on their sides, forming perches for the bowls. She rearranged them, squinting in approval at the effect. But now the furniture seemed all wrong, ill placed for anyone to appreciate the splendid display on the bookshelves.

She swung an armchair toward the picture window and pulled the couch forward. It was an improvement but still was not quite satisfactory. She pushed and pulled and shoved some more, and by the time Suzanne walked in, the couch was in the center of the room, facing the picture window. An armchair angled toward it, sharing an end table, arranged to take in the view. A second arm-chair had been pulled up to the bookcases near the kitchen counter, with an end table and a lamp next to it, as if it were a reading nook.

Suzanne gave it all a cursory glance and sank into the reading chair as if it had always been there.

"I've got it," she said. "You wanted to design your own Cliff House but settled for messing up my living room."

"It looks a lot better this way, you have to admit."

Suzanne dropped her briefcase onto the floor and kicked off her shoes. "I won't admit anything." She pointed at Mara's glass of sherry. "Can I have some of that?"

Mara fetched the bottle and another glass and poured a drink for Suzanne.

"You see," Mara said as she handed Suzanne her sherry, "this way the couch gets the full view out the window. And I've changed all your traffic patterns, they're much better. And the chair by the bookshelves makes a separate little space, like a reading nook. It's perfect."

"Perfect," Suzanne echoed. "I'm never here to see the view, I don't entertain, and I'm not going to live here forever. It's only temporary, but at least it's perfect."

"Temporary or not, you should live with comfort and con-venience."

Unimpressed, Suzanne pulled herself off the chair and disap-peared into the bedroom. She came back in her terry-cloth robe to find Mara in the reading chair, with the lamp switched on and an open book in her lap, as if the apartment were a model home and Mara was demonstrating its charms to a potential buyer.

Mara flipped the pages of the book. "See how cozy?"

"Have another sherry and you'll calm down," Suzanne advised.

"But this is your home," Mara protested. "Like it or not, it's where you start and end each day. What could be more important? If your surroundings are depressing, you'll be depressed. If they're comfort-able and pleasant, you'll feel good about your whole day." She stopped, frowning. "I sound like Guy."

Suzanne fixed a pot of hot tea. She carried it to the coffee table and set it on a magazine next to the sherry bottle. "Did you finish your article?"

"No, I've changed it—no more walking tours. Lowell had a better idea—a feature on Cliff House being brought back to life, a kind of living ghost story. The pictures alone are fabulous. It could really sell, but I'll have to do lots of research."

"A new article?"

"You sound disapproving."

"Do I?" Suzanne shrugged. "I'm not. It just doesn't seem logical to switch." She made a rueful face. "Maybe logic doesn't always work."

"You're saying that? The Queen of Logic? I'm shocked," Mara teased.

Suzanne made a disparaging face. "I've been logical and sensible and cautious all my life, and where has it gotten me? I'm as bad as you. You make up rules and think you have to follow them. We should both know better by now; the only thing we have to do is make ourselves happy, right?"

Mara laughed. "Is it that easy?"

"I don't know. I've never tried it." Suzanne laughed too. "But you've got promise, Brightie. At least you picked up Guy on the beach. That's an improvement. The old Brightfield never would have done it."

"Please stop saying that. It wasn't a pickup, and it isn't very funny."

"I'm not trying to be funny. I think it's great. I think it's exactly the kind of thing you should do. And look, your first time out, you picked up—sorry—one of the most eligible men in town. If it was me, he would have been an ax murderer. Talk about beginner's luck."

"It wasn't luck. It wasn't anything," Mara insisted. "And I don't like it. I don't like getting involved in people's lives like this. I'm not used to it. I never get involved in this kind of intrigue, not even with the people who are supposed to be my friends. A few days here and I'm embroiled in mystery."

"What kind of mystery?"

Mara told her about the rock-throwing explosion at Guy's studio.

"That's serious," Suzanne exclaimed. "Guy should do something about Manelli. He's crazy not to."

"He won't, so that's that." Mara sipped her drink. "It's not my business. I'll be going back to New York soon. It has nothing to do with me."

Suzanne gave her a queer look. "I thought you were starting a new article."

"I can start it here and finish writing it at home."

Suzanne went to the window and stood with her back to Mara. "Oh, well, you never were good on follow-through."

"What's that supposed to mean?" Mara demanded, stung. "All I said was I'll finish at home. I never said I'd stay here forever."

"Well, I've got to get to bed," Suzanne said brusquely. "See you."

"No, wait." Mara called her back. "I'd like to know what you mean. I can follow through. I've had long friendships and long relationships. Look at you, look at Dan."

"And look at your brilliant career," Suzanne said sarcastically.

"I know it's a mess—I'm the first one to admit that. Don't you think I know it? Why do you think I'm trying to change? That's what this is all about, Suzanne."

"How can you change as long as someone always bails you out?"

"Okay, I'm lazy. I admit that. And, yes, I always had Dan to bail me out. And before Dan . . ." She shrugged. "I don't even remember."

"How can you admit it? You make me so angry. You and your million little jobs, with Dan always lurking in the background, letting you hop from one thing to another, like a silly little rabbit, a little hopping bunny. Hop, hop, hop."

Mara stared at her, taken aback.

Suzanne flopped onto the couch. "I'm sorry," she mumbled. "Bad day at work." She lifted her sherry. "When are you going?"

"I don't know. Soon." Mara paused. "Suzanne, please don't act like I'm letting you down. I came out here to do some work. It was never supposed to be more than that."

Suzanne got up and gestured at the couch. "Need help with the sofa bed?"

"No, I can do it. You going to sleep?"

Suzanne nodded. She dumped the last of her sherry into her tea cup and drained it. She got up and promptly bumped into the armchair. "Ow!" She rubbed her ankle, throwing the chair a dirty look. "Listen, Brightfield, just let me know when I can put my living room back the way I like it. Oh, well, pleasant dreams."

When the phone rang, Mara had been lying there, wide-eyed and sleepless, for what seemed like hours, staring into the darkened room. She waited for Suzanne to pick up, but when she hadn't by the third ring, Mara flung off her blanket and stumbled to the kitchen counter, grabbing the phone before it could ring again. Somehow Dan's voice on the other end was no surprise.

Without preliminaries he plunged into the inquisition. "Where the hell have you been? Don't you know how to use a phone anymore?"

"I'm sorry," she apologized, "I've been meaning to call. I just got involved in things."

"Well, good," Dan said, placated. "You're okay, then?"

"Of course I'm okay. I would have called if I wasn't." Mara calculated that is was nearly three in the morning in New York. "Why are you up so late?" she asked.

"Work. Then I couldn't get to sleep."

"Me either. I've been lying here awake for hours. But, Dan, I do have some news—a terrific idea for an article." Briefly she described Cliff House and how she planned to approach the topic.

"Just a minute," Dan cut in, "I'm getting a pen. Okay, spell those names for me again."

"What names?"

"The developer and the architect. I'll run them through research. Might get you some good dirt."

"I don't want any dirt." She laughed. "Dan, I'm doing my own research."

"I've been thinking of a spread on new building designs, all the hot names, what the current controversies are. This could fit in nicely, if it's big enough."

"Hold it, I don't want to fit in anything. This is my own article, I want to sell it on my own. You know that."

"Sell it to me, it's the same thing."

"It's not big enough. It's a local controversy, Guy's not—"

"Who?"

"Guy Levin, the architect, he's not a nationwide name. It's not for you; it's a local article, Dan. All the controversy is local, connected with Cliff House."

"You never know. I might find a bigger angle."

"You won't," Mara insisted. "Are you interested in local cranks throwing rocks through windows?" Mara halted, instantly regretting her words.

"Rocks through what?"

In an offhand way she described the rock throwing at Guy's, making it sound as if his studio were in the office, not his home, and downplaying her own shock at the mundane violence.

Dan inhaled sharply through his teeth, a habit he had, an unconscious signal that something had caught his interest. "Rocks through a window—that's nice. That's a nice angle. That might mean there's something at stake there, more than you know about."

"A nice angle? Dan, it was a nasty threat. Someone could have been hurt."

"But you're fine. You said nothing happened."

"I *am* fine," she assured him. "Only you're twisting things around. This article isn't for you, or for any of your magazines. It's too small."

"Hey, I'm trying to help you here."

"I know you are, and I'm sorry. It's late. I've had a busy day. Maybe we should talk about it some other time. I don't know, I may be coming home soon, anyway. Sooner than I thought."

They said their good-byes, and Suzanne came into the living room, bleary-eyed and yawning. She sprawled over the foot of the sofa bed.

"You heard?" Mara asked.

"I tried to, shameless eavesdropper that I am. Tell me if I have this straight: Dan thinks the rock business makes it a good story?"

Mara nodded.

"What's he want you to do now, hang around my picture window hoping someone will smash it in? Some white knight."

"I never expected a white knight, Suzanne. I was never looking for that."

Suzanne grabbed Mara's toes through the blankets and shook them. "Don't kid yourself, cookie. We're all looking for that." She paused. "Does Lowell know you're leaving soon?"

"No."

"Guy?"

"I'll tell him tomorrow, when I return his books. My mind's made up, there's no use hanging around here any longer than I have to."

Suzanne tugged on the hem of Mara's nightgown. "You're not going," she said.

"Don't try to talk me out of it. I can't stay."

"Okay, princess, but I have a feeling you're not going anywhere." Suzanne stopped at the bedroom door. "You know, when you called to say you were coming out here, your voice sounded scared. Now that you're talking about leaving, it sounds the same way. Funny, isn't it?"

Seven

IT WAS LATE AFTERNOON by the time Mara got to the site. The first thing she saw was Paddy Manelli and his demonstrators, grouped outside the wooden fence that separated the construction site from the road. Mara stormed up to him furiously. "You! You have some nerve showing your face after that rock-throwing stunt. What if I had been hurt? You didn't even know it was me there, not Guy. You couldn't even do it right!"

Paddy gazed at her mildly. "I don't know what you're talking about."

"Are you denying you smashed Guy Levin's windows?"

Paddy shrugged.

"Did you really think you could stop him that way? It's pathetic that you couldn't come up with a better plan!"

Paddy threw back his head and laughed. "A plan?" His eyes twinkled in delight. "I don't need a plan. This project is doomed. Cursed. It'll never happen."

Mara felt a blaze of disgust, then realized the site was strangely quiet. There were no sounds of demolition. She pushed Paddy aside and hurried onto the site. The huge yellow construction trucks stood idle, ringed around Cliff House, as if drawn up to an imaginary boundary line. As she watched, a driver climbed down from the cab of a front-end loader, and another man took his place behind the wheel, reaching to turn the ignition key. The engine caught, coughed, and then died. He tried again with the same results, gave an exaggerated shrug, and climbed back down. The first driver slammed his hat to the ground, but the second driver, and the rest of the men, seemed vastly amused.

Mara spotted Danny Epstein in the crowd and hurried toward him. "What's going on?"

Epstein scratched his head. "Damned if I know. Damnedest thing I ever saw."

"Where's Guy?"

Epstein jerked his head toward the trailer. "Phone. Trying to find another crew, but that's not going to help."

"I don't understand."

"Guy has it in his head that the men are balking, stalling on purpose. Thinks they're Paddy's stooges, or worse. That's crap," Epstein swore. "I hired this crew, I know these guys. If they say the trucks won't go near that building, I believe the trucks won't go near the building."

Mara felt a chill. "Paddy says it's the curse. You don't believe that, do you?"

"What—voodoo? Witchcraft?" Epstein laughed. "I'm not superstitious, but I've checked the trucks and I've checked the ground, and I'm damned if I know what's causing it. Yeah, I'd call that some kind of curse. And curse or not, it's not good news, get me?"

Guy slammed out of the trailer and hurried to Epstein's side. He nodded curtly at Mara. "Who let you on-site? You shouldn't be here without a hard hat. It's dangerous."

"What's going to hit her? Air?" The young driver who had failed to start the truck eyed Mara appreciatively, grinning at his own joke.

"Shut up, Delgado," Guy murmured.

"Hell, no," Delgado answered, sobering. "My dad's been in this business all his life, and he has stories about things like this."

"What stories?" Epstein asked. Guy winced.

"Good God, don't encourage him, Danny," Guy said.

Delgado pointed at the stalled truck. "That truck there, is it moving?" he asked. "Could anyone get it to move? No. So there's a good explanation, right?"

As Guy watched, expressionless, the men gathered near Delgado. "My dad tells this one story," Delgado began. "I'll never forget it. See, there was this old place, huge, a mansion, way down the coast. And this woman, see, she loved the place. Grew up nearby, always wanted to live in that big old mansion. So years go by. The place is bought and sold a dozen times, someone is always gonna tear it down and put up something new. But nothing ever happens. As soon as the trucks roll in, disaster. Someone croaks, the company goes bust, or"—Delgado paused, his eyes roaming the faces before him—"the trucks stall and won't go near. Just like this. That place was cursed, too."

"Hell, Delgado—" Guy said interrupting.

"Wait," Delgado commanded. "That's not the story."

Imperceptibly the men drew even closer. Mara moved along with them.

"So finally," Delgado continued, "this girl, the one who loves the place, let's call her Jane Smith, she goes to the latest contractor and makes a deal. If he can't tear the place down, he'll sell it to her, reasonable. Well, he tries again and again, but finally he gives up, too. So Jane Smith buys the house, her lifelong dream. She turns it into a boardinghouse for college types. It's right near the state college. See, this is a true story. So that was okay, things are fine.

"But the boarders keep claiming the place is haunted, claim they see a ghost clomping down the hallways at night, and they all describe her the same way, a beautiful young girl in an old-fashioned dress and long, long hair. But what can you do about a ghost, right? Nothing. So one day Jane Smith, she goes up to the attic to go through the boxes and trunks up there. She never had time before, I guess. And she opens a trunk and it's full of old clothes, just like the kind the ghost is supposed to wear. And there's a book inside, and she picks it up and it falls open to a photo, see, and in the photo is a lady who looks exactly like the ghost. She's dressed the same, her hair's the same—it's definitely the ghost. And Jane Smith, she turns back to the front of the book, to the very first page, and there on the page is an inscription, and it says 'To my darling niece, from your loving aunt, Jane Smith.' "

Delgado paused to gauge the effect on his listeners. "See, it was a long-lost relative, the same name as Jane Smith, her own great-great-aunt or something, and she never even knew her relative once lived in that house."

Guy stared at Delgado in disbelief. "What the hell is that supposed to prove?"

"That was a true story," Delgado said. "What it proves is that this is for real. This place is cursed."

"I'll give you a true story." Guy jabbed a finger into Delgado's chest. "A true story is, you're fired. Get the hell out of here."

"Guy!" Epstein jumped in between the two men, but Guy leapt for the stalled truck, vaulting into the driver's seat. "It's okay," Epstein told Delgado. The men stood silently while Guy turned the ignition and pumped the gas. The engine flooded and stalled.

"It can't be all the trucks," Mara said quietly to Epstein. "They can't all be stalled."

Epstein squeezed her arm sympathetically, then motioned to the men. "Okay, fellas, that's it for now. Come back in the morning."

There was some grumbling, mixed in with a string of curses from the stalled truck. Guy jumped down from the cab, slamming the door behind him. He glared at the men's backs as they walked away. There was a loud, single cackle of laughter, and then a familiar voice, speaking in a lilting, phony Irish brogue.

"And mebbe it's the little people come to darken your door." Paddy Manelli grinned.

Guy's body tensed and his face darkened. Mara wouldn't have been surprised to see his feet paw the ground like a bull's, for in the next instant he had charged at Paddy in a blaze of comic rage. Paddy danced backward, keeping one step away from him. Guy chased Paddy to the edge of the wooden fence.

"Come on, have at me," Paddy taunted. "Come and get me—give me grounds for a warrant—I'll have you arrested for assault. Go ahead!" He made an obscene gesture and ducked through the fence. Guy stalked back to where Mara stood with Epstein.

"If the damned place burned to the ground tomorrow, I wouldn't complain," he muttered darkly.

"Me, either," Epstein answered. He clapped Guy on the back and went to check the equipment one more time.

Hands on hips, Guy gazed at Mara, shaking his head. A faint smile played about his lips. "You know, some people say women are a curse on a construction site."

Mara smiled uncertainly. "Are you angry at *me* now?"

"Me, angry?" Guy swept at the air with one hand, and magically his good humor was restored. "So we didn't get a blasted thing done all day. Why would I be angry? What are you doing here, anyway?"

"Your books." She lifted the canvas bag. "I came to return them. But if it's a bad time . . ." She trailed off.

He took the bag from her hand. "Pretty fast research," he remarked. "When will you need them back?"

"I won't. I got down all the basic facts."

"Don't you need more than that?"

"No, I—the rest is in the writing," she stammered. "And I can always call you or Lowell for more information. I'll need photos, but you can mail them when I've placed the article. Anyway, thanks a lot for your help." She extended her hand, but Guy ignored it.

"What are you talking about? Are you going somewhere?"

"Back to New York. I'm finished here."

"This is pretty sudden. When?"

"Soon, I'm not sure exactly. But thanks again. I'll call if I have any questions."

"You're not going tonight, are you?"

"No, I . . . not that soon."

He looked away, frowning. "There's something you should see before you go. It won't take long, and I think it's important. Come on." He led her to his parked car, stashed the books behind the front seat, and motioned for her to get in.

Mara hesitated. "Where are we going?"

Guy smiled. "To sunny Sausalito. Right across the bay."

He was right about the sun. It had been absent in San Francisco, but here it glared off the water and warmed the air, heightening the colors of the boats bobbing nearby. The ferry had let them off alongside a small marina. Overhead, the sky was clear and dotted with white clouds. A sea gull skimmed past shrieking, and came to an abrupt landing on a wooden pillar, ignoring them as he poked busily at his feathers.

Mara lifted a hand to shield her eyes from the low-slanting sun. "Is it always this picturesque, or did you arrange this somehow?"

"I have inside influence."

They crossed the long dock to a sort of wooden boardwalk.

83

"You didn't mention taking a ferry," Mara said.

"I was afraid you wouldn't have come. It is possible to drive here, but this is the best approach."

Guy rested a hand lightly at her elbow, guiding her out of the marina proper into a large, adjoining square. There was more wooden decking underfoot, and benches lined up along the waterfront and flowers and trees planted in abundance. They strolled past a flower cart and the vendor called to Guy, pointing out her most impressive bouquets. Guy reached obligingly into his pocket, pulling out money for a spray of wildflowers. Mara liked the easy give-and-take of the exchange, pleased with Guy's casual manner. She was pleased that he was so easily charming now, when he had been so fiercely angry before. She was pleased by the easy swing of his long stride, the warmth of his voice, and their casual intimacy and she accepted the spray of wildflowers.

"They're lovely, thank you."

"You inspire me. I like the way you enjoy things."

She bowed her head. "I didn't know I had that quality. Caution, I know I have that. I'm very cautious."

"Caution has its virtues, I suppose. But sometimes I wonder if it isn't beside the point."

"Is it?"

He glanced at her and she felt a tension between them, like a physical thing, at once holding them apart and yet drawing them together.

They followed a narrow wooden path that passed between two buildings and emerged in another courtyard amid a cluster of low wooden buildings. All the units faced into a central courtyard, paved with wooden slats like a boardwalk. There were more benches on platforms rising to different levels, planted with young eucalyptus trees that in time would spread to form graceful overhead canopies. At first she thought the complex was a renovation, a restyling of an old dock factory, like the famous Monterey canneries. She asked Guy about it.

"No," Guy told her, "it's all new. Three years old now."

She looked more closely, examining how the squat buildings hugged their site, how the vibrant colors of the docked boats and their swaying masts in the marina beyond formed a backdrop to the clustered housing. There was a homey air about the place. Each of the units had wide-paned windows and generous window boxes. They seemed to have always been there, yet there was an unmistakable freshness about them. The courtyard was at once public and private, gay and sedate, new and yet already comfortably broken in. A carved sign, painted like a ship's masthead, arched over the entry gate: THE LANDING AT MARINA BAY.

"It's charming," she said.

"It's all right—for its kind."

"It's yours, isn't it?"

"For better or worse. It made me a pile of money."

"I like it. It's dramatic and comfortable at the same time. Very livable. I like the feel of it. I should have recognized your touch at once; it's a lot like your house, kind of spare and cozy. But the window boxes and all the flowers, they seem a bit fussy for you. Whose touch were they?"

"I'd take credit, but it was a deliberate ploy to get buyers. I knew people would go crazy for those boxes. Believe me, more than anything, it was those quaint window boxes that put me over with the planning board. They capitalize nicely on the area's image— Bohemian chic."

"Don't act so jaded. They are nice."

"But fussy. Sometimes what the public wants and what I want are two different things. The point is," he said seriously, "I can compromise. I can do whatever's needed to get the job done."

"I already knew that."

"Did you? Because I won't compromise with Cliff House. That's too important."

"Maybe you're a snob," she said tentatively.

"I don't believe in snobbery. I want the best for the most people, for my clients."

"I can't decide if you're closer to Paddy or Lowell," she mused. "They way you talk sometimes, you could be an old-liner like Paddy. But the way you lord it over your clients, you're an elitist. I can't fit the pieces together. You're too full of contradictions."

"So is everyone. I don't have a problem with that."

"I guess you don't."

They fell silent, strolling back to the waterfront. Mara leaned against the railing, staring at the water as it slapped gently against the wooden pier.

"I like our conversations," Guy remarked. "I like that we both say what needs to be said, and that's it. Have you noticed? We both cut off at the same point."

"Is that so rare?"

"Very." He looked at her intently. With a start she realized that his hand lay cupped over hers on the railing. In the instant that she thought of pulling her hand away he increased the pressure, holding hers more firmly. She meant to protest but found herself examining the curve of his upper lip, the corner where it lifted into his habitual wry grin; she found herself tracing the line of his jaw and the angle of his cheekbone. She had a feeling of breathless excitement and was strangely calm, content, yet yearning.

"I want you to know me," Guy said. "I want you to see what I've done so that you know what I could do. I'm not all bluster. I don't want you secretly thinking I'm ineffective."

"I don't think that."

"But you feel better now that you've seen a real building, now that you're standing here."

She was about to deny it politely, but their eyes met.

"Yes. Now that I've seen something solid, something you built yourself, it makes Cliff House more real."

"Good." He smiled a slow smile, and she was aware that her own smile mirrored his. Their fingers locked together on the railing. They both looked at them, as if their hands were foreign objects, somehow detached from them.

"Are you leaving because of me?" Guy asked.

"You have nothing to do with it."

Guy lifted their clasped hands and bent them behind her back. His other hand circled her waist, pulling her against him. Her breath caught. His scent mingled with the scent of the water and the salty air. He pressed the side of his face against her cheek, and she felt the slight roughness of his skin. People were passing by, their voices sounding muffled and distant and unreal. With her hand still entwined in his, Guy suddenly pulled her across the courtyard and onto the narrow streets of downtown Sausalito. The pavements were lined with boutiques and restaurants and galleries and pubs. Shoppers strolled past leisurely, laden with bright parcels. A bell rang as a bakery door open and closed behind them, and the smell of fresh baked goods was tantalizing. They passed crooked wooden buildings and climbed up steep, angled streets.

They stopped finally, in front of an old Victorian inn, weathered and ramshackle and inviting. Mara was dimly aware of a prim lobby, a dull wooden counter, and an officious clerk as a room was taken and a key exchanged and the clerk's discreet but knowing look as Guy led her to the stairway, all dim and unreal but for the pulse in her throat. She pressed her fingers lightly against it, as if she could calm it.

"Are you all right?" Guy asked.

She nodded, unable to speak, and he opened the door, and then there was only the square, old-fashioned room and the door closing behind them; and then her hands learning his face, and his finger-tips and the smell of him; and his arms wound tightly around her, and his slow, lingering hands and his lips brushed softly past her lips and eyes and throat and she felt a sense of relief and bliss. And a sense that this was right and this was expected and this was what she'd been moving toward and running from. And a sweet, delirious oblivion in the salt breeze lifting the crisp white curtains, and the sun in a square on the fresh white bed. And the smell of sunshine and warmth and sun-dried sheets. And Guy's hands and mouth and the pulse of sweet, firm skin and a jumble of arms and legs and her knowing it all and wanting him to know all. And all of her awak-ened to him and every sensation a surprise, and all mixed with the low angled sunshine and the breeze through the open window. And in the distance the low, piercing cries of the sea gulls hovered over the waves.

The water lapped at the ferry. It ebbed and swelled, and blotches of early-morning light glinted and jumped off the crests of the tiny waves. The sun was already uncertain, but the chilly air and the stinging cold spray kicked up by the ferry's motion were briskly refreshing after the long, tumultuous night.

Bursts of sporadic conversation came from the other passengers; early-morning commuters huddled together, clutching their news-papers and their briefcases and trying to keep out of the wind and the spray. Mara was alone at the railing, except for two small children who raced past with piercing laughs, playing a raucous game of tag as their sleepy-looking mother made halfhearted noises imploring them to stop.

Guy made his way back from the snack bar, carrying two steaming cups of coffee and balancing against the roll of the ferry. "Here," he said, putting both cups down on the nearest bench. "This will wake you up."

"I don't want to wake up," Mara said with a languorous smile. "I like the way I feel."

Looking sleepy himself, Guy held out an arm, and with a small burst of gladness she curled herself to him. His arm tightened around her shoulders.

"You're a perfect fit," he whispered.

She craned her head back to look at him. "Am I?"

"Can't you tell?" he answered gravely. "You're my miracle."

She studied the lines of his face. "The first time I saw you on the beach, I was a little afraid of you. But I liked your mouth." With one finger she traced its outline. "Like a snapping turtle's. Pointy, right here in the middle. But I like it," she added hastily. "I love the way it curves."

Guy laughed. "And I like your worried eyes. They're sweet and pretty and so worried-looking."

"Are they worried now?"

"Let me see." He tilted her head to gaze into her eyes. "Very."

"I'm frightened," she whispered.

"Yes," he said calmly. "It is frightening. Is it too fast for you? Faster than with Dan?"

She felt a slight shock at hearing Dan's name. "Things were different with Dan."

"You knew him a long time?"

"Yes. But I wasn't interested in him at first."

"He pursued you?"

"Not exactly. We worked together."

"He was your boss?"

"No, but he was on the fast track."

"Not you?"

"Me? I kept getting fired and free-lancing and getting hired and quitting again. I'm not made for regular jobs."

"Me, either."

The ferry lifted and slapped down with a thud. Their coffee cups rocked and threatened to spill. Guy swept them off the unsteady bench, hoisting one in each fist. "Whoa! Better drink these before we lose them."

Mara felt she would burst with each small happiness. Everything seemed new—the sun, the sea, the fresh hot coffee. She reached for a cup, but Guy said, "Wait a minute," and took a plastic packet of black licorice from his pocket. He ripped it open with his teeth and pulled out two long pieces.

"What's that for?"

Guy chortled. "You'll love this. It's an old Paddy Manelli trick. A Black Irish coffee, he calls it. One black coffee, stirred with one black licorice stick. No cream allowed. If it gets too cool, the water can't melt the licorice. It's good, really. Try it." Guy nodded toward her cup while he took a careful sip from his own cup and grimaced. "Ummph," he grunted, "hot."

Mara gaped at him. "Paddy's trick? I thought you two were enemies."

Guy looked amused. "Paddy's not my worst problem, believe me. He's a crank. He's good publicity."

"You don't believe that. That doesn't sound like you at all."

Guy sipped steadily at his coffee. "I know Paddy. There's a lot of history behind us. Most of it bad," he admitted wryly. "Street fights, rivalries, things like that. But someone you've fought that hard and that long, they're family." He paused. "My problem is, I believe what he's saying. He's right, in theory, about taking money from the mouths of the needy. There are people hurting out there, with no place to live, no decent job. They don't need another Cliff House. But that's not the way the world works. Not building Cliff House won't get them jobs or houses. No, Paddy's not my problem. Delays are my problem, and Paddy's not the one causing the delays."

"Oh, I see," she said sardonically. "Not Paddy. Then the curse was responsible for those stalled trucks yesterday?"

"The curse, or Ned Deets," Guy said.

"Deets? Because you wouldn't pay him off?"

"Stranger things have happened."

"Then what are you going to do about it?"

"Nothing to do. By now Lowell has another permit. We'll start construction on time. No problem."

"You're already behind on demolition."

"We'll catch up. Epstein probably has the crew going already. We lost a day, but we'll catch up with overtime."

"Isn't that bad for your budget, paying for overtime right away?"

"Are you my accountant now?"

"Sorry." She turned to face the water. "You told me you were willing to make compromises when you had to. Don't you think a compromise is in order with Deets?"

"Not with Cliff House."

"What good is Cliff House unbuilt?"

He grasped her shoulders. "Mara, this is something that started a long time ago. I'm not going to give in now, not when I don't have to."

Mara took a stabbing sip at her coffee. "I know I don't have much right to talk. I don't have much to show for myself, but I do have ambition, Guy."

"You're fine with me. You don't have to prove a thing."

"That's not what I mean. I mean I'm not that different from you. It's taken me a lot longer to figure out what I want, but at least I see now that compromises are worth it. You have to bend sometimes. It's like Lowell says—"

"Lowell?" he interrupted. "Let me tell you about Lowell. He seems impressive. Hell, he *is* impressive. But that doesn't make him automatically right, not always. He's human, too. Oh, his accomplishments are real, but it's not like he's a hero and the rest of us are just scurrying around down here, with all our imperfections hanging out. He's got imperfections; he's just better at hiding them."

"But he—"

"Let me finish. I know about compromise. When I started in this business, I was naïve. I didn't know how to work things. I made mistakes and spent a lot of years paying for them. Then I built Marina Bay. And that was the last compromise I'll make. I made it for a reason: so I wouldn't have to compromise with Cliff House. Because once you start selling out, where does it stop? I don't want everything I ever do to be a compromise. There may be only one great building in me—if there's anything great—and I think it's Cliff House. It has to be Cliff House.

"Marina Bay proved I was a commercial success, a safe risk. But Cliff House will prove something else, and right now it's the only thing I want to prove."

"Then what happens now?"

"Now we replace the crew if we have to, or replace the equipment."

"Suzanne said you could get an injunction against Paddy for blocking your work."

"I'm not worried, Mara. Nothing's going to stop me now. Nothing—human or inhuman."

"I do admire you." She laid her hand on his arm. "I really do."

Guy looked at her hand. "All right." He covered her hand with his own, then removed it and downed the last of his coffee and crumpled the empty cup. Impatiently he checked his watch. There was a sudden bustle of activity as the ferry neared its slip.

"You're disappointed in me," she said.

"I'm not."

"Yes. You wanted me to tell you not to compromise, at any cost. But I still see you as the hero."

He looked at her gravely. "I'm not looking to be a hero. I just can't compromise, no matter what. Not for anyone. If there was a curse, I'd take that on, too. If I don't build Cliff House now, then all my compromises were for nothing. This is my time, Mara. There's going to be a Cliff House, my Cliff House. That's the only thing, Mara." He put his arms around her and pulled her close. "That's the only thing," he whispered.

Guy halted in the parking lot. "I nearly forgot." He reached into his pocket. When he withdrew his hand, a key lay on his palm.

"What's that?"

"A spare house key," he said. "I had it made so you could get in to use my books." He folded her hands inside his, then lifted them to his mouth and kissed them. Mara felt the cold of the key on her palm and the warmth of his hands capped by the soft brush of his lips across her fingers. She realized suddenly that Suzanne had been right; she wasn't leaving San Francisco. She'd run from Dan, searching for something, and it had been Guy. Accepting that, she wasn't frightened anymore.

"We'd better see if your car made it through the night unharmed," she said when they broke apart.

"You've been living in New York too long," Guy cracked. "The car is fine. Where can I take you?" he asked.

"Where are you going?"

"To check the site. Make sure the trucks are rolling again."

"You're not going home to change first?"

He eyed her in amusement. "I was going to go put a shine on my new suit, but there isn't time."

"Very funny. Let's go, then."

"Where are you going?"

"To the site with you. I want to see a demolition in action. I've never seen one up close."

"You'll have plenty of time. We've got three days left on our demo permit."

Guy maneuvered easily through the early-morning traffic.

"And you absolutely refuse to make peace with Deets?" she asked.

Guy gave her a scathing look.

"Okay." Mara paused. "I guess it doesn't matter what I think."

At the site the men were waiting, but the trucks hadn't moved. Mara spotted Epstein and Delgado bent over one with wads of rags in their hands, as if they were wiping it down.

"What is this, cleaning day?" Guy frowned, looking perplexed. "Come on." He hurried closer, one arm lightly under Mara's. Epstein did his best to hide his surprise at seeing Mara again, first thing in the morning and wearing the same clothes she'd had on the day before, but a sly grin tilted one corner of his mouth. Mara flushed and tried to maintain a dignified expression.

"Morning," Epstein said gruffly.

"What's happening, Danny?" Guy demanded.

Epstein stepped directly into Guy's path, feinting from side to side when Guy tried to duck around him.

"What the hell?" Guy exploded in exasperation.

"Just take it nice and easy," Epstein said soothingly. "It's all under control."

"What's under control?" Guy's voice was grim, his eyes steely.

92

"The situation. I don't know who did it—you tell me—midnight visitors? Elves? I don't know. But someone got in here last night and smeared the trucks with some kind of goo."

"Goo?" Guy looked as if he didn't know whether to laugh in Epstein's face. "What kind of goo?"

"Beats me." Epstein lifted his hands. They were stained with a blackish-green grease. He touched his fingers together lightly and they made a little popping sound as he pulled them apart. "It's some kind of grease or glue. No one knows what it is," Epstein said. "It's all over the trucks—doors, seats, steering wheels—a real mess. It'll take hours to clean it up."

"Manelli," Guy muttered. He pushed Epstein aside to take a look for himself. Mara followed. Delgado backed away from the truck to give Guy room. As he said good morning to Mara his eyes flicked to Epstein's, and they both seemed amused. Mara did her best to ignore them.

"What's the story, Delgado?" Guy demanded.

"See for yourself." Delgado held up the rag with which he'd been wiping the truck. It was a stiff, soggy mass of coagulated grease. "It sticks to everything." He shook the rag and it stuck to his fingers. He gave it a disgusted, helpless look.

"Are you going to blame this on a curse?" Guy taunted.

Delgado blinked innocently, as if he didn't know what Guy was talking about.

"Why don't you throw sand on it?" Mara suggested impatiently.

"Huh?" Delgado looked blank.

"Throw sand on it. It will absorb the grease or whatever it is, and then you can scrape it off."

Delgado gave Epstein a dubious look.

"Well, what are you waiting for?" Guy scooped up a handful of sand and rubbed it over the truck's greasy door handle. The sand rolled into grainy pellets.

"Hey, that's cool." Delgado winked at Mara. "Good thinking."

"Don't mention it," she drawled.

Guy wiped his hands off on his pants. "Epstein," he barked, "in my office." He stormed toward the trailer, Epstein and Mara following.

"Any word from Lowell?" Guy demanded.

Epstein looked uncomfortable. "Yeah, there was word," he said evasively.

"Well?" Guy asked.

"Ling has the flu."

Guy's face went blank. "The flu," he repeated flatly.

Epstein shrugged. "Lowell said he'd check back later."

"All right, Danny." Guy's voice had an echo of defeat. "Go rub down the trucks."

Epstein retreated, leaving Mara standing helplessly. "Is there anything I can do?"

"Yeah, get an inspector's license. Damn," he whispered. "Deets got to Ling."

"Or Ling really could have the flu," Mara suggested lamely.

"Right." Distractedly Guy searched through the papers on his desk.

"I'd better be going." Mara reached for the phone. "I'll call a cab."

"I'll do it for you," Guy said.

"Thanks. I'll wait for it out front, by the highway, where I can be seen." She started to leave the trailer.

"Mara, wait." Guy reached for her. "I'll catch up with you later. That's a promise."

He kissed her, not a brusque good-bye kiss but a kiss with lingering warmth, his hands caressing her as if he couldn't bear to break away. She was surprised. She'd learned not to expect such attention from Dan, not when he was involved in work. She returned the embrace, grateful that Guy could surprise her in such a welcome way.

When she finally left the trailer, the men were still hard at work, scraping clotted sand off the trucks.

Eight

MARA PUSHED OPEN the apartment door. Suzanne was in the middle of the living room, dressed for work in a blue suit, her briefcase tucked under one arm.

"I thought you'd be gone already," Mara said, surprised.

"I was just leaving. But I had this weird idea I should be worried about you."

"I'm sorry, I should have called," Mara said guiltily.

"Where have you been? Or is that a stupid question?" Suzanne tossed her briefcase down and perched on the arm of the nearest chair. "I know you weren't with Lowell. I just called him to find out."

"How embarrassing." Mara colored.

"Don't worry about it, he's a big boy. No offense, but until now I wasn't completely sure who the lucky winner was. I can't say I'm disappointed it was Guy." She peered at Mara closely. "It was Guy, wasn't it? Am I right or not?"

"We were in Sausalito."

"How'd you end up there?"

"Blame the curse of Cliff House," Mara said flippantly. "Is there any coffee?"

"No, but make some for me, too. I think I want to hear about this."

Mara measured out the coffee as she told Suzanne about the stalled trucks on the site the day before.

"And grown men—construction workers—really believed there was a curse?" Suzanne shook her head in disbelief. "I don't buy it, that's crap. They were paid off, probably by Deets, as Guy says. It's crude, but I guess construction types aren't too subtle."

"Not subtle at all," Mara agreed. "But I think it was Paddy." She described the vandalism they'd found that morning, adding that Guy had cursed Paddy under his breath.

"Speaking of curses," Suzanne interrupted, "Dan called. Last night. He wanted you to call him right back. I said you couldn't, though I didn't think it'd be an overnight wait." She settled onto a stool at the counter, staring impatiently at the coffee machine.

Mara glanced at her watch. "It's almost eleven in New York. Do you think I should call now? I don't want him to think I'm avoiding him."

"Oh, I don't know," Suzanne said dryly. "He might just think you were out with your new lover."

"You didn't tell him anything, did you?"

"This is your party. You can tell him that. You should enjoy it. Deep down, I don't think you ever liked Dan very much."

"I loved him, Suzanne."

Suzanne made a skeptical face. "I admire your loyalty but not your taste. Look, Brightie," she said more seriously, "just because you've been making a mistake for years doesn't mean you have to go on making it. I mean it. I know it was fun being with Dan, very glamorous and all. I was always jealous of that."

"You were?"

"Don't act surprised. You enjoyed making me jealous. Anyway, you've come to your senses now. And don't get me wrong, even if Guy isn't Mr. Right, what matters is you've made the break from Dan. If you get Guy in the bargain, that's great. In fact, I'll be glad to be jealous this time. There's a lot more to Guy than there ever was to Dan. Just don't go back to Dan, promise me."

"But he has a right to expect something from me."

"Not too much. Don't give him too much. Anyway," Suzanne continued with more energy, "Dan had some sleazy information for you. I took notes." She rummaged through her briefcase.

"It's the research. I told him not to bother."

"Well, he doesn't take orders, does he?" Suzanne waved a legal pad in the air. "Here it is. You're not going to like it." She threw herself across the couch, frowning as she scanned the hastily scribbled lines.

"God, my handwriting stinks." She squinted. "Let's see—the stuff about Lowell was no surprise. He's made tons of money in speculation, and his hands are always clean, and he's well respected."

"And?" Mara prodded.

"Well, the juicy stuff is all Guy's. I knew he had some kind of local notoriety, but I never knew he was a figurehead. He's very well known in architectural circles, more for his writing and theories than for actual buildings, but he's got a reputation as a real purist. Noble ideals and all that."

"Yes, Cliff House is a monument to his ideals," Mara said.

"Well, a lot of his colleagues thought he was a sellout for doing a fancy condo project."

"Yes, in Sausalito—that's where we were last night. The Landing at Marina Bay. He dismisses it, calls it his compromise, but I thought it was beautiful. Nothing like Cliff House, but I'd be happy to live there. Anyone would."

"That's the place. And there's an ex-wife angle."

"What angle is that?"

"She's a society girl, very big bucks. She mostly financed the Marina project for Guy, and then, when it was done, they were divorced. There were some messy finances involved, with Guy fighting her for his share of the profits. Some people accused him of using her, and it kind of dented his reputation as a saint. Dan wants you to play that up, use all the dirt you can get. He also said he thought Guy was dumb to let all that money get away. Dan was always such a romantic," Suzanne added sarcastically, "but I've got to hand it to him—he's right out there. He's so up front in his evil, it's almost endearing."

Mara wandered aimlessly across the room. "I should have taken my research more seriously," she finally said. "Dan is right, of course. The scandal makes it a stronger story."

"But you wouldn't use that, would you?"

"I won't have to. It's not the type of article I'm doing. But Dan knows his business. It's a good hook, and I hope he doesn't get someone else to use it. It's lucky for Guy I'm on his side. My article will have to show how special Guy's work is. I'll have to do that for him."

"I don't know who to feel sorrier for—Dan, because you're dumping him; or Guy, because you're helping him. I think Guy has more to worry about." Suzanne ripped the sheet of notes off her pad and gave them to Mara.

"Thanks."

"Maybe that's the real curse, Brightfield, you helping Guy." Suzanne laughed.

"Don't joke about it. I almost wish there were a curse," Mara said wistfully. "I'd understand Guy better then."

"What's wrong with Guy?" Suzanne asked in surprise as she measured out coffee.

Mara frowned. "It's like he's being deliberately unrealistic. He talks about compromising and doing what's best for the project, but at the same time he refuses to do anything about the delays."

"What could he do?"

"He could deal with Deets, for one thing."

"I disagree. That's extortion. He doesn't have to pay any bribes."

"But everyone does. Lowell says so, and I believe him."

"You're wrong, Brightfield," Suzanne said stubbornly. "Guy can find another inspector. I'm sure there's a lot of graft that goes on, but he doesn't have to go along with it. I admire him for that."

"Well, what about Paddy, then?" Mara pressed. "You said Guy could file charges against him."

"Did anyone call the police?"

"No," Mara admitted. "No one actually saw Paddy do anything. Though he's been on the site."

"No good, there's no evidence. You have to have some evidence before you file charges for vandalism or criminal mischief, and then the district attorney's office would get involved and they'd investigate."

"I have to do something," Mara said anxiously.

"Forget it, it's out of your hands."

"But there must be something. Paddy was on the grounds yesterday. Isn't that evidence?"

"Possibly criminal trespass."

"Okay, then let's do what you said, get a temporary restraining order to bar him from the site."

"Guy would have to sign the complaint."

"And he won't." Mara slumped onto the couch, dejected. "He'll never do it. He's got his own warped ideas about loyalty. We'll have to work it some other way. Help me, Suzanne."

"What can I do?"

"You're the lawyer, you tell me. Can't we at least scare Paddy somehow?"

"Now wait, Brightie. I don't really know criminal law. I'm guessing at these procedures. But I know you need real evidence, which you don't seem to have. Next time file a complaint with the police."

"I can't wait for the next time." Mara sprang off the couch. "I've got it. It'll be simple. You won't have to do anything illegal. We'll just visit Paddy and talk over our options." She broke into a wide grin. "Yes, that should do just fine." She pulled her sweater over her head. "Just give me one minute."

"To do what?"

"To grab a quick shower before I drive in to work with you. I can't see anyone looking like this."

Mara leaned into the elevator, holding the doors open for a last word with Suzanne. "I'll be right back down. You'll only need to take a few minutes off—just call it an early lunch."

The doors closed before Suzanne could protest. Mara strode impatiently to Lowell's office. His secretary told her she could go right in. As she entered the office Lowell closed a heavy file and dropped it into a deep desk drawer.

"Mara! What a nice surprise."

"May I?" Mara pulled a side chair up to Lowell's desk. "First tell me, have you gotten another building permit?"

"I'm expecting a phone call on that," Lowell said.

Mara glanced toward the outer office and leaned forward. "Can I speak freely in here? Or are there certain names best unmentioned?"

Lowell laughed. "Shut the door if you'll feel better. But I think you can speak out loud."

Mara got up and closed the office door, ignoring the secretary's resentful look. "Okay," she said, seated again. "Now tell me the truth, Lowell. How harmful was it for Guy to refuse to pay Deets?"

Lowell leaned back in his chair. "Without being melodramatic?" He gave an exaggerated shrug. "Things could happen. A matter of, oh, a delay here and there, work held up while we wait for paperwork. An inspector finding the work below code and forcing us to do it over.

"You want the truth, and the truth is, we could hit real snags. We're starting out behind schedule, and I'm not thrilled with our budget. Let's say I'd rather avoid any further inconveniences," he finished.

"Then you think a compromise is in order?"

Lowell cocked an eyebrow at her. "What do you mean by compromise?"

Mara settled back in her chair. "What I wondered was, suppose you find another inspector, and suppose that inspector has an agreement with Mr. Deets. If Deets was happy, then I assume the project would go smoothly?"

Lowell gave her a grudging smile. "It's an interesting suggestion."

"And Guy wouldn't have to know anything about it? Not ever. I mean this, Lowell, it matters to me."

"It matters to me, too."

"Can you arrange it?"

Lowell eyed her closely. "Are you sure you know what you're asking me?"

"Lowell, it's a good project, isn't it? A really special project." She got up and walked to the window staring unseeing past the impressive view of the financial district. "If Guy every finds out, I'll take responsibility."

"You're not in a position to take responsibility."

"I know. I have no authority to say or do any of this. And I don't mean to give you orders or act like I'm giving you permission to do anything. But I thought it was something that should be considered. I thought you might feel the same way."

"I know you feel involved," Lowell said seriously. "Guy has that ability, he brings that out in people. And it is a special project. Special to me, too. But I told Guy I wouldn't go against his wishes."

"And not pay Deets, you mean. But that's not getting you anywhere, is it?"

Lowell shrugged. "If I were going to be as devious as you're suggesting," he said slowly, "I might be able to use my privilege as a partner. I might re-channel certain funds. If a check came from an investor, I could cash that check and deposit it to the company account for a slightly smaller amount, keeping the difference in cash. I might send Deets the cash. The investor would get back their canceled check as a receipt, and the missing cash would disappear conveniently into an accounting oversight."

"And everyone would be happy," Mara said shrewdly. "You have thought about it."

"Guy wouldn't like it at all."

"Guy doesn't have to know. You said we have to take care of him, Lowell. In some ways he's unrealistic."

"But very lucky." Lowell gave her a meaningful look.

She brushed it off. "Well, the important thing is that you get to build Cliff House. It means everything to Guy." She laughed ruefully. "He would hate me doing this behind his back."

"Now wait—I'm doing it, not you," Lowell corrected.

"No, I want it clear that I'm doing it, too. I'm in it now, Lowell."

"Okay. This is business as usual. Just business as usual. You believe me?"

"All right."

"Do you really believe me?"

"You're being very kind," she said thankfully. "Yes, I believe you."

He nodded, satisfied. "Why don't you wait outside while I make some arrangements, and then I'll take you for an early lunch."

"I'd like that," she said, "but I have other plans."

"You're not going to hang around the site, are you?"

"No, of course not." She hesitated. "Actually I'm going to throw a scare into Paddy Manelli."

"Good for you. We think a lot alike." Lowell extended a hand. "Unofficial partners." He grinned in complicity.

"Partners," she repeated, shaking his hand.

Paddy lived on exactly the kind of street, in exactly the kind of house, that Mara had expected him to live in. One of San Francisco's "painted ladies," a three-story Victorian, slightly dilapidated, leaned against its close-set neighbors as if they had slid down the gently sloping street and come to rest at the bottom of the hill. With every flourish and geegaw brightly painted in garish colors, the houses had the look of faded old women trying vainly to revive their looks with false cosmetics. As she and Suzanne got out of the car Mara had the feeling Paddy was lurking inside, peeking through the curtains at them. When the front door creaked open before they had finished climbing the steps, she knew she'd been right.

Paddy stepped onto the sagging front porch. His scowl was fierce, his red hair wildly askew, but his eyes seemed unfocused, as if they'd caught him napping.

"You're home—good. We won't have to waste time with this." Mara waved a white piece of paper under Paddy's nose, keeping it carefully out of his reach.

"What's that?"

"Legalities." Mara smiled enigmatically. "This is Suzanne Shafer; she can explain the specifics to you. Shall we go inside?"

Paddy wavered, and for a moment Mara thought he was going to order them off his porch, as he had every right to do. She could sense Suzanne's resolve wavering, too; she hadn't come without many resigned protests, and Mara knew she would have taken Paddy's dismissal glady. But Paddy stepped aside, waving them through the front door with an almost gracious bow. They entered ahead of him, trailing down a long center hall. One side of the hall was lined with piles of old newspapers, tied and stacked into bundles nearly four feet tall.

Paddy waved at them vaguely. "Don't mind those. I'm throwing them out soon."

"What do you do with those papers?" Suzanne regarded them with a mixture of awe and disdain.

Paddy seemed surprised by the question. "Keep up with current events. Don't you?"

"I throw the paper out when I'm done with it."

"So do I."

In close quarters Paddy's eager nervousness was more engaging than threatening, and Mara found it hard to believe that this man whisking newspapers and magazines off the couch, clearing a space so she and Suzanne could sit down, was anything but a good-natured host caught off-guard by unexpected visitors.

They sat, and Paddy sat across from them, in an old armchair that was losing its stuffing. Mara could see that Suzanne, reluctant to begin with, was growing more uncomfortable by the minute.

"We appreciate your hospitality," she said hastily, "but we're not here to be social."

"No, you want to wave a piece of paper at me." Paddy's manner was mild, but his eyes danced shrewdly. Next to Mara, Suzanne did her best to stifle a smirk.

Mara spoke crisply. "Your threats and destructiveness are dangerous and illegal. We're giving you a chance to stop before we take legal action."

"On whose behalf?" Paddy asked.

"What?"

"On whose behalf are you taking legal action? Guy Levin didn't send you. Isn't he the party of the first part, if we want to sling around legal jargon?"

He grinned boyishly and Suzanne guffawed. Mara glared at her, doing her best to control her annoyance. "Okay, I'll be plain. You've destroyed private property, attempted an assault on me, even if it was by mistake, hindered Guy's project, and generally acted irresponsibly. You can't go around doing those things without reprisals. Isn't that right, Suzanne?"

Suzanne sobered instantly. "It's true. You have destroyed private property and committed criminal trespass. We can hit you with a temporary restraining order or a permanent injunction."

"But you're missing the point," Paddy said reasonably. "Guy is never going to press those charges. He's got far too much guilt."

"Guilt? Why would he have guilt?" Mara scoffed.

"For taking food from the mouths of hungry children."

"Oh, please, give me a break. Yes, there are problems in this city, and people are unemployed and even homeless, but Guy isn't taking bread out of anyone's mouth. If anything, he's giving men jobs, or are you against that, too? Look, Paddy, maybe your cause is valid, but you're way out of line, and I think you know it. I think you're doing this for other reasons. For yourself, so you can be somebody."

"I *am* somebody. We're all somebody," Paddy answered, as if by rote.

"No," Mara said with sudden insight. "No, Guy took his feelings and his political ideals and he's made something real from them. And you couldn't do that. I think you're jealous, that's all. Ideals or not, I think you're just plain jealous."

"Brightfield, come on." Suzanne rose as if to go.

"Jealous?" Instead of acting angry, Paddy became thoughtfully subdued. "Hunh. Jealous. I've known Guy all my life, you know."

"I know that," Mara said.

"We grew up together. He was a snotty kid, you know that? Or maybe I was the snotty one, I forget. We fought a lot, but there was something between us. Our fathers worked together sometimes, did you know that? His was a foreman, mine a stonemason. An old Italian stonemason—what a cliché, huh? Things were different then. Not so many skyscrapers ruining the look of the place. This used to be a perfect city. Really sublime. Oh, Guy's all right, he doesn't fool me."

"Paddy, Guy is trying to do something good for people, the most good for the most people, to put it in terms you'd understand. But that's not it, either." Mara paused, "The truth is, you're using him, riding on his coattails, because you think he'll let you stage your little protests without doing anything to stop you. And you were right, up until now. But you're not going to get away with it anymore."

Paddy gazed past her dreamily, oblivious of her anger. "You think I'm jealous, that all this is mere jealousy. Let me think about that." To her astonishment he lowered his chin into his hand, scowling. "Guy is misguided, that's a fact. Still, you're right, I have a lot of admiration for him, yes I do. He knows his job. Always has, I'll say that. I'll say he has the knack of getting things done. I have a lot of admiration for the man. But jealousy? Now, I don't know. I'll have to think about that one." He looked genuinely disturbed, and Mara was annoyed to see Suzanne give him a look of sympathy.

Mara stood. "You have to stop the harassment, Paddy. Lowell Musselman will press charges. You can't rely on Guy's good graces anymore. We have evidence against you, evidence that Guy hasn't wanted to use, but Lowell doesn't share your history. Stop now or you're going to find yourself in trouble, and you'll have to spend a lot of time and money to get out of it."

"Hunh. Well, I'll think about it, I really will." Paddy ushered them back down the hall, holding the front door for them. As it closed behind her, Mara had the uncomfortable feeling she'd been indulgently dismissed.

She glared back at the house resentfully before following Suzanne down the steps to the car.

"Don't you ever tell anyone I gave you any legal advice on this," Suzanne warned. "I don't want anyone to know I ever said a word."

"Who's going to tell? Paddy? I don't think he heard a word we said. We would've done better to threaten his newspapers. I should've come with a lit torch and threatened to burn them up. That would've made an impression."

"He knows exactly what we said. He's no dope, Brightfield."

"Are you kidding? He's totally wacko. I only hope he has the sense to respect a court order, or the threat of one."

"He has a lot of sense." Suzanne paused. "What does he do for a living? Do you know?"

"He's a professional pest, I don't know. Suzanne, please don't act like you're taking his side. Remember the rock throwing. He's guilty as sin. And Lowell was thrilled I wanted to do this."

"Lowell was? Well, I don't mind Paddy's eccentricity; I think it's interesting. But throwing those rocks was more than eccentric."

"He's a zoo specimen. I hope you're right, I hope we really accomplished something."

The front door slammed. Guy called out curiously. "Mara? Are you here?"

"I'm here." She surveyed the living room with a surge of satisfaction, then hurried to meet him in the hallway.

"Thought so," Guy said, shrugging off his jacket. "I saw the light on."

"Is it all right? I thought I'd surprise you." She felt a moment's trepidation; she'd gone too far, invading his privacy to prepare her childish surprise. Her sense of anticipation wavered. But he reached for her, and she leaned to him for a welcoming kiss. When she broke away, he pulled her back, holding the kiss even longer. "That's the kind of welcome I like," he said.

"Come see what I've done." With renewed excitement she tugged him to the living room, pausing on the threshold, watching closely for his reaction. His eyes narrowed critically, and she held her breath.

"What's all this?" His tone was bemused, not offended.

"Cliff House. Or a vague facsimile."

The living room had been transformed. She had scavenged around town, gathering bits of Victoriana; there were the photos of Cliff House propped on the pedestals, and lengths of gauzy fabric draped in swags over the front window. She'd polished silver vases and filled them with lavish flowers. She'd pulled the round table from the corner into the center of the room and draped it with a thick lace tablecloth. The good silverware, usually stashed in Suzanne's linen closet, had been polished and set out on heavy linen napkins. She'd bought heavy lengths of brocade and spread them over the couches. With the lights set on low the living room could have been any Victorian dining room, though Mara thought of it as a replica of Cliff House. The recorded sound of the ocean in the background completed the effect.

The novelty and silly daring of the idea had kept her flushed and exhilarated through the afternoon; now she felt timid, worried she'd overstepped some bounds.

"I searched the house a bit for things, I hope you don't mind."

Guy loosened his shirt collar and walked to the cassette player. He pushed the eject button, and the sounds of the ocean ceased abruptly. "Mystic Moods—ocean breakers?" He laughed, reading the label, and inserted the tape again, pressing the play button. The ocean commenced rolling again. "What else did you think of?"

"Everything, I hope."

"Well. Let me get cleaned up a bit, then I'll be able to appreciate all this." He eyed her dress, the white linen sheath she'd worn to the dinner dance. "Is this a formal affair?"

"Very formal."

"Then it'll take me a little longer to get ready." He kissed her again. "What smells so good?"

"Me, I hope."

"No, this is in the food category. Are you cooking?"

"I have many skills and talents unknown to you."

"I can see that." He hooked an arm around her waist, and for a while she thought the dinner might burn, gladly forgotten. But she pushed him away, laughing. "First things first," she said. With a push she sent him up the stairs.

"Any new today? Anything happen at the site?"

"Don't even ask."

While she waited, she puttered happily in the kitchen, checking on the food. Guy reappeared, twirling like a model to show off his tuxedo. He scooped her up and carried her into the living room, lifting the measuring spoon from her hand and laughing at her pleased surprise. He slipped a record onto the stereo, leaving the ocean tape roaring gently in the background. She leaned her head against him.

"Now you smell good," she said, inhaling the scent of soap and cologne.

He nuzzled her neck. "Were you busy with this all day?"

"Not all day."

"What else did you do?"

"Not much. I saw Lowell, but just for a minute."

"Is he stealing my time?" Guy teased.

"Not likely. He, um, helped me with research."

"How could he help?"

"Oh, he knows a lot about this town. I can use it for background."

"Background?"

"Don't act jealous. It's silly."

"Is it?"

"Of course. You don't have to be jealous of Lowell."

"Who do I have to be jealous of?"

"No one." She leaned back, gazing steadily into his eyes.

The phone rang. "Let it ring," Guy murmured.

"No, you'd better get it." She turned down the music as Guy lifted the receiver. He spoke only briefly, then hung up and turned the music back on, holding his arms open for her.

"Now we really have something to celebrate. That was Lowell—we got the permit."

The sound of the crashing waves was like a faint applause. She accepted it smugly. She had stepped in and resolved his problems. Now nothing could go wrong.

Nine

THE FACADE HAD A BLANK, startled look. The windows, devoid of glass, were dark and gaping holes. With nothing to soften the look of the place it was only an ugly squat box, a mean shell, deserving of destruction. Around it there was bustle and activity and, she noted with satisfaction, no sign of Paddy. She was impressed with the swift action she had bought. She was proud. And the best part was, Guy would never know.

"Mara!" Guy strode toward her. "Get back. There are explosives planted around here."

She waved toward the entrance gate. "Epstein said you're not ready to blast."

"Soon," Guy said. "It's barely controlled chaos." He settled his hard hat onto her head.

"This is exciting. I've never seen a demolition."

"Well, you're about to." He signaled toward the building, and she saw a man scamper out of a doorway, waving his arms.

"That's it," Guy said. "Better get back."

He led her beside the trailer, where a group of the men had already gathered.

"Aren't we awfully close?" she asked.

"Those are demolition experts," Guy assured her. "They made sure we're in a safe place. Traffic will be stopped on the highway, they'll set off the blast, and it'll be over before you know it." Guy checked his watch and nodded. "Now," he said.

The explosion was like a long, steady roll, a rumbling from deep

108

in the earth. Despite herself, Mara cried out as the walls imploded, sliding slowly inward.

"Let's take a look," Guy said.

Where the building had been a moment before, there was nothing but a thick cloud of dust. As the dust settled, lumps of concrete and piles of brick and twisted steel beams showed in the wreckage. The demolition experts checked the ruins carefully and gave the all-clear. The trucks moved in to clear away the rubble. Mara was somehow disappointed. It was over so quickly.

"I expected something more," she said lamely. Guy was speaking to the demolitions men, ignoring her. When he was done, he seemed to remember she was there.

"Should I be jealous of Cliff House now?" she chided.

"Jealous—why?"

She followed as he inspected the site. "What time did you leave this morning? Dawn?"

He answered distractedly. "We have to make up for lost time. Every minute counts." He glanced at her, catching her disappointed expression. "Sorry. I'm sorry, honey—I can't waste time now. We can't waste any time."

She smiled broadly at him.

He looked perplexed. "What are you smiling about?"

"You called me honey. It's nice."

Epstein exchanged brisk shop talk with Guy, shouting above the noise. Then he saluted and headed toward the trailer, leaving Guy staring moodily after him. "Come to the office," Guy shouted at Mara.

He closed the door behind them. The noise was muffled. "That's better."

"I'm not trying to be a pain," Mara apologized, "but when are you getting off tonight? I mean, do you keep regular hours now or what?"

"Regular?" Guy peered out the window. "Near enough," he said vaguely, still staring out the window. He nodded and Epstein came in. The phone rang and they both went to answer it. Epstein reached it first.

"Hello? Yuh." He held the receiver out to Guy. "Arnold Ling— you called him?"

Guy nodded, tight-lipped. Mara's heart gave a jump of fear. "Ling? The building inspector?"

"That's right."

"You called him?"

"I called him."

Epstein interrupted. "Before you start with Ling, I need you to sign this." He held out a clipboard. Guy reached for it while holding the phone. Surreptitiously Mara reached behind him, depressing the receiver button and disconnecting the call. Guy scribbled his name, and Epstein left with a grin and a quip, throwing Mara a salute. The door slammed behind him.

Guy cradled the receiver to his ear. "Damn," he muttered, jiggling the button. "No one there."

"Why did you call Ling? You have your permit."

Guy moistened his lips. "Yeah, we got it." He glanced at the closed trailer door. "There's something going on, and I don't like it."

She tried to look neutral. "What do you mean? What's going on?"

"I think Epstein paid off Deets."

"Epstein?" Her surprise was genuine.

"He swears he didn't, but I have a bad feeling."

"Why Epstein?"

"Because suddenly all our permits cleared. It's too fast."

"You're the one who said it would be fast. Besides, Deets didn't do the inspecting."

"No. Arnold Ling did. And Ling is clean."

"Well, then, how could it be Deets?"

"Ling could have fronted for Deets. He could have paid off Deets himself. Happens all the time."

"Oh." Her confident smile faded. She felt chagrin; her plan hadn't been so brilliant, after all. Guy had seen through it immediately, and he might soon guess her part in the deception. She squared her shoulders. "Well, I don't see what Epstein could have had to do with it," she said, bluffing. "Lowell arranged the permits. You're the one who told him to go to Ling. He did exactly what you said, and now you're making accusations. You're paranoid."

Guy sighed, knocking a pencil against the edge of the desk. "Maybe I am."

"How would you even find out? If you asked Ling, he'd just lie, wouldn't he, and say he hadn't taken a bribe. That wouldn't prove a thing."

With an expression of disgust Guy flipped the pencil across the room. "You're right. Sometimes I hate the truth, you know that?" He gave her a piercing look, then picked up a walkie-talkie. "Epstein, I've got to go out for a few minutes. You're in charge." To Mara he said, "I'm going to talk to my dear partner. My dear crooked partner, Lowell."

She swallowed. "Wait. Before you accuse Lowell of anything, let me, I mean, I can—"

"You're right," he interrupted. "That's a better idea. You can talk to Lowell."

"Me?"

"Why not? You can find out some way, mention something like Deets must be happy now, or something like that, and see how he reacts. See if he looks guilty."

"I can't do that."

"Sure you can. But it'll have to be phrased just right, with the right words."

"I can't do it. I wouldn't be able to. Besides, I'm sure Lowell didn't pay off anyone. He promised not to. And it's lousy of you, suspecting your partner."

"It'd be easy enough for him to do it. He'd just take cash from the company account. It's easy to sell your partner down the river."

"You're being ridiculous."

"Am I? We'll see about that. Come on, we're going to check up on Lowell."

Suzanne looked up in surprise as they burst into the offices.

"We're here to see Carter," Guy barked, passing by her desk without slowing down. Mara threw her a desperate look, and Suzanne leapt up, following them to Carter's office. Carter was with a client. When he saw the look on Guy's face, he excused himself quickly, shutting his office door behind him to face Guy in the corridor.

"What's going on?"

"I'll ask the questions." Guy poked a finger at Carter's chest. "Lowell took money from the account, didn't he? Money to pay to Ned Deets."

Carter drew back offended. "Who's Ned Deets? Lowell gave me some checks to deposit late yesterday, and I wrote him a check from the account to cover unexpected expenses. That's all I know."

"What kind of expenses?"

"He didn't tell me and I didn't ask."

"Okay. That's enough to know. Okay." Guy pushed Carter aside.

"That's not the way we conduct ourselves in this office," Carter raged after him. Ignoring him, Guy trooped out of the office.

"What is going on?" Suzanne asked Mara.

"Tell you later." Leaving Suzanne staring after her, Mara rushed after Guy. She caught up to him at the elevator, where he was angrily punching the call button.

"Stop this, Guy. You're going to embarrass yourself."

Lowell seemed oddly unsurprised as they burst into his office. Behind Guy, Mara made signs to Lowell, trying to warn him, signify somehow that Guy had figured out their plan to pay off Deets.

Lowell stayed calm as Guy took a confrontational stance, facing him squarely, arms out, hands at the ready, like a gunfighter—as if he were ready to draw.

"What about Deets?" Guy asked quietly.

There was a long silence. Behind his desk, Lowell tensed slightly, but his hands lifted and opened, as if to show himself unarmed as he finally met Guy's eyes. "You got me," Lowell said. He pushed back his chair, his eyes still on Guy's so as to spot any quick moves as he eased out from behind his desk, his hands still raised in a gesture of surrender. Instinctively Mara stepped back and to the side as they faced each other.

"It wasn't Deets," Lowell said.

Guy gave him a disbelieving look. One hand began to rise, pointing. "Don't give me—"

"It was Ling."

Mara gasped. Lowell shot her a quick look, as if apologizing for his confession.

"Ling?" Guy repeated doubtfully.

"Just enough to sweeten the pot. I didn't want to get you involved," Lowell continued, "knowing how you felt."

Guy's shoulders sagged. His anger seemed to fade into resignation. "Dammit. I liked Ling. Did you pay yourself a little something on the side, too?"

Mara was shocked. "Guy!"

Lowell's head jerked back. "You want to check up on me? Fine. Check with Berenson, then."

"I will, don't worry." Guy made a move as if to leave, but Lowell stopped him.

112

"Whatever I've done," Lowell said, "I made the choice that would expedite the project. And I would do it again. By the way"—he reached for a sheet of paper on his desk—"assuming no further delays, you might want to okay this press release."

Guy took it reluctantly, reading it quickly.

"What is it?" Mara asked.

"Announcement of a groundbreaking ceremony," Lowell answered. "We're still underinvested. I think this might help. A little public show always does."

Mara took the paper from Guy. "A champagne reception . . . it sounds nice."

"I think it will be."

"Fine," Guy snapped. He grabbed the paper back and flung it onto Lowell's desk. "Pay bribes and drink your damned champagne. That's the way to do business." He stormed from the room. Mara went after him, throwing Lowell a look of gratitude for not mentioning her part in paying the bribe. Lowell nodded, as if he understood perfectly.

In the hall Guy kicked at the elevator doors. "Feel better?" he taunted. "You were right, he didn't pay Deets. He paid Arnold Ling."

"At least he admitted it. Now will you calm down?"

"I told you, I wanted to keep Cliff House out of all this."

"But he had to do it. The project is going again, isn't it? And if it's what's usually done—"

"Nothing is what's usually done. Every situation is different."

"But this was fastest. This was the best way. And Lowell didn't try to lie or pretend. I understand you don't like the way he managed things, but he told you what happened. He tried to do what was best for Cliff House."

The elevator arrived and the doors opened. Mara placed her hand on Guy's arm, but he threw it off and stepped into the elevator. Mara remained in the hall.

"Please, Guy," she said, not knowing what else to say. "Please. I love you."

The doors slid shut. Mara watched helplessly. A moment passed, the doors slid open again, and Guy beckoned her inside.

Ten

Smoke, thick and dark and evil, billowed from the third-floor windows. The pointed turrets, the soaring corner towers, their windows taller than two men, the sharply peaked eaves and the fancifully carved and molded and painted trim, the large central tower with its spires and arches, the peaked churchlike facades, all the roof above, vanished behind the flames, obscured by the smoke.

The lower floors, square and squat, nestled against their base of rock and earth, as if hunkering down for a fight. Diminished, without the soaring grace of the upper floors and spires above, it seemed a smaller building, square and routine, perhaps not even worth saving.

On the flat sand of the slightly sloping beach below, near the rocks and rubble strewn about the lower cliffs and on the upper road, along the embankment, they were gathered to gape at the flames and the smoke.

Of the group on the beach, the tallest of the men posed languidly, his body curved in an elegant slump, hands behind his back grasping his hat, staring inquiringly into the camera. A group of boys gathered around a bicycle gazed at him reverently. One man and woman stood apart, their stolid backs expressionless, showing no evidence of loss or lamentation. None of them, none of these few on the beach, looked at the building, as if it were any longer important. As if, already, it no longer existed.

But farther up on the sand, standing alone, her body alertly attentive, a small girl stood; knees locked, elbows raised, absorbed in the spectacle of the engulfing flames, absorbed in the magnificence of the loss.

There were other photographs, of course, photos of Cliff House, standing noble and dignified in striking silhouette against a luminous nighttime sky; of Cliff House, grandiose and serene, reflected in the still pond of low tide on the beach; of Cliff House, inviting and gay, welcoming a horse-and-buggy parade of visitors. But of all the photographs, it was the one of the fire that Mara turned to again and again, and the little girl standing alone. That would have been her, Mara thought, standing alone, drawn to the terrible and wonderful and noble destruction.

Mara set the photographs down on the desktop, next to the computer. Idly she lifted her hair off the back of her neck in the turn-of-the-century style. She checked the effect in a mirror, searching her bag for a barrette with which to fasten it securely. In the bottom of the bag was a small package; earrings she had bought earlier that day, new to her, but antique earrings of Victorian filigree set with a single stone. The woman in the shop had said there weren't many earrings left from that period; many pins and bracelets but not many earrings. Mara had insisted on the earrings. With her hair up, they gave the most authentic effect. With the earrings on, all she needed was an antique dress—something in lace, perhaps, with a sharp waist and a delicate high neck to complete the look.

Downstairs, the key turned in the lock. Mara patted her hairdo and hurried down to greet Guy. The living room was still set up as before, with its charming Cliff House vignette, though there was now a more permanent look about it. Guy sank onto the couch, letting out a long sigh.

"On schedule?" Mara asked.

"On schedule." Guy stretched his legs and arms, unkinking his back. "What have you been doing all day?"

"Still trying to get a first draft finished before the ceremony tomorrow."

"You're not going to hand it out there, or are you, my little publicity hound?"

"No, I'm just trying to set myself deadlines."

She poured them each a drink and carried them to the couch.

"I guess it's a good idea," Guy said. "You finish up and we can really enjoy the rest of the week."

"Enjoy it? Aren't you working golden overtime, or whatever you call it?" She snuggled next to him.

Guy gave her a self-satisfied grin. "As a matter of fact, two very hardworking people in this room are giving themselves a treat this week. They are going to get away from all thoughts of work."

"Are they?"

"Absolutely. As a reward for keeping on schedule." Guy lifted his glass in a toast.

"To schedules."

Guy kissed her lightly and tilted his head back, squinting curiously. "A new hairdo?"

"Homage to Cliff House. Do you like me as a Victorian lady?"

"Let's see." He pulled her head down for a kiss of lingering softness, and her own quick excitement caught her by surprise. His hands moved restlessly against her until they each responded without thought, the way it was with them.

The computer squawked, rearranging a sentence, as Guy came into the kitchen. His clothes were rumpled from having slept on the couch. He bent and kissed the back of Mara's neck. "Why didn't you wake me?"

"Because I wouldn't get any work done if you didn't sleep occasionally."

"Um-hmm." He kissed her neck again. Mara laughed and pushed him away.

Guy peered at the computer screen and compared the text to the notes scribbled on a piece of paper at her elbow. "This your article?"

"Um-hmm." She finished typing and pressed the keys to save what she'd written. The text flickered and then reappeared on the screen.

Gesturing grandly, Guy began to read it out loud: "Christmas night, 1894, the second Cliff House burned. In its place, on the rugged, desolate coastline in a city where others were building in the whitewashed Mediterranean style, Sutro elected to build a monument to his Bavarian past, a wedding-cake castle. But this Cliff House, the most majestic of all, this vision, this dream, also burned to the ground. There has been nothing since to rival either Sutro's vision or ambition—to build a palace of leisure and recreation for the people of this city. It's taken almost a hundred years for a comparable Cliff House to take its place. A Cliff House again envisioned by a dreamer and an idealist—a Cliff House that, once finished, will again fulfill Sutro's vision."

Guy whistled. "A little heavy on the purple prose, isn't it?"

"Too much? Oh, well." Mara yawned, rubbing at her eyes.

"Too much if it's me you're describing. Dreamer and idealist fulfills Sutro's vision—why don't you just say I had this neat idea for a groovy building?"

"Funny. If it reads that badly tomorrow, I'll change it."

"Come to bed now, anyway."

"Okay. One minute." She bent over the keyboard. "I'll knock out a few extra adjectives. And the opening sentences could stand rearranging, and then the last paragraph."

"Uh-huh." Guy picked up the page of notes she'd used, knocking the pile of photographs to the floor. Mara picked them up and propped the one of Cliff House burning in front of the computer screen. "My inspiration," she said.

"Not my fate, I hope." Guy crumpled the page of notes and tossed it into the wastebasket.

"Oh, don't do that."

"But you've finished with this bit."

"Sutro never used a wastebasket." Mara fished out the page and smoothed it over, then placed it neatly under her other notes.

"You're going to keep every scrap of paper?"

"Only until I'm done with the article."

"So now you're not only a Victorian lady, you're Adolph Sutro?"

"Oh, no, you're Sutro. I'm the aspiring journalist who admires you."

"Well, admire me upstairs."

"I will, soon." She held up the photo, studying it solemnly.

Guy paused in the doorway. "Lady journalist, let's keep the time travel to a minimum, okay? I mean, let's not redo the entire house and our wardrobes in the Victorian mode, all right?"

"Don't worry, I have at least one foot firmly rooted in this half of the twentieth century."

"Come to sleep soon. It's a big day tomorrow."

• • •

Suzanne pushed through the milling crowd, calling Mara's name. Mara spotted her and hurried over. "Suzanne—over here. I'm glad you came."

Suzanne rushed up, breathless. "Am I late?"

"Not at all. Come up front with me."

Mara led her to a cleared spot on the site; a large, grassy area near the cliffs that had been cleared for the ceremony. Tables were set up there to hold trays of champagne and tiny cakes.

"Thanks for remembering to ask me." Suzanne glanced at Mara's hair, which was arranged on top of her head in an elaborate Victorian style. "That's new," Suzanne remarked. "And so is that." She turned to gaze at the building behind them. "It's really coming along, isn't it?"

The beginnings of the new Cliff House spread under the clear sky. The foundations of the main buildings were laid and the first framework completed. Even in its rough stage the outlines of the finished building were evident, and the skeleton had its own peculiar grace.

To their right, where the baths once stood, the ground had been cleared for construction. The trucks and cranes stood on the broken ground like benign giants standing guard, watching over the stacks of steel beams and lengths of girders and the thick electrical lines that snaked everywhere.

"Good crowd," Suzanne noted. "I recognize some of the people from the dinner dance. That wasn't very long ago for all this to have happened." She gestured toward the buildings.

"Once they started building, it moved really fast," Mara agreed. It caught her by surprise, too, when she thought of it; how fast things had changed. She wasn't even sure when she had begun to think of this as her new life, but it seemed to her as real as Suzanne's familiar face, and as natural.

"We must have thrown the fear of God into Paddy and his bunch," Suzanne remarked. "At least they're not here. Where are Guy and Lowell?"

Mara pointed them out in the center of the crowd, where Lowell was calling for attention. The talk spattered into silence.

"Welcome, friends," Lowell called into the crowd. "Technically

118

I can't welcome you to a groundbreaking since, as you can see, the ground has already been broken." There was a spattering of polite laughter.

"But being unorthodox is nothing new to us," Lowell continued. He clapped Guy on the shoulder. "This so-called groundbreaking is symbolic. Where one outmoded building perishes, a new one begins. Breaking ground is a metaphor for growth, for clearing out the old to make way for the new. I'd like to think of today's ceremony as a premature dedication—dedicating these buildings to their future users, to travelers from every corner of the world, but most of all to the people of San Francisco."

Lowell picked up a shovel resting on the ground. Guy placed his hand over Lowell's and together they stabbed the blade into the earth, scooping up a mound of dirt. There was a burst of flashbulbs as a photographer recorded the moment, and the crowd surged forward to offer its congratulations.

Suzanne turned to Mara. "Your suitcase is still at my place. Don't you need fresh clothes?"

Mara looked away, embarrassed. "Oh, I, uh, stopped by to pick them up. You were at work. Sorry, I should have come by when you were there. We could have had dinner or lunch or something."

"That would have been nice."

There was a burst of applause from the crowd as Guy made some particularly amusing comment.

"He's Mr. Charming today, isn't he?" Suzanne gazed at Guy, handsome in his suit, offering smiles and handshakes to well-wishers. She sighed. "Maybe I would've done the same thing—holed up with a gorgeous man and never been heard from again. Who am I kidding? Of course I would have done that."

"Let's make a date for dinner," Mara said as the crowd spread toward the refreshments. She and Suzanne trailed along. Guy was not far ahead, deep in conversation with an older couple. A woman in an expensively cut pink suit approached them, tapping Guy's elbow. The couple broke into wide smiles, greeting the woman with familiarity. An almost visible tension between Guy and the woman in pink caught Mara's attention. Dark haired and slightly older than Guy, she was one of those well-tended women who would have been brightly pretty in the flush of youth but whose prettiness seemed to solidify with age into a distinguished presence, demonstrating not beauty but an impressive self-confidence. Lowell joined their small group, excusing himself a moment later to approach the refreshment table.

Mara felt Suzanne's elbow in her side. "Let's grab some champagne before it's gone," Suzanne whispered.

They reached the table at the same time Lowell did. "Suzanne, how nice of you to come," he said graciously, lifting two glasses of champagne. "How have you been?"

"Fine, thanks." Without thinking, Suzanne reached for one of the glasses of champagne. Lowell released it, and she sipped eagerly.

"This deserves a special toast," she said. "To Cliff House, long may it stand."

Obediently Lowell drank the toast as the woman in pink appeared at his elbow. Hurriedly he set his own glass down and reached for another, which he handed to her with flourish. "To Cliff House," he repeated, clinking her glass with his own.

Suzanne's smile wavered as she realized the glass she had taken was meant not for her but for the woman in pink. Mara quickly raised her own glass and clicked it with Suzanne's to cover her awkwardness, and then was obliged to click her glass against Lowell's and the woman's, who obediently repeated the toast with Suzanne, gazing at her with openly bemused curiosity.

"We haven't met, have we?"

"No, uh, I'm Suzanne Shafer."

"I'm sorry," Lowell interrupted, "let me." He nodded to Mara. "Mara Brightfield, and this is my dear friend, Julia Levin."

Mara felt her hand grasped firmly and quickly released. "Levin?" she repeated stupidly.

"Are you Guy's Julia Levin?" Suzanne blurted.

"His ex." Julia laughed, seeming not at all taken aback. "The only one, I believe."

Mara was glad Suzanne had expressed the shock she was feeling. She had no idea what she'd expected the former Mrs. Levin to look like; if anything, she'd pictured a stereotyped debutante, young and slim and sleek. She'd never guessed Julia might be older than Guy, and she chided herself for letting her reaction show. Knowing Julia's background, she should have been prepared for anything.

Mara stole a glance at Suzanne. Imperceptibly Suzanne managed to convey that yes, she was shocked, too, and no, Mara hadn't looked like she'd just had the surprise of her life. Most likely Julia had no idea who Mara was, or what her relationship was to Guy.

"Yes, I knew there was a divorce," Mara said, flustered, instantly regretting the remark, though she assured herself there was no shame in what she'd said. But Julia was so collected, so aggressively restrained, that Mara felt gauche and clumsy, regretting her lacy blouse and the silly Victorian hairdo. She'd thought them flattering and amusing but now felt certain she looked both absurdly old-fashioned and overdressed.

"Yes, there are so many divorces nowadays," Julia said politely.

Mara glanced at Suzanne again, suddenly tongue-tied. Guy appeared, and she felt an unaccustomed stab of insecurity, but he curled one arm around her waist, claiming her, and she felt such a burst of gratitude and relief that she realized how worried she'd been that he might not show any sign of knowing her at all. She allowed herself a small feeling of triumph; she wanted the former Mrs. Levin to know how important she was to Guy.

Julia, of course, took in the meaning of Guy's gesture at once and, if anything, became even more cordial. Mara couldn't help admiring her poise.

"It's a wonderful turnout," Julia said, congratulating Guy. "Lowell's a brilliant organizer."

"Levin!" a voice boomed. Mara recognized Dr. Macy. Without his white hospital coat, dressed in a suit, he seemed smaller and more frail than Mara had remembered. He shook Guy's hand, then peered into her face. "Hello there. Still taking good care of our patient?" He grabbed both Mara's hands and winked at Guy. "Is he giving you any trouble?"

"None at all." Mara laughed, aware of Julia eyeing her curiously.

"Are you a nurse, Miss Brightfield?" Julia asked.

"No, it's a long story. A silly story, actually."

Dr. Macy beamed a smile from Mara to Guy, with the self-satisfied look peculiar to people who think they've helped bring a couple together and are proudly possessive of their accomplishment. Lowell intercepted the look and linked his arm through Julia's. "There's someone I'd like you to meet." Making his excuses, Lowell steered Julia into the crowd. Dr. Macy plucked a glass of champagne from the table and moved on to gather a plate of food.

"Very interesting," Suzanne blurted. "Does your ex-wife attend all these functions?"

"Julia's an investor," Guy told her. "You might have met her at the dinner dance."

"I didn't notice her there," Mara said. "And she's not the kind of woman you don't notice."

Guy made a dismissive gesture. "I'm sorry."

"It doesn't matter." Mara exchanged her empty glass for a full one.

Suzanne gave Guy a sharp-eyed look. "She's invested in Cliff House? Is she still interested in real estate or is that her way of staying tied to you? I mean, I thought she made enough money from your last project?"

Guy was taken aback. "You seem to know a lot about it."

"I read the papers." Suzanne set her champagne down. "Well, folks, this has been great, but I've got to get back to the office. A lawyer's work is never done. Thanks for the champagne." To Mara she said, "Call me." She reached up to give Guy a quick kiss. "Good luck." Darting Mara a questioning look, she was off.

Mara felt lost without Suzanne's blunt honesty. "Maybe this is none of my business."

"Julia deals with Lowell, not me," Guy said.

"Okay, that's fine. You don't need to tell me everything."

Guy frowned and took her arm, guiding her away from the crowd. "I wasn't trying to hide anything from you."

"It's okay, really. You didn't think it was worth mentioning, and that's fine. I happened to know about Julia through something I read, and I guess I'm just surprised you never mentioned it."

"It didn't seem important."

"I guess not, if you've been divorced for a long time."

"Well, three years."

"That's all?" Mara didn't hide her shock. "Somehow I thought it was longer than that."

"No."

"Well, I guess it doesn't make any difference. I'm just surprised. I'm surprised you didn't mention it or talk about it more."

"There's nothing to talk about."

"But, Guy, there's a lot. You loved her once, enough to marry her. Something happened to that, and that's a lot to talk about."

"I made a mistake. You should understand about that."

"Yes, I know about that."

"Mara, with me, when a thing is over, it's over. I have no intentions of being friends with my ex-wife. I'm not that civilized."

"It might be better if you were. You know how it is, the more someone means to you, the stronger your feelings are about them. If you were friendly with her, it might mean she didn't mean much to you. Isn't someone more important when you hate them than when you're neutral about them?"

"I don't hate Julia. What do you want to hear? That I'm weak?"

"No, that's not it. I was weak, staying with Dan, always waiting for something more but afraid to break away." She placed her hand in Guy's. "I suppose I wanted some kind of closeness, needed it, and even pretended it was there when it wasn't. But it's there, with you." She gave a little laugh. "Before, when peopled talked about being in love, I thought they were making it up. I thought they were lying or exaggerating, because I never felt that way. I was willing to go along the way I was, telling myself I had enough. I thought there wasn't anything more—until you."

He folded her into his arms, dropping his head on hers. "Am I enough?" he whispered.

"You're everything."

"Mara . . ." He put his head down for a kiss.

"Not here," she protested, embarrassed.

"Why not?" he challenged, but he kissed her on the cheek instead of the lips, laying his hand gently against the side of her face. She placed her hand over his, as if to capture the sweetness of his touch.

"You'd better get back to your guests," she said.

He sighed. "I guess so. But remember where we left off. I'll see you later." He released her, turning to go back into the crowd.

Mara folded the white linen dress and laid it carefully in the bottom of Guy's big suitcase. She puttered about the bedroom, gathering the things she was taking with her for the weekend and setting aside those to be left behind. The packing was taking longer than it needed to; she didn't have that many clothes at Guy's to begin with, and she needed only a few things for the few days they'd planned, up the coast in Mendocino. But the preparations gave her such an enjoyable sense of anticipation that she was deliberately less efficient than usual, prolonging each small task, humming cheerfully and mindlessly as she worked. The ringing doorbell startled her. Instinctively she glanced in the bureau mirror; her hair looked a mess. She tucked up the loose ends hastily and hurried downstairs.

"Guy?" she called. "Is that you?" She suppressed a childish premonition: Guy was back with a special surprise for her; that's why he rang the bell instead of letting himself in.

The bell rang again, and she flung open the door. "Suzanne!"

Suzanne burst into the small hall, dropping her briefcase on the floor. "Hi! Is he here?"

"No, he's still at the site. He went back to work after the ceremony."

"Great. Tell me everything," Suzanne said eagerly. "What happened after I left?"

"Nothing happened."

"Really? You're okay about meeting the mystery wife?"

"I'm fine."

"Oh," Suzanne said with some disappointment. "I thought it was a pretty big deal. After all, we knew he was married before, but we didn't know they were still connected. That bowled me over. She must be a real money hound, investing in one of his projects again."

"She knows a good thing when she sees it," Mara said lightly.

"Are you kidding? After what they went through? Guy did everything but sue to get his share of the money from her."

"What does it matter now? Come upstairs. I'm in the middle of packing." She smiled, unable to hide her pleasure. "We're going away, first thing in the morning. There's a music festival in Mendocino, and we're going for a few days. It's a special treat."

"What's this?" Suzanne had stopped in the hallway, peering into the living room where the Cliff House setting was still in place. Without background music and the dim lights and the force of Mara's fantasy behind it, the neglected table and chairs and the throws over the couches looked like sad leftovers from an amateur play.

Suzanne examined it silently and then gave Mara the same

piercing examination, taking in the hair falling out of its elaborate Victorian pile, and the lacy blouse and her old-fashioned looking outfit.

"Is something a little strange going on here?"

Self-consciously Mara patted her hair. "It was kind of a joke."

"Uh-huh."

"But you've never seen the house before! I'll give you the grand tour. All the renovation is Guy's design," she boasted, showing Suzanne around. On the second floor the kitchen had been turned into Mara's work space, and she tried to hurry past, but Suzanne made a thorough examination of the room. Books about Cliff House were piled on the work island, her stack of notes overflowed the desk in the corner, and postcards of Cliff House were taped to the wall surrounding the computer. Suzanne bent over the photographs of Cliff House burning.

"You're really working, huh? I'm glad. Now show me the site of the famous rock throwing."

Mara led her up the spiral staircase to the studio. The broken windows had long since been replaced, and the room was in its usual pristine order. Mara felt a sense of proud ownership as she raised the shades to show off the view.

"It's cute, Brightfield. Having the kitchen in the middle is a little unusual, but I suppose you get used to that. It's kind of fun. I like it."

Back in the bedroom, Suzanne sat on a side chair while Mara finished packing. "I thought you'd be more upset," she said, "about Julia."

"Guy is allowed to have had a life before me."

"What about her investing in Cliff House? That's his present life, and he never mentioned it."

"You can't tell everyone everything. He didn't think it was important."

"What's this—forgive and forget?" Suzanne raised an eyebrow. "That isn't like you, no offense. You're more the slow-burn and hold-a-grudge-forever type."

"I am not."

Suzanne was silent for a moment. "When are you coming back from your trip?"

"First thing Monday, unless Guy can't stand being away. It is a long time. But now that things are getting back on schedule, I guess he wanted a break."

Suzanne gazed around the bedroom, at the intimate disarray of Mara's things mixed in with Guy's. "Well, as long as you're okay."

"I really am." She sank onto the bed. "You can't imagine how wonderful it is, being with Guy."

Suzanne hesitated. "Can I ask you something? Did you ever tell Dan it's over between you?"

"Not formally—no, I guess not."

"And you're not having any second thoughts?"

"No. How could I? Being with Guy is a—a revelation. He's really doing something meaningful. Someday Guy could be a great man."

"What do you mean by great?"

"Great. Famous."

"C'mon, Brightfield, I know he's got some good ideas, and I love his Cliff House design, but he's not a revolutionary. He isn't going to change the way the world looks. He's not creating a whole new vocabulary or anything like that."

"He could. He really could, Suzanne. A whole new architecture of design for people. It's something the world needs."

"Most of the world is trying to feed itself. It doesn't give a fig for architecture."

"You're wrong. Guy could explain it so even you would see."

"I see what you mean, I just think you have an exaggerated view of Guy's importance."

"No, what he says is right. Our surroundings matter more than anything. To put it simply, if we live in mean streets, we become mean. Doesn't that make sense? Look, if you find yourself in a sinister place, don't you run to get out of there? What makes it feel sinister? Blank-faced buildings and deserted streets. Think about it. You're saying design doesn't matter, but we know it does, we know how it affects our—"

"Stop, please. I don't need the art appreciation lecture. I'm just trying to get you to put things into proportion. Guy may be important among other architects, but I don't think he's going to be world-famous."

"What difference does it make, anyway?" Mara said crossly.

"Let's not fight. You had a—"

The doorbell rang again. "Now what?" Mara exclaimed. "No one ever comes here." She hurried to the door.

"I'll protect you from door-to-door salesmen and Girl Scout cookies but nothing violent," Suzanne called after her. "I'm not about to get caught in a lover's quarrel, am I?" She followed down the stairs.

"I don't think it's Guy, and I told you—I'm not angry about Julia. I couldn't care less about it." Mara opened the door and Lowell stepped inside.

"Something's happened," he said. "I thought I should see you right away."

"Come in."

Lowell spotted Suzanne on the stairs. She made an awkward gesture. "I was just leaving."

"You don't have to go," Mara assured her.

"It's about the project," Lowell said.

"Well, Suzanne can hear that. Let's all sit down, though."

Lowell glanced into the living room, and Mara flushed. "Maybe upstairs would be better."

She led them to the studio, pulling chairs up to the big table and switching on the automatic coffeepot.

"I'm sorry to barge in," Lowell apologized. "But I thought you'd want to know right away." He hesitated, and for the first time Mara felt a spurt of alarm.

"What is it, Lowell? Is Guy all right?"

"Oh, yes, nothing like that. No, it's a financial problem. I left Guy in the office. He's making phone calls, but I'm afraid that may be a wasted effort."

Mara gave Suzanne an uneasy look, afraid Lowell meant there was some new trouble over the bribe money paid. That would explain why he'd wanted Suzanne to leave. Mara's conscience pricked. As if he understood what she was thinking, Lowell placed his hand over hers, patting it to reassure her he wouldn't breach that particular confidence.

"It's about Julia," he said quietly.

"Julia! I knew it." Suzanne leaned forward expectantly.

"I don't understand," Mara said.

"You'll have to understand something about Julia first," Lowell explained. "She's not just an ex-wife. She's a member of San Francisco's elite."

"We knew that," Suzanne interrupted. "She's high-society."

Lowell smiled. "Yes. With all the money and privilege that implies. I hate to say it, but she made Guy's career. At least his early career. Julia brought him connections, valuable connections, and the kind of commissions a beginning architect needs if he expects to make a name for himself. And a living."

Mara nodded. "I see."

"Guy had nothing of his own. No clients and no potential clients. No connections at all to the type of people who might commission his kind of designs. But Julia did."

"You seem very impressed with Julia," Mara said coolly.

"That's beside the point. What matters is that Julia has withdrawn her investment in Cliff House and taken others with her. It comes to a very substantial amount."

"Julia," Mara repeated nonsensically. She blinked. "I didn't know . . . Had she invested that much?"

Lowell's shrug implied it was a very large amount. "It's no one's fault. No one knew what delusions she might have had. Guy had no clue."

"Delusions? But not . . . Lowell, you don't mean it's because of me? I can't believe that. Are you saying she withdrew her money because she saw me with Guy?"

"I guess we can draw our own conclusions."

"But that's ridiculous. She wouldn't be so petty. After all, she invested for practical reasons. She expected to make money. She couldn't have pulled out just because of me."

"Don't give people too much credit."

"No, I can't accept it. I can't believe it." She turned to Suzanne. "You should be happy. I guess you were right."

"What's that?" Lowell asked.

"Suzanne thought Julia expected something for her money, more than just a straight investment. She thought Julia was staking a claim to Guy, trying to buy him back."

"I guess it's been known to happen," Lowell said.

"But not with Guy. Surely she'd know that better than anyone."

Suzanne held up a hand. "Hold on a minute. Lowell, you men-

128

tioned others. Are you saying that Julia used her influence to make other investors take their money out?"

Lowell gave the same patient, slightly disbelieving shrug.

Mara pressed a hand to her forehead. "What are you going to do? Can you get new backing?"

"I'm working on that already. We can try to float a loan from a foreign bank. Guy's against it; he's always wanted to keep us funded locally. And I've agreed, up until now. It won't be easy, scrambling for money at this stage. We may have to bring in new partners."

"Partners?" Mara's voice was alarmed. "They'll leave the design alone, won't they, Lowell? They have to at this point, don't they?"

"You would think so."

Mara stared, unseeing, at the windows. "Poor Guy."

Suzanne leaned forward. "But what does Guy say about it? There must be something he can do. He could talk to Julia, for one thing, and ask her to reconsider."

Lowell smiled. "To quote Guy roughly, before he'd do that, he'd blow the project off the face of the earth."

"Great."

"He'd do it too," Mara muttered.

"He won't beg from Julia or any of her friends," Lowell said. "And he refuses to let me try. No, it will have to be all new investors."

"Does this happen often, that a project gets stopped like this?"

"It happens, but not often. No, I can't say that."

"Then it's a disgrace," Mara said. "For Guy—and for you. It's a disgrace."

Lowell shook his head. "I won't kid you, it's not the best thing that could have happened. But business is business. Sometimes even losses can be profitable."

"Not for Guy," Mara insisted. "Not when he was trying to get his vision down in steel and concrete. A big tax loss wouldn't mean much to him."

"Maybe not," Lowell said kindly. He stood, scraping back his chair. "If Guy okays the idea, I may be leaving tonight or tomorrow morning, to try to scrape together foreign financing. Meanwhile I told him you should take your trip, as planned. You're not going to do much good moping around here. It might be best for Guy to

129

get away. You know him, he'll just haunt the site, and there's not a damned thing he can do."

"You're right, we'll get away." Mara found it hard to speak. "This will destroy Guy. After everything he's gone through, all the compromises, to have them all be for nothing . . ."

"Don't think that way. We're stalled, that's all. It's not over yet. It will take some time, but we all have time."

"Thanks for coming to tell me, Lowell." Mara walked him to the door. She came back upstairs to find Suzanne pacing impatiently in front of the windows.

"I don't buy it," she said. "It doesn't make sense. You said it, Mara: Money is money. People, especially rich people, don't throw it away. They don't change their minds over nothing."

"It's hardly nothing—at least not to Julia."

"Oh, please, Guy having a girlfriend? Believe me, that's nothing."

"Thanks a lot."

"You know what I mean. Think about it. Be realistic. What would Dan do in the same situation.?"

"Oh, Dan," Mara said dismissively. "Guy isn't Dan, that's the whole point. To Guy this project is everything. It's not a business deal."

"We won't argue. Do you want me to stay with you until Guy gets home?"

"No thanks. It wouldn't make it any better."

"Well, try not to dwell on it. I know how you dwell on things."

"I don't dwell on things."

"Okay." Suzanne got ready to leave.

"Suzanne, wait. I did something pretty terrible. I did something— Guy doesn't know it, but we paid off Ned Deets. He knows we paid someone, but he thinks it's Arnold Ling. Only it wasn't Ling. We lied."

"Hold on. What are you talking about?"

"Construction was stalled, and I told Lowell to go ahead and give Deets the money he wanted through another inspector. Guy knows about Ling, and he's pretty upset. It would be worse, though, if he knew I was in on the plan and that it was really Deets. And now, with this Julia thing . . ." Her voice trailed off.

"Since when does Lowell listen to you?"

"Well, I confirmed what he was already thinking. It made sense, Suzanne. It wasn't worth jeopardizing the project by refusing to pay some petty bribery."

"That's very cute. Now I get it. You think Guy is going to be world-famous, and that justifies any actions you like by claiming some public good that I don't even see."

"Forget about that now. I'm just afraid the whole project will fall through and Guy will find out it was compromised from the beginning, and that I helped compromise it. And now, with Julia, well, I've made the whole thing fall apart. Don't you see? I've single-handedly destroyed him. I've destroyed his work."

"Wait. It's hit a snag, a real snag, but I don't think you've destroyed anything. First of all, you're not that powerful. You couldn't be."

"Suzanne, please don't be angry."

"I'm not angry. I'm just amazed at your self-delusions. It's a nice fantasy, and very flattering. Mara Brightfield, tragic heroine—she makes a mistake and nations shatter."

"All right. I get your point. I'm just afraid of what this will do to Guy."

"Whatever this Deets stuff means, if Lowell did it, it can't be as bad as you think. And as far as Julia's money goes, I still can't believe you're the cause. She probably had other reasons to take back her money. Maybe she heard of a better deal." Suzanne got ready to leave. "You're right about one thing, though: Guy is the one who really matters. Anyway, before I completely forget, there was another reason why I came here tonight. Dan is in town. He left about five messages on my machine. He's at a hotel downtown, and he wants to see you. You'd better give him a call before you leave town."

Eleven

THREE DOORS FROM DAN'S hotel room, Mara halted. Behind her, the elevator doors opened again, and an older couple got off, passing her. For an instant Mara considered getting on the elevator and riding back down to the lobby. But then what? Stoking her courage with a drink? Leaving the hotel and not seeing Dan at all? She had deliberately led Dan astray, pretending her only interest in Cliff House was professional; background research for her article; the article that lay unfinished on the table in Guy's kitchen, in Guy's house, which she already thought of as her own, while Dan belonged to her past.

She'd dressed in a proper and unassuming way so that Dan couldn't accuse her of leading him on, as if she were coming back to him, as if this meeting were a reunion and not a farewell. Still, as the older couple walked by, the woman's eyes brushed over Mara obliquely while the man gave her a more forthright look. Mara wondered what she looked like to them, a nervous woman lingering by the elevators, afraid of approaching a room. She felt nervous and unsure of herself; as if Dan had the right to claim her, as if Dan had loaned her out for a while but now she had to return to her rightful owner.

She took the last few steps to the door. She rapped and it opened almost immediately. On seeing her, Dan inhaled sharply through his teeth.

"I was expecting you to call first," Dan said.

"I knew you'd be here."

Dan didn't look accusing, as she'd expected, but somehow disappointed, as if he already knew she had let him down. And he seemed so shockingly familiar that she realized she'd expected him to have changed in her absence.

He was not much taller than she was, and he wasn't slender, but there was a peculiar grace to his movements; he used almost a gliding motion as he walked. He tossed his head back nervously now, and a sandy fringe of bangs fell over his eyes in a gesture that made him seem younger than he was. Dan's looks were deceiving. The thing you had to realize about Dan was, the more innocent and childlike and unassuming and nonchalant he appeared, the more rigid and uncompromising and ruthless he actually was.

Some were fooled. Others were not but preferred to be commandeered and manipulated by a sweet-looking, boyish-faced tyrant than by an obviously cruel one. And Dan's authority never actually felt tyrannical; just unswervingly single-minded. One thing people knew about Dan: He never compromised. He had never compromised where Mara was concerned.

He'd always wanted her. Once, she had liked being the object of so much desire. If Dan was proudly possessive, she'd felt no cause to complain. After all, she had the certain knowledge of his constant admiration. On her part, she hadn't meant it to last forever, though she'd never planned on ending it. Dan was simply a fact of her life. And truthfully, it was exciting to be around him.

She stepped into the room, and Dan closed the door behind her. She walked to the point farthest away from him, to an upholstered side chair by the window. Outside was a wide view of Nob Hill. She wondered if he had taken the time and trouble to specify a room with a good view. But then, his secretary would have made the arrangements. Dan rarely got personally involved in the details of his life.

He stopped at a bar set up on a side table. "You look tired," he said. "Want a drink?" His hand hovered over the bottles.

"No. Yes—no."

Dan poured himself a dark whiskey, adding ice cubes carefully, one at a time. "Were you afraid to call me?"

"No."

"You haven't called the whole time you've been here."

"I told you, I've been busy, working on my article. I got involved. After all, you get involved in your work." She smiled falsely. He knew her so well that it was possible he could read her mind, or at least read her face and her gestures, and see the lie there. It was offensive, that he knew her so well. The weight of his knowledge, the years they'd spent together, were like a solid thing weighing on her.

He carried his drink to the coffee table and set it there while he perched on the edge of the couch. Abruptly he leaned over and kissed her. It was a casual kiss, a greeting, almost dutifully affectionate. He leaned away abruptly and rubbed a hand over his face. With a shock she realized he looked haggard around the eyes. She felt a stab of sympathy for him, then quickly suppressed it.

"I'm surprised you were able to get away," she said.

"It wasn't easy."

His voice was flat and diffident.

"Did you come on business, then?"

He looked at her sharply, offended by her pretense that things were normal. He looked so uncharacteristically defenseless that she moved next to him on the couch, reaching for his hand, which lay innocently open between them. For an instant his hand seemed so familiar that she almost couldn't tell them apart. She felt repugnance at such familiarity, at their too long intimacy. But she slipped her cupped fingers under his and pressed them with gentle reassurance. "I guess we have to talk."

"You've got me there. I'm afraid to talk to you."

There was a long silence. "Was your flight okay?" she finally asked.

"Fine. How's your friend? Sorry . . . Suzanne, how's she?"

"She's fine. Everything's fine. The piece is going well. I'm doing more research than I expected, but I think it really adds to it."

"What are you doing, taking all the walking tours before you write about them?"

She looked at him in surprise. "I'm not doing that anymore. I'm not doing the walking tours, I'm doing the piece on Cliff House. You know that."

"You sometimes change your mind mid-stream."

"Not about this. Why did you go to all the trouble of looking things up for me, about"—she hesitated—"the architect and Lowell Musselman if you thought I was going to drop it?"

"I thought you might lose interest."

"I haven't. It's a wonderful story."

"Then come home and finish it."

134

"I can't." She sounded alarmed and continued more carefully. "There's a problem, a financial snag. You'd understand the details. I'm not exactly sure what's going to happen, if the building will continue or not. I don't feel I can leave until I know."

"You could always call to find out."

"That's not the same. It's not the same as being here, being involved. I'm involved in this project. I can't let it go."

"I'd like to see this magical site. You're so fascinated by it."

"There isn't much to see yet. They're just beginning construction."

"And what's the snag?"

"Oh, money. It's always money, isn't it? Some backers dropped out, and they need to find new financing."

"A lot of financing?"

"Almost all of it, from the way it sounds."

"It sounds like no one in charge is very bright. It's a little late in the game for that kind of chaos."

"It was circumstances, nobody's fault."

"Maybe I could help." Dan gathered her fingers in his and squeezed them gently. "Is that what you want me to do? Do you want me to bail out your new lover?"

Her head jerked to the side with a small, quick movement, as if she'd felt a sharp blow. She had an impulse to gasp but realized that she wasn't really surprised. "How did you know?"

"You're not half as mysterious as you think. Actually, Mara, you're not mysterious at all. Sorry to disillusion you. In case you've forgotten, we were supposed to be getting married. Were you planning to come back?"

"Not right now."

"Ever?"

"Maybe not."

"Well, then. I guess it could have been anyone. Not just your architect."

"You're wrong, Dan, it wasn't like that. I wasn't looking for anything like this to happen."

"Oh, I think you were, one way or the other. You have been for a long time. It's just that you're the last to know. You're not very perceptive about yourself."

"I'm sorry I'm so transparent."

A grimace flickered over Dan's face. "I didn't do anything to deserve this."

"I know that. I know you didn't. You're innocent in all this."

"Am I?" Dan half laughed. "I never thought of that, of innocence. I just felt stupid."

"I wanted to tell you. I would have, but I didn't know how."

"What would you have said?"

"Dan, I don't know."

"Tell me. I want to know. Tell me about him."

"I couldn't."

"I want to know. Tell me."

"In some ways he's a lot like you. Maybe you should be flattered. You'd admire him. He's dedicated and ambitious, and yet he has this vision, this dream of enriching peoples' lives."

Dan laughed. "I would have expected the opposite. Some stay-at-home type, a cozy domestic partner."

"No, he's unique, he's like Cliff House, like everything I've said about the project—visionary and unique."

He inhaled. "You're heading for a big letdown. I think you're confusing the man with his dreams. No, we're not the same type. I'm not a dreamer. I'll fight to get you back. I'll do anything."

"Why can't you let it go, Dan? Let's both be honest: I'm not that special. I never understood why you wanted me so much. I never trusted you, thinking I was so special."

"I don't know what I did to make you so determined to hurt me, but you're doing a good job. You're the most special thing in the world to me, and this man doesn't know the first thing about you, has no idea what you're capable of. I should never have pushed this marriage. You hate making decisions."

"But I made a decision. I came here. I chose a new life. I chose to want something else."

"What you mean is, you tried to find someone new to take care of you."

"I'm taking care of myself."

"Oh? How are you doing that?"

"I'm writing. I'm going to sell articles."

"Unfinished articles? You've been telling me that for years. I've never seen a finished piece."

"I'm a good writer."

"That's easy to say."

"I'll find other work in the meantime, if I have to. I've always found other work."

"Exactly—other work that kept you from what you say you really want to do. I know you blame me, Mara, I know you think I kept you from this great work of yours, but I never did. You stopped yourself. You could have finished dozens of articles in the time I've known you."

"All right, maybe I let things get in my way, but I won't anymore."

"Have you finished this piece?"

"We're not really talking about articles, are we, Dan?"

"Oh, now I'm the bully. The villain. That's how you want it. I'm the villain, keeping you from the work you love."

"Don't mock me."

"I'm not mocking."

"You say I've found excuses for my life, and I'm saying that's what I want to change."

"I see you trying to exchange me for someone else, thinking you automatically become a better person. Is that it? And you're going to work hard enough to afford the things you want, all the things you like."

"I don't need that much."

"Mara, I'm not attacking you. I'm saying I know you. I know what you are, what you need, what you'll settle for. Just like I know why you need this . . . this distraction right now."

She bristled. "You know, Dan, I think you're right. I was scared of marrying you. I was afraid of settling for less than I wanted. I wanted something more. I wanted to love someone the way I never loved you."

He cupped the back of her head, pulling her to him roughly. "You don't know what you're talking about."

She pushed against him. "I'm not coming back."

"I love you. That's the only reason I ever wanted you."

"I'm sorry."

He released her abruptly. "Stop saying that. Stop apologizing. I miss you, and I want you to come back with me."

"I can't."

"There's nothing for you here. Nothing that you don't already have."

"If everything was so perfect, Dan, why did you suddenly need to marry me now, after all these years? You didn't suddenly love me more."

"Why do you think?"

"I think you were embarrassed. I think times changed and we got older, and you found it embarrassing socially."

"Is that your excuse? You think I didn't take you seriously enough? I hurt your feelings—Is that what this is all about?"

"You don't even listen."

"I listen. I hear you saying it would be simple if that were true. And you like things simple. But it isn't that easy. You have to decide."

"I decided. I'm staying here."

Dan took a sip of his drink, studied the glass, and set it carefully on the table. He drew his thumb through the beaded moisture on the outside of the glass, rotated it, and drew his thumb around it again, leaving a black ring. The drops of displaced water slid down the sides of the glass, pooling on the coffee table. Automatically Mara slipped a clean ashtray under the glass to protect the table. Dan shook his head, bemused and despairing.

He pulled out his checkbook and slapped it once against his palm. He leaned forward and wrote, drawing in his breath sharply as he signed the check.

"I'm giving you the money," he said.

"What money?"

"The money you need for Cliff House. As an investment." He slid the check in front of her. "You fill in the amount. I don't care how much."

"You're crazy."

"I don't care how much. I've done my own investigating. It's a great location. With the right management it can't miss. Anyway, I'm willing to speculate." He tapped the check with his fingertips. "This is the price. Enough money to finish Cliff House. And you come back with me. That's the deal."

She had an impulse to laugh. "That's insane."

"It's a good deal," he said mildly. "I'm investing in you. Think of it as an advance, what you would have cost me over a lifetime together."

"You can't buy me."

"Did you really think I'd let you go?" He reached over suddenly,

138

loosening her hair. "I don't like this, though."

She slapped his hands away and pinned her hair back hastily. She scooped up the check and held it out to him. "Take this. It's crazy. I'm not for sale."

"Think about it. Take your time. It should appeal to you. You can always look back on this as a tragic interlude, a sweet, suffering memory. Very dramatic. You always did dramatize whenever things were dull. That's what I like about you most, I think. We're both so easily bored." Tenderly he caressed the side of her face.

She drew back. "There are other ways to get the money. There's money out there. It will come from somewhere."

"Where?"

"I don't know. Lowell knows. He may already have found new backers. Or I could try. I could find backers somewhere. I know people."

"Who?"

"People, connections. There's a doctor I met, and—" She stopped.

"You don't know anyone."

"Even if I can't help Guy, I won't walk out on him." She stood up. "I'd better leave."

He held out the check. "Take the money. Save the project. You can hold it against me for the rest of our lives. You'd like that, wouldn't you?"

"Have you gone mad?"

He got up and placed his hands around her waist. "I know you, Mara. I know it appeals to you. You'd like to save the project. You don't want him as a ruined man."

She pushed against him, but he only smiled and tightened his grip. "When the dream starts to crumble, the man has a way of crumbling, too. I know you, Mara, you don't love him, you love his dreams. You wish they were your own. You tried to make them your own. If you stop thinking of your life as a grand drama, you'd see you had an affair. That's all. An ordinary little affair. You don't like to be ordinary, so you put it in grandiose terms, saying you found a new life. But this man doesn't need you. It's his dream, not yours. You'll find out you're not needed, and where will you be? I love you, Mara. I need you."

Dan's grip loosened. She felt her certainties eroding. She sank onto the couch and Dan sat beside her, stroking her head. "Nothing has changed for me," he said. "I don't suddenly want you less. I didn't meet anyone new."

"You haven't mentioned my happiness," she said bitterly.

"Oh, happiness is it? Happiness. You think I have nothing to do with that anymore, your happiness?"

"I never loved you as much as you loved me," she said flatly. "I think you've always known that."

She heard a peculiar sound and was startled to see he was trying not to cry. She'd never seen him cry. She was frozen with a new idea; maybe he was right. Maybe she was only trying to hurt him. Maybe her idea of breaking away had been tied to a desire to break him. Was that all she wanted? To break his hold on her because she had never loved him enough to justify everything she'd taken from him? If Dan was right, then it was all a bargain. What you gave and what you took was only decided by conscience. When she totaled her debts, she owed Dan.

He burrowed his head into her shoulder, and she stroked his hair and wiped the tears from the side of his face. To her amazement she realized it wasn't impossible to think of going back to him. She already had the habit of loving him.

He fell back, stretching full length on the couch and pulling her across him. His fingers grasped and intertwined with hers. She felt raw and capable of treachery, as if Dan had become the other man and her knowledge of him was forbidden. With a mixture of horror and resignation she recognized the old force between them, tangible and undeniable. His free hand moved down her body. She reached to stop it, and her eyes locked into his and she was unable to pull hers away, as if they were bound together by their weaknesses and their failures. He did know her.

"Don't worry," he whispered. "Nothing could shock me."

"It shocks me." She pushed herself away, scrambling off the couch and straightening her clothes.

"You haven't decided anything," Dan said softly. "You don't want to admit you're capable of this, of going back to me. But you are capable of it. You've never really left. Think about it, Mara. I'll wait for you. I'll be right here."

The cab lurched, braking sharply at every corner. The streets swooped and zigzagged, ending in sudden dead ends at brick walls. The cabbie must have thought she'd enjoy the novelty of it, but in the darkness, in her agitated state of mind, it seemed only like he had made a mistake.

"Couldn't you go another way?" she complained.

The cabbie twisted in his seat to stare at her in exaggerated disbelief. "Tourists eat this up."

Mara gripped her armrest, bracing for the next sharp turn. "Forget it."

In a way she was comforted by the comic journey. It made it seem as if the night was only a nightmare and not really happening at all. But she had a lingering sense of Dan's presence, as if he had enveloped her in a layer of tainted air that she couldn't escape. The cab lurched to a stop. Lowell's house was starkly modern and impeccably kept. To her relief the ground-floor lights were still bright. She paid the driver quickly, overtipping, and hurried up the front path, feeling furtive as she rang the doorbell.

Lowell's shirt was eased open at the neck, but otherwise he was fully dressed. He drew back in surprise. "Mara! What are you doing here so late?"

"Can I come in?"

"Of course." He stepped aside, waving her past. Inside, the house was modern and spare, expensively furnished but somehow impersonal. The living room was littered with stacks of papers.

"You're working late," she said. Her voice sounded strained. "At least I didn't wake you." Lowell was gazing at her peculiarly, and she lifted a hand to straighten her hair, giving him a forced smile.

"Sit down." He swept a pile of folders off the couch and motioned her over, slipping the folders into an open desk drawer.

Mara perched on the edge of the couch, rocking slightly, her hands clasped tightly together.

"You need a drink." Without asking what she wanted, Lowell poured out a whiskey and soda. She took it obediently, sipping it gratefully, imagining it was a purifying liquid.

"I'm not sure why I came here."

He pulled out a desk chair and swung it around to face the sofa. Mara cupped her hands around her drink and finished it off. "You don't seem very surprised to see me. I guess I am the type to barge in, unannounced."

"Is this about Julia?"

"Julia?" She blinked. "I'd almost forgotten about that." She laughed weakly. "This is some night. But maybe that's the answer. Maybe we all go back where we started, back to our original partners. Maybe that's the answer."

"I don't follow you."

"Dan Wallace is in town. He offered to finance the project if I go back to him."

She got up unsteadily, went to the bar, and poured herself another drink.

"Whoa," Lowell cautioned. "You'll knock yourself out."

"Oblivion sounds pretty good right now." Mara took a sip off the top, filled the glass back up, and carried it carefully to the couch.

"It's a lot of money," Lowell said. "Does he have it?"

"He has it." Mara lifted the glass to the light, trying to see through the whiskey. "I don't trust myself, Lowell. I don't know if I've made it all up."

"Made what up?"

"Loving Guy. Loving Cliff House. Dan sees me as some sort of parasite, living on borrowed dreams. I'm not sure he isn't right. I have a terrible feeling he's right." She shut her eyes and gulped at her drink.

Lowell brushed the back of his head with one hand, then sat beside her. She shifted slightly away from him. "Don't—I'm not a very nice person, Lowell. And I'm a coward. I thought I left Dan, but it seems I forgot to tell him. Then I wormed my way into Guy's life, trying to be important, and managed to ruin everything for him, ruin his life's dream."

"Are you saying you want to go back to Dan?"

"I don't know. I would, if it would save Guy. It sure couldn't hurt him." She slumped against the couch. "I don't know anything, Lowell—you tell me what I want. Hell, it's all business, isn't it? And all's fair in love and business. I should take the money. Guy needs it. You need it." She shut her eyes again. "Besides, I deserve Dan." She laughed. "We're both rotten."

"I find you very touching."

"I find me pathetic."

She moved restlessly to the fireplace. Crumpled papers were

mounded over a bed of kindling. "Were you going to light a fire? It's chilly tonight."

Lowell pulled several logs from a brass bin and arranged them on top of the papers. He struck a match and touched it to the kindling, and bright flames leapt up. Mara knelt in front of them, rubbing her hands together.

"At least Dan answered my question," she said.

"Which question?"

"Was all this too good to be true? Finding Guy, and his work, finding Cliff House." She glanced at Lowell shyly. "It was too good to be true." She stood abruptly.

"Let me make a suggestion," Lowell said. "Forget Dan's offer. It's passion talking, an easy promise. He could take it back tomorrow. Don't tell Guy about it, just get away."

"I'm afraid." She dropped her head into her hands. "I don't deserve Guy."

"Don't put him on a pedestal. You'll be disappointed."

"That's what Dan said."

"And don't judge yourself too harshly." He paused. "Give me some time. In a few days this will all be straightened out."

"It's not that easy, Lowell. It's not the same now. Dan was smart, coming here with his offer. He knows I was tempted. He knows I'll never be sure of myself now, if I'm doing the right thing or doing it for the right reasons. To give Guy up would be noble, and I'm not noble. I never have been."

"No one is." Lowell poured himself a drink. "Listen to me, Mara, nothing happened tonight. You were tempted and you said no. We've all been tempted and you're no different from any of us."

"Guy is different."

"Offer Guy the money." Lowell sounded mildly annoyed. "Go ahead, see what he says."

"He wouldn't take it—if he knew I'd gone back to Dan for it, he'd burn that money."

Lowell poked the fire. "You go up to Mendocino. Forget about the money, forget about Cliff House. Guy's had a severe disappointment, and he doesn't handle disappointments well. He doesn't need to be disappointed in you, too."

She walked over to him and leaned her head against his back. "You make it sound so easy."

"You make it too complicated."

"Lowell"—her words were muffled against him—"what if I lie? What if I tell Dan I'll go with him and take his money but stay here instead? Would that be terrible?"

Lowell laughed. "You amaze me. You'd do it, too, wouldn't you? It wouldn't work. Dan would cancel payment. You'd never get the money."

"Of course not. You must be shocked that I even asked."

He turned, and she slipped her arms around him briefly, taking comfort in his acceptance of her.

"Does Guy know where you are?"

"No. He wasn't home when I left."

Lowell dialed Guy's number. Mara heard the phone ring repeatedly on the other end. Lowell hung up. "I think I know where to find him," he said.

He fetched Mara's purse from the floor by the couch and slung the strap over her shoulder, leading her to the door. "Tomorrow morning, you'll go to Mendocino. If things work out, this crisis will be over by the time you get back."

In the middle of the abandoned site, Guy sat silently in his car. Behind him, the occasional whoosh of a car down the esplanade highway was muted by the louder and more incessant roar of waves crashing against the rocks below. Before him, the large construction crane, a long girder hanging from its jaws, stood like some ungainly prehistoric giant savoring its prey. Beside the crane, his building, barely started, seemed to glow in silhouette against the sunset sky.

Occasionally the barking of the sea lions on the rocks below threatened to override the gentle thunder of the surf. Or perhaps he only imagined their barking, and it was some pounding in his own head that he heard, some insistent and unwanted thought begging to be acknowledged.

Unfinished, the structure had all the majesty and grandeur he would have wished; all the power and dignity that the site deserved. Perhaps this was the way his Cliff House should remain; as raw as girders soaring against a night sky, a rude slash of a man's intentions and nothing more—not the certain disappointment sure to follow, because, after all, a building, no matter how majestically conceived, was always eventually limited by the prosaic needs and demands of those who would use it. The dream was always dulled by the never-ending details, by the placement of heating ducts and adequate ventilation and insulation and plumbing and electrical outlets and everything up to code so that people could enjoy the comforts of home, their necessary but so unmajestic comforts of efficient storage space and proper sanitation. But all that really mattered, all anyone could hope to create, was this, that which was already before him, majestic and raw and brutal against the sky; as glorious as the site itself. A tribute. A tribute that made him dream undreamed of possibilities. And all the more ironic, because the sweet beginning before him was already tinged by the specter of his certain ruin.

His right hand gripped a takeout container of coffee. A licorice stick drooped over one side. Mechanically he lifted the cup to his mouth, blowing a thin stream of cool air across the open rim before taking another sip. Cooling and sipping, cooling and sipping, he raised and lowered the cup with his right hand while his left hand fondled the steering wheel, gripping and loosening, gripping and loosening, in a steady but separate rhythm from the rhythm of the hand that raised the cup. Unconscious of the stinging burn of the coffee, unconscious of his hands or of their steady, opposing rhythms, he stared at the dark skeleton of his building, barely begun and already abandoned, a stately ruin atop a lonely cliff.

Lowell parked outside the fence. The sound of the car door slamming was lost in the roar of the waves. A fog bank hung low over the cliffs. There were no stars to be seen. Mara shivered as she and Lowell walked side by side through the main gate. On the site, the security lights pierced the fog dimly. Mara grasped Lowell's arm, stumbling over coils of cables and scraps of lumber. Lowell halted, and Mara saw that Guy was just ahead of them, standing next to his car, gazing toward Cliff House. Lowell drew his arm away from hers and gave her a gentle push. Mara turned back, watching as Lowell disappeared into the fog. When she turned back, facing Guy, he was watching her, his unbuttoned coat blowing gently in the chilly wind. She walked to him slowly and began to fasten the buttons. He grabbed a handful of her hair and pulled her against him, murmuring against her hair.

"Know any spells to break a curse?"

Twelve

THE CAR SWUNG INTO another of Route 1's sudden curves, heading north. It was a glorious day. Away from San Francisco's cloud banks, the sky was clear and sunny and the air surprisingly warm. The vista beyond the highway was wide and commanding, with a peculiar gentleness. Golden mounded hills rolled into the distance, dotted with stiff green bushes standing primly upright. Each bush cast its own separate shadow, a distinct disc of shade against the gold grass. Compared to the tangled, lush and dense green foliage of the East, this landscape was calm and composed, warm and dry and clean, low-lying and compact and neat.

Guy eased the car through the curve. There was an unexpected drop in road level, and Mara reached out, straight-armed against the dashboard, to steady herself.

"You shouldn't do that," Guy admonished. "If we ever hit something and you did that, you'd break your arm."

"It's a reflex. A self-protective reflex."

Mara glanced past Guy and the outside lane of traffic to the sea beyond. Her stomach lurched and tightened. Although they were on the inside lane and nowhere near the edge of the highway, she felt precarious, as if the car were riding a thin crest and could easily and unexpectedly plunge over the cliffs and down to the rocks and water below.

The sudden lurching turns accented her anxiety. There was no shoulder on either side of the road, and no barriers to separate them from the sometimes shocking slope down to the sea.

146

"I thought you wanted to see Route 1," Guy said.

"I did."

The car swung into the next curve, and Mara shut her eyes against a spurt of dizziness. She opened them again to the sight of a placid ocean. Still, her throat tightened. "I didn't expect it to be as bad as its reputation. I'm not used to such curves. Could you slow down some more?"

"There are people behind me. I can't go any slower."

"You could be the slowest car on the road. Someone has to. There's nothing wrong with being cautious."

"I've driven this road a thousand times. I'm not planning on driving us over the edge."

Nervously Mara wet her lips. "I'm sorry. I don't know why I'm so scared."

"Exposure," Guy said. "Mountain climbers call it exposure."

"What's that?" she asked.

"Sudden fear of open spaces. Lots of climbers get it. I've had it."

"While you were driving?"

"No. But it happened to me once on a construction site. There was a wooden plank that spanned a foundation trench. I'd walked back and forth over that plank all day, but one time, all of a sudden, I happened to glance down. We're only talking eight or ten feet here, but I looked down and suddenly I couldn't move. I'll never forget that feeling. My legs really went rubbery. Someone pulled me off the plank. For the rest of the day I had to go around the far side of the site to get into the building. I tried to talk myself out of it, but nothing helped. That's exposure—you don't sense the ground you're standing on. We're on high ground here, and to one side there's a huge drop. It's the openness that's getting to you."

"I feel sick."

"Your equilibrium is off. Ignore it. It's just one of those things. You feel the most at risk when there's the least chance of harm."

Guy eased the car into the wide curve of a shallow basin. Mara pressed her right foot forward, as if she were pressing down the brake. They had reached a point where the road curved back on itself. Directly across from them, on the opposite side of the horseshoe-shaped basin made by the coastline, Mara saw a truck pinned crazily on the rough weeds of the hillside embankment. It clung to the side of the hill as if frozen in a slow-motion fall. The cab was jackknifed at a sharp, impossible angle away from the long trailer, and it seemed as if a strong gust of wind might send it hurtling to the rocks below.

Guy glanced over his shoulder to see where she was staring. "Look at that." He whistled softly. "Must have happened last night. You hate to see a driver miss the curve."

"This is not comforting to me."

"We're in no danger. This car maneuvers a lot better than any truck. But you can't compare the view."

"I think I've had enough view."

Guy was silent a moment. "I get the feeling something else is bothering you—besides the driving." He gave her a searching look and she dropped her eyes.

"Nothing else is bothering me." She sensed Guy's eyes on her and felt as precarious as the fallen truck, as if she were balancing on a thin line between the lies she had told and the truths she had aimed for, caught between wanting to help Guy but hurting him instead. She felt turned around and unsure of herself, and her fear of the road's tortuous curves seemed to be an expression of her larger fears. Every word of her conversation with Dan the night before came back to her, and in the light of day, carefully considered, his arguments sounded more convincing, more truthful than her own.

An exit loomed ahead, and with a sudden, sickening swerve Guy took it. Mara hung on to her door handle as they spun off the exit onto a deserted-looking road. Guy pulled into the weeds on the side of the road and turned off the motor. The buzzing, grinding sound of insects filled the air. There were no buildings in sight, and no other cars in either direction, only dry fields spreading to either side around them.

Now that they had stopped, the heat was intense. Guy lowered his window, and the pulsing drone of the insects swelled and ebbed inside the car, as thick as the heat.

"We could turn back," he said.

Mara turned her eyes away, unable to answer. She felt a deep uneasiness and tried to empty her mind of any thoughts. After the night's swift decisions she felt weak and formless, with fresh uncertainties. She was afraid of what might happen once they got to Men-docino but had no idea why.

"If we turn back, we'll have to drive in the outside lane."

"Are you that scared of the driving?"

Her voice barely cut through the drone of the insects. "I forget, sometimes, that we're just starting out. Sometimes I feel I know you as well as I know myself. But I couldn't. No one knows another person that well. No one really knows another person at all, or what they're capable of."

"You know me," Guy said.

"I know *about* you. But people aren't just facts."

"You knew me the first day we met. You knew exactly what to expect from me. You know me now; you just have to trust yourself."

"It's not that simple." The dread moved up from her stomach and gathered in her throat. She forced herself to breathe over it.

"I just wonder," Guy said softly, "if the project fails, if I've blown the whole thing, which would be worse—what I'd think of myself or what you'd think of me?"

No answer seemed safe. "Tell me about Julia," she said abruptly, surprising herself. "You've never said anything about her. Hiding someone is like a confession."

"She's no threat to you. I don't even like her much. Julia is the type who needs to own things, exotic things, including people. She loves artists and musicians and creative types, anyone the least unusual in her eyes. She collects them. She didn't marry me so much as collect me. Then she found out I wasn't so exotic."

"And now she wants you back?"

He looked at her queerly. "Maybe once but not now. Not anymore."

"Do you mean 'not anymore' because I'm here? Because of me?"

"Well, she's no good at sharing. But more because she doesn't need me anymore."

"Needing isn't the same as wanting."

"Forget about Julia. She doesn't matter now. The only thing that matters now is fixing the harm she's done."

"Lowell can do that, can't he?"

"If anyone can." Guy paused. "I never asked what you were doing with him so late last night."

Mara forced a smile. "Well, I didn't have a better offer."

Guy took it as a reprimand. "Once this is all settled, one way or the other, I'll be around more."

"Once you're working again, I won't mind seeing you less."

"Never less." He folded her hands into his. "Never less, I promise. Don't be so afraid."

He put the car in gear and swerved it in an erratic U-turn, bumping down the road before accelerating into the curves of the highway.

A discrete sign, fancifully lettered THE FARMHOUSE, pointed down a long, graveled drive bordered with spreading eucalyptus trees. The wide lawns were dappled with sunlight and sloped toward the sea. At the center of the compound, between the main building and the cottages tucked among more eucalyptus, mild-mannered deer grazed peacefully. Squat white ducks ruffled their feathers and beat their wings, their quacks punctuating the dull background roar of the waves.

Guy pulled around the circular drive and stopped in front of the main building. Two stories high, of weathered clapboard with a trim chimney and crisp shutters and wide, deep porches, it looked like a perfectly preserved New England farmhouse, homey and welcoming. Instinctively Mara knew it was the wrong place for them. They needed lights and movement, noise and activity around them, a blinding swirl that might envelop them. Here, their own thoughts and feelings were too exposed. It would take an effort to pretend things were normal.

Guy greeted the desk clerk with forced cheerfulness. The woman responded effusively.

"I'm Sonia, your hostess. Welcome to The Farmhouse." Her blond head bobbed in approval. "You have reservations?"

Mara let Guy take care of the arrangements while she looked the place over. The downstairs room was decorated like an old-fashioned parlor. There were comfortable couches and a scattering of rocking chairs. A deep brick fireplace centered on one wall. There was an upright piano and an old-fashioned phonograph. Books filled the bookcases and plants stood atop every available surface. A lone guest sat at a sunny window, reading.

"Have you stayed with us before?" Sonia asked. "No? Well, let me tell you about the amenities." Her head nodded a vigorous accompaniment. "You'll be staying in a bungalow, and, of course, every bungalow had an ocean view. There are no phones or televisions, though there is a phone in the lounge in case of emergencies. Are you anticipating any emergencies?" Sonia nodded at her routine joke. "Of course not. You can take your meals in our dining room, or of course, try the restaurants in town. Mendocino itself is about five miles away. Well, that's about it, unless you have any questions."

They had none, and Sonia assigned them to a bungalow, handed them keys and brochures, and wished them a pleasant stay.

As promised, the bungalow was charming. The small front room was taken up by a flowered sofa and matching armchair, reading lamps, and wicker baskets filled with magazines. In the bedroom a double bed was covered with a thick comforter. White, ruffled curtains hung at the windows, and a crock filled with fresh flowers perched on the chest of drawers. A rocking chair angled invitingly toward the view. An ocean breeze chilled the room, and Guy moved past Mara to shut the window.

Mara put her suitcase on a wooden chest at the foot of the bed. "It's lovely," she said dutifully.

Guy swung his suitcase up next to hers. "Let's unpack later," he suggested.

"What do you want to do now?"

Guy held out his hand. "Let's go for a walk."

Mara looked at his hand with misgivings, imagining it leading her to a path along the sea, where their conversation would lead directly into her guilty conscience.

"I'd rather drive into town."

In town there would be bustling crowds; the crowds would lift her mood and distract Guy, she thought. She was right. The happy little town was crowded with weekend tourists. Clumps of people clotted the wooden sidewalks, browsing and chatting. Teenage boys stopped to taunt teenage girls; the girls giggled coyly and hurried ahead, waiting for the boys to catch up. Older couples strolled arm in arm, bickering gently in front of shop windows. Families nudged their reluctant children into cafés and boutiques, while toddlers

151

grabbed expectantly at the colored balloons and banners and swirling pinwheels tacked onto porch rails and balustrades.

The town itself was like a tiny New England crazy quilt. The houses clustered together—miniature Victorians with gay paint highlighting intricate designs; saltboxes with their distinctive, steeply slanting roofs; and prim Cape Cod cottages painted white with weathered trim in green or black, their crooked shutters bordering window boxes that overflowed with flowers and vines trailing onto the ground.

Mara and Guy moved restlessly among the crowds, unmoved by the profusion of craft shops and galleries, the old-fashioned general store and quaint cafés, until Guy suddenly pulled her to a halt outside an antique store. Its window was crammed with Victoriana, and the centerpiece of the display was an elaborate Victorian dress, a masterpiece of intricate lace and soft, billowing fabric.

"It's you," Guy said. "I'm buying it."

"Oh, no, Guy."

He reached behind her head to hold her hair up in the back, squinting his eyes. "What happened to that other hairstyle?"

"Nothing. I got tired of it, I guess."

"With your hair this way, you'd look great in that dress." Guy pulled her into the shop, asking the clerk, a short woman in a peasant skirt and blouse, to take the dress from the window. The clerk glanced at Mara's slim figure with tired eyes.

"You're just small enough," she said. "Not everyone could wear that. And it's in beautiful condition."

Ignoring Mara's protests, the shopkeeper climbed into the window, pushing aside vases and shawls and a stack of picture frames.

"Let's go, Guy," Mara whispered. "I don't want it."

"I want you to try it on."

The woman lifted the dress from its metal stand and climbed out of the window, holding the dress carefully. She lifted it against Mara, cocking her head to one side. "Definitely." She eyed Mara's antique earrings. "See? You already have jewelry to match. Go on, try it." She pointed toward a cubicle draped with velvet curtains that served as a dressing room.

"I'd rather not," Mara said firmly.

The woman held a fold of material out to Guy, urging him to

feel the fabric. "Beautiful condition and first-quality. Only the best things last, you know. No one saves ordinary clothes. This dress was special to someone."

"I'm going outside," Mara said. The woman's insistence and the closeness inside the shop were suffocating her. "I don't need the dress."

Outside on the sidewalk, she pushed her way to a clearing by the fence and leaned against it, feeling upset without fully knowing why. Her annoyance at the saleswoman was already fading. She recognized that it wasn't the hard sell that had upset her but the fact that Guy hadn't listened to her protests. She didn't want Guy to buy her the dress. Vaguely she felt that the ties between them were breaking, and it seemed wrong to add a new tie, even one as insubstantial as the gift of a filmy white dress. She felt a sense of alarm. She hadn't concocted any plan, nothing she could have put into words, but in the back of her mind there was an awareness that she was on the verge of taking some action that would prove irrevocable. She was frightened by herself, by not knowing what she was about to do, yet feeling certain that something would happen.

Guy appeared in a moment, carrying a shopping bag with the white dress inside. "What's with you?" he asked irritably.

"I just don't need a dress. It was probably overpriced."

"It's done, so forget about it."

"I'm sorry. I don't know what's wrong with me. I don't really feel that well."

"You look kind of pale. There's a tea shop—let's get you some tea. And don't say no."

Heavy lace curtains shielded the quiet room from the fading afternoon sun. A table by the wall emptied, and Guy set the dress on an empty chair and pulled out two chairs for them. A waiter appeared with handwritten menus. Guy scanned his quickly. "The tea for two," he ordered.

"People always get a kick out of that," the waiter said, grinning.

"I'll bet they do." Guy turned the menu over. On the back was a handwritten summary of the history of Mendocino. Idly he read it out loud. "Mendocino, originally known as Mieggsville, after 'Honest Harry' Meiggs, who established here the first sawmill in Northern California. When Honest Harry absconded to South

America with his fortune, leaving the mill bankrupt, the town changed its name to Mendocino." Guy scowled cynically. "There's a pretty story. Honest Harry is a thief. Nothing's changed, I guess. People were never honest."

It took an effort for Mara to make conversation. Her head had begun aching, and she leaned it against her hand. "What put you in a bad mood?"

"This town, I guess."

"The town? I thought it would cheer you up. It's the kind of place you love—human and quaint and intimate." She suppressed a shudder.

The waiter set a ceramic teapot in front of them, along with an elaborate plate of breads and cakes.

"Let's have some good old honest tea," Guy joked.

"I'm not very hungry."

"Then just have tea. You look like you need it."

She made a show of buttering a muffin and washed it down with tea that was still too hot to drink.

Guy stretched an arm along the wide windowsill, peering at the people jostling past on the narrow sidewalks.

"But it's sad," he said, speaking quietly, almost as if he didn't care if she heard. "Anyplace like this, any little downtown or side street with some kind of charm, or what people *call* charm—any kind of distinct design is what they mean—is immediately branded a tourist spot, as if it's a given that we can't expect this in our regular lives. No, we expect to live in nameless, faceless, meaningless places, as if that's what life is all about. Take anyplace with distinction, think about it, any town or neighborhood that people like to go to because it feels good to be there, well, that proves it, doesn't it? We need this, we crave special places. We make them into minor shrines, and all they are is the way every place should be." His fingertips drummed against the windowsill.

"I saw a photo the other day—downtown Moscow, I think it was. All modern apartments and office buildings. Big, bland rectangles, what we call modern. What a disservice that label is. You couldn't tell Moscow from Cincinnati. What's the point? Why travel anywhere if it's all the same? And that's what we're getting to, everything being the same.

154

"The next time I have to give a talk somewhere, I'm going to do a slide show—the most exotic cities in the world, and you know what? You won't be able to tell them apart. Rio, Lisbon, Bangkok, they'll all look the same, a world filled with Holiday Inns. What's the point? All the garbage talk of stealing from the past, like it was some great sin—well, musicians use notes, don't they, over and over, the same notes for centuries, and we speak with words that evolve slowly, but by and large they're the same words, and no one says throw out the notes, create new words, they've been used before. It's a language, and architecture is another language. A porch is a porch, not a criminal throwback to some ignominious past. Not a sin. A porch or a turret or a window lintel—they're just words, notes, a part of the language. Why not use it again and again? There's no shame in perpetuating something that works. We don't have to reinvent the language every time we speak, so why this ban against repeating a style that works? Especially when the choice is between something human, something that speaks to us, or something bland or harsh or anonymous? We really got off the track."

He finished his tirade, his mouth tight, his fingers still drumming on the windowsill. She thought he was merely throwing up a wall of words, separating them, hiding behind it. They drank tea in silence until the waiter put their check on the table. Guy paid, weighing the money down with the teapot.

"Ready?"

They walked back through the town to the parked car. Once in the bungalow again, Guy gave her an apologetic look. "Sorry, this weekend wasn't supposed to be a punishment. Let's try to save it."

"I want to. I want to be with you. It's just that—"

He covered her mouth with his, as if he wanted to stop her from saying things he didn't want to hear. She knew she should push him away, but there was sweet comfort in the way he held on to her, crushing her to him. There was comfort and an edge of desperation in the way his hands stroked restlessly across her back, the way his cheek rubbed against hers as he murmured her name and kissed the side of her face and her neck and throat, as if he drew comfort from the feel of her, too.

"I want us to be happy together," he whispered.

"Oh, Guy, I *am* happy with you."

"I need you, Mara." He kissed her throat over and over again while she cradled his head in her hands. "There's only you . . . only you."

She clung to him, taking reassurance from his tenderness. Her mind was silent now, her fears and misgivings stifled by the sweetness of being with him. He could make her feel that everything was going to be all right. There were no barriers between them, no history of disappointments or shortcomings. Guy was everything she'd always wanted, and this moment, with its soft, lingering touches, was like a confirmation that everything she'd once thought impossible really was possible. He bent her backward, leading her toward the bedroom, and she went with him gladly, forgetting herself, forgetting everything.

The sound of a car driving past the bungalow roused her. She leaned up on one elbow. Guy was alert beside her on the bed, watching her with an amused, but tender, smile.

"Was I sleeping?" she asked.

"Just for a little while. We both kind of drifted off." He brushed her hair back from her forehead, leaning over her as if to kiss her awake.

She turned her head. "Don't, Guy."

"What's wrong?"

She shook her head. All the doubts had flooded back, coupled with a new sense of confusion. She loved him, yet she was the worst kind of fraud; leading him on, wanting him, having him while the only answer for them was for her to break away, to leave him.

"Guy, I . . . I really need some time alone. Just a few minutes. I'd like to take a walk."

"I'll come with you."

"No, I need to be by myself."

"I don't want you to go, Mara."

"But I'm not going anywhere. It's just a walk. I'll be back soon, and then I'll feel better. I'm sure. Then we'll go out and have a nice evening. I promise."

She slid from the bed, grabbing her scattered clothes. She took them into the bathroom, dressing hurriedly.

156

Guy looked at her oddly when she emerged. "Don't take too long," he said.

"I won't. Just a few minutes," she promised. "Guy, I'm sorry. I'm sorry for the way I'm acting. I didn't mean to be—" She stopped, unable to think of the right words. With a helpless, apologetic look she left the bungalow.

Mara took the path that led past the main house to the cliffs over-looking the ocean. When she was directly behind the main house and couldn't be seen from the bungalow, she cut back across the lawn, entering the house from the back porch. At the desk, Sonia seemed happy to see her. Mara asked for the telephone, and Sonia's face crinkled with expectation. "Nothing serious, I hope?"

"A small emergency."

Sonia led her to a short hallway where a closet had been con-verted into a phone booth. An old-fashioned wooden wall phone had been remodeled to accommodate a push-button dial. Sonia waited until Mara assured her that she was fine. She pulled the door shut and dialed Lowell's number. His answering machine was on; he had already gone. She hung up without leaving a message. She hesitated, then called Suzanne, making an effort to speak gaily, as if nothing were wrong.

"How are you?" Suzanne demanded. "I tried calling Guy's, but you'd already left. What's happening?"

"Nothing. I don't know. We just got to Mendocino," Mara said. "Did Lowell call?"

"Lowell? No. Was he supposed to?"

"I just thought he might have."

"How did Guy take it, about Dan being in town?"

"I didn't tell him."

"Well, what did Dan want, as if I didn't know?"

"He was trying to make things difficult."

"Did he?"

Mara was silent a moment. "You were right, Suzanne—I should have cut it off before I came out here. I guess I was fooling myself—again."

Suzanne was silent for a moment. "What are you going to do now?" she finally asked.

"We have a concert tonight."

"Well, try to make it through the weekend."

"I'll try. Suzanne . . . never mind. 'Bye."

Mara nodded to Sonia, went out by the back porch, and looped around the house to the side path, as if she hadn't been in the main house at all. She walked to the ocean overlook, spending longer than she realized staring out at the sea.

Back in the bungalow, she heard the shower running. The white dress was spread out on the bed, the arms arranged in a gesture of welcome. She pulled it over her head, and it fit perfectly, clinging and skimming over her body. Pinning her hair loosely into the old-fashioned style, she pivoted in front of the dresser mirror. The bathroom door opened and Guy came out, wrapped in a towel, catching her reflection in the mirror.

"Wow, that looks great." He bent and kissed her neck. "How was your walk? Do you feel better now?"

She rested her face against his chest, closing her eyes. "I don't want to lose you," she whispered.

He kissed the top of her head, holding her extra tightly for a moment. "I'll be ready in a minute," he said.

"Take your time. I'm going to shower, too, and put on fresh makeup." She opened her suitcase, digging out underclothes and toiletries and cosmetics. She felt suddenly gay and lighthearted. The rituals of bathing and dressing gave her something to look forward to, something normal and familiar that she could take comfort in. When she finally emerged with her hair and dress and jewelry perfectly arranged, approval shone in his eyes.

He bowed and offered his arm. "To dinner, madam?"

Mara dropped a curtsy. "Anywhere but here. I couldn't bear Sonia beaming at us."

They drove past the main house like conspirators and found a restaurant with a view of the shoreline, not far from the music festival, where they had tickets for the evening concert. Guy ordered extravagantly, and the waiter kept their wine glasses filled. Their only topic of conversation was the food they were eating, and they ordered more courses than they could finish, as if to avoid topics that existed outside the meal. Yet with each course Mara felt her gaiety becoming more strained.

When the meal finally ended, they found a path that wandered along the edge of the cliffs. A strain of music floated past. At the same time a brightly striped tent appeared ahead.

"The festival must have started already," Guy said. "We'd better hurry."

The drifting notes of music became more frequent as they neared the tent, competing with the sounds of the sea. A sea gull's cry was interspersed with a strain of melody; a sudden, thunderous chord was nearly lost in an equally sudden crash of waves on the rocks below.

The path narrowed, squeezing between clumps of sea grass and scratchy, nettlelike bushes. The breeze off the shore was brisk, and Guy pulled Mara to his side, trailing one hand over her shoulder, as if to warm her. His hand rose and lingered, stroking the back of her neck and caressing the tendrils of hair that had escaped their pins. He turned her to face him, and his hand stroked the side of her face and moved toward her lips.

She shivered involuntarily—Dan had touched her that way only the night before. She caught Guy's hand, stopping it, holding on to keep it from touching her again. He stared at her.

"I guess it's the curse," he finally said. "The curse of Cliff House is on us." He was only half joking. "I'm losing you and I don't know why. I don't want to lose you."

"Guy, if you had to lose something, which would you choose— Cliff House or me?"

"That's a crazy question."

"It's the only question."

"I can't answer that."

"Then I'll answer for you. You'd choose to lose me, not Cliff House."

"What are you talking about?"

"I'm talking about everything that's been wrong between us. There's a lie here, my lie, and it's been growing all along. I see what it is now. It's that if I really loved you, I'd want what's best for you. Wanting you is selfishness, but giving you Cliff House, that's what's best for you. I see it now. This is all about truth, Guy. I've always wanted things to be easy. I always let someone make things easy for me. When I met you, I was pretending to manage on my own, but all I did was transfer my needs to you, hoping you'd manage for

159

me. I'm always letting someone else straighten out the messes I make, letting them make things easy for me again."

"You're not making any sense."

"The thing is, you don't want me, not the truth of me. You don't see the real me. I didn't even see it. The real me is just like Julia, getting close to people who do things that matter so that I'll start to matter. But I don't matter, certainly not as much as Cliff House. Don't you see?" She grabbed his shoulders. "*I'm* the curse."

"You're crazy."

"Yes, I'm crazy. Everything would have worked out for you, but I came and interfered where I didn't belong. I tainted everything."

"You don't know what you're talking about. You don't make any sense." He began to shake her, as if he could shake out other words, words that he could understand.

"It's over now. I'm leaving, leaving you and Cliff House."

"Are you trying to break me, break all my dreams at once?"

"I'm giving you back your dreams. You said it yourself, you've said it all along. Cliff House is from your heart to your city. Julia took back her money, but I can replace that. I can get it back for you. I'll give you the money."

"You're raving. You can't get that kind of money."

"I already have it. Think of it as a wedding present, from Dan and me. We're giving it to you."

He stared at her in astonishment. She dropped her eyes.

"The truth is, I'm supposed to marry Dan, and I'm going to. I never said I wouldn't," she added quickly, before he could protest. "I said I loved you, but I never said I wouldn't marry Dan. I'm too selfish for that."

"You don't love him."

"But I do. I'm in the habit of loving him. He knows me. He knows me exactly and completely. He even said this would appeal to me, giving you up to save Cliff House. He was right; it does appeal to me. It's the one thing I can think of that will mean anything in my life. You don't know me that way. You don't know the harm I can do, the damage I've already done. This is the only way I can fix it."

"You're talking nonsense. You haven't done any harm, and you won't."

"I paid Ned Deets," she said calmly. "Not personally, but I went to Lowell and told him you were being foolish and stubborn. I told him to pay the bribe. You were right to be suspicious about it, but it wasn't Lowell's idea, it was mine. Lowell wasn't going to cross you, but I begged him. It was stupid to antagonize Deets, and it was stupid to antagonize Julia."

"I don't believe any of this."

"Yes you do. Because this answers all your questions. We're a lot alike, Lowell and I. He said that last night, and he's right, Guy. And there's another lie I told. I wasn't with Lowell all night, I was with Dan. He came to town to take me back with him. Oh, Guy—he's what I deserve—don't you see? I know I've hurt you, Guy, but you should have known. You should have seen what I was, right from the start. And there's more. I—"

"You've said enough." He grabbed her arm so tightly it hurt. She cried out, not sure if he was pulling her close or trying to push her away. Instinctively she yanked her arm from his grasp. Her foot slid on a loose stone and skidded sideways, and she lost her balance, staggering backward. For an instant she was flailing at empty space. Her heartbeat and the pounding of the surf below combined into a single pulse. She caught a glimpse of black waters swirling over villainous rocks as she began to fall. Guy lunged at her, and she clawed at the air between them in a panic. Her dress caught on a thorn. Guy pulled at her and a patch of fabric tore away. He was yelling, and then his hands were on her and she was back on the path and he was holding her, and she could feel his heart pounding. She caught her breath. Guy dropped his arms and stepped away as she tried to steady herself. He plucked the scrap of cloth from the bush and it slipped from his fingers. It caught in the breeze. It rose and hovered and then fluttered away slowly, in a lazy zigzag, down to the rocks below. They both watched it.

"We'll leave here in the morning," Guy said. "It's too late to go back now."

In the darkness of the bungalow Mara lay on the bed alone. Beyond the closed bedroom door, Guy lay on the sofa, awake or sleeping; she didn't know which. She felt she no longer had the right to know. The sound of a tinkling piano drifted in from the lounge in the main house. Someone was picking out show tunes. From time to time boisterous voices burst into bits of song, a remembered chorus here and there, lapsing into silence again until the next chorus came around.

She dozed fitfully. Her sleep swirled with images of Dan, his face and mouth and hands over her, her skin feverish as he touched her, as he pulled and pushed and tortured her to a shameful excitement. She woke with a start to find the white dress tangled and pulling at her arms. She thought she should get up and undress and wash properly, thinking that then she'd be able to fall into normal sleep, but it seemed too big an effort. Instead she lay back in the dark and was soon asleep again. She saw high cliffs and dark, swirling waters, and Cliff House battered by waves and sinking into darkness. She had a feeling of drowning and heard the crashing ocean sweeping over everything; and always in the background was the tinkling, sinister music.

When she awoke at dawn, the ocean seemed to be pounding inside her temples. Her skin was damp and chilled. She stretched her cramped hands, and her fingers were cold and her hands seemed to be numb and separate from the rest of her body. She stumbled out of the bed and went to the window and closed it, muting the sound of the ocean. She dragged the white dress off over her head, unmoved by the sound of ripping fabric, and left it in a jumble on the floor. She got back into bed, hiding herself under the blankets and sheets, wishing for more hours of darkness.

A knocking at the door woke her again. The room was filled with the hard, bright light of morning. Guy entered, fully dressed. He looked strained and unrested.

"I'm packed," he told her. "We'll leave as soon as you're ready."

"I can take a bus back."

"Get packed. I'll wait."

At his insistence they stopped for breakfast in the dining room. He said it was a long trip back, and there was no sense being hungry on top of a bad night's sleep. They each picked at their food but took extra cups of coffee. A strained truce existed between them, allowing for polite chatter and even ironic humor, as if they were new and casual acquaintances eating together for the first time.

Her mind was racing, but she was unable to concentrate and so didn't know what it was she was trying to think about. Part of her mind was disconnected, as if someone else were there, taking breakfast with him. She felt as if someone else had taken this trip and that when she got back home, she would find that nothing had happened, nothing had changed between them.

At the desk, Sonia was no longer on duty. Her replacement was a young man with a full beard and a neatly trimmed mustache who was briskly impersonal, asking only if they were leaving early because they were dissatisfied with the service. Guy answered that there was a personal emergency.

In the car, Guy checked the road map. "There's a road that cuts inland. It picks up the highway near Ukiah. You won't have to face Route 1." He handed the map to her so she could keep track of their progress.

At the beginning of the drive the road was wide and smoothly paved and the scenery was pretty. They drove through heavy woods into lumber country. The paving disappeared then, and the road became little more than a pair of dirt ruts, apparently an old logging trail. Mara scanned the map nervously to see if she had taken them in the wrong direction. But this was the only road. It widened then and picked up again as the forest thinned. They were in marijuana-growing country, Guy said. They passed dirt driveways closed off by heavy metal chains and no-trespassing signs. It was a strange community, turned in upon itself and forbidding amid the pleasant greenery, which no longer seemed pleasant, but treacherous in its lushness and somehow perverted, with an air of illegal activity. Out of nowhere they came upon an outdoor spa, an old hippie outpost of wooden saunas and meditation tanks. There were peace symbols painted on the surrounding trees.

Everything seemed strange, unfamiliar, and out of kilter. The drive seemed to be taking much longer than it should have. She checked the map again and again, but it was always the same. There was no other road.

The road climbed still higher, and the landscape changed again. The forest fell back, and they were traveling along a high, narrow ridge. Deep valleys opened out to either side of them, showing golden, rolling, mounded hills. She felt a queasy terror as they rounded a tight curve, wrapping around the mountain in a single lane. If a car came in the other direction, and assuming they stopped in time to avoid colliding head-on, one of them would have to back down the narrow, tortuous curve to let the other pass. She wished Guy would sound the horn in warning, but she was afraid to ask him to do it. He was staring grimly at the road ahead, showing none of the trepidation she felt. They passed a road sign planted in the crumbling dirt of the narrow shoulder: EROSION AREA. USE SINGLE LANE.

What had once been the outside lane was now part of the sliding embankment. Glancing out her window, the shoulder seemed to disappear completely under the car, as if there were nothing between her and the deep, open valleys. Her fear returned—exposure again—and she had to swallow repeatedly to control a wave of fear. Her heart leapt at each swerve the car made. Each adjustment of the wheel seemed to bring them to the edge of a precipice. Out her window, the ground sped past with sickening speed. "Slow down! Slow down!" she wanted to scream. The valley was less than a tire's width away. The wheels skidded over loose stones, the way her foot had skidded on the stones on the path the night before. Her stomach dropped and she had a sensation of falling. She felt the car pitch as it rushed blindly around the next curve, felt it spin out to the shoulder of the road, felt the shoulder of the road narrowing, felt the narrow strip of crumbling, eroding dirt falling away, saw it disappear, and the deep, empty valley loom closer and closer.

She grabbed the wheel, afraid he meant to kill them both. The car swerved sickeningly and skidded sideways, and Guy wrestled for control of the wheel. They came to a halt inches from the side of the precipice.

"Are you trying to kill us? Kill me?" he cried.

Her voice was pitched high, edged with panic. "We were going over the edge!"

"We were nowhere near the edge! Look!" His voice was tinged with cold fury. "Look!"

Mara raised her eyes. Ahead of the car, the road widened slightly. A road sign was planted there: SCHOOL BUS TURNAROUND.

She heard her own nauseous laughter. It wasn't possible; there couldn't possibly be room enough for a big yellow school bus to turn in that narrow, unsure space. A yellow school bus, so heavy and solid and ordinary, filled with children, was part of ordinary life. Then this wasn't a ride into terror; this was an ordinary road, high in the mountains, but ordinary and even somewhat safe, despite the crumbling lanes and posted warnings.

Guy was staring at her in disbelief. "What are you trying to do?"

"I was trying to help, to save us."

"Like you wanted me to choose between you and Cliff House? Is that your idea of helping me?"

"But I only meant . . . you don't understand. If we could only talk . . ."

"We've already talked too much."

She hesitated. "Yes. I remember what you said about severing ties. That once you're done with a person, you're really done with them. I won't talk. I won't bother you again."

He slammed the car into gear and backed it carefully onto the road, his hands tight on the steering wheel. After a distance the road dropped to level ground and became smoothly paved. A sprinkling of houses appeared, and then a sprawl of subdivisions. Billboards sprang up, then gas stations and shopping malls. The road widened into a highway, and there were four and then six lanes of traffic. Everything around them was mundane and ugly, yet familiar and comforting in its familiarity. Everything between them was changed, but everything here was the same.

Thirteen

THE HOTEL LOBBY WAS large and grand, with pink marble walls and floors carpeted in deep rose. Tall fluted columns and scattered adornments touched with gold filled the spaces between floor-to-ceiling windows framed by thick velvet drapes. The front desk, bearing enormous vases of fresh-cut flowers, was a deeply carved mahogany counter. Dan stood at the counter, his suitcase leaning at his feet. He had just finished his transaction and was bending to pick up his case, half turned toward the door, when she saw him from the entryway. He straightened and came slowly across the vast space, deliberately taking his time.

She lifted a hand in greeting but, at his look, let it drop again. He reached her but only paused momentarily, then made a move as if to go out through the main doors. She grabbed at his arm.

"Wait—what are you doing?"

"What does it look like?"

"But I'm back."

"Did you come to say good-bye?"

"No, I was . . . I'm going with you."

"Where's your suitcase?"

She had changed her clothes at Suzanne's but left her suitcase behind, thinking she and Dan could pick it up some other time.

"It's at Suzanne's. We can get it when we're ready to leave."

A look of disgust crossed his face, followed by one of quick disdain. "I'm ready now."

"But you said to take my time. You said you'd wait. You said I had

166

time to say good-bye." She was aware of people in the lobby staring at them.

Dan pushed her into a small alcove off the lobby. He threw his suitcase onto a chair. "You look like shit, you know that?" His head tossed defensively.

"What did I do, Dan? You said to take my time."

"Do you think there's a revolving door out there, Mara? You leave, then you come back, then you leave and come back again? How many times did you expect to do that?"

"You said you'd wait."

"Not this long."

"Two days! You said to take weeks. You said you'd wait."

"I didn't think you'd do it—go off with him. I can't trust you anymore, Mara. You've let me down, and it's not that easy. You can't just come back, waltz in here like . . . You can't have it both ways. Ten years, *ten years*, Mara. Doesn't that mean anything to you? You're unstable, Mara. You know that? You're unstable."

She recognized the start of a tirade and knew the best thing was to sit it out, to be patient. He would rant and rave, his anger swelling and abating, and somewhere in the midst of it would be the real point of his hurt.

"Your trouble is, you have no honor. You're cheap, Mara. In business, Mara, I may be tough, but one thing I'm proud of, damned proud of, I've always had honor. I've *always* had honor. I don't cut a deal and walk away from it."

"You said I could take time to think."

"Alone! I never said to go away with him."

She looked at him in surprise. "What difference does that make?"

"What difference does it make?" His mouth tightened and he inhaled sharply. "You know, I honor the terms of a deal, Mara. You come waltzing back in here . . ." He rubbed his hand back and forth over his hair. "Your weekend didn't work out, is that it? You changed your mind again?" His right hand clenched into a fist and smashed onto a tabletop. She jumped involuntarily. "You don't have consistency," he said, as if that were the worst that could be said of anyone.

He took a moment to gather his composure. "I couldn't believe it. I couldn't believe you went with him, actually went with him. I guess that was your answer. I guess you didn't have the courage to tell me.

But no—I take that back. You don't plan that far ahead, do you, Mara? You don't have the logic. You just go with the moment, take the easy way." He drew a long breath. "You can forget the money. You can forget the money, Mara. Or did you think you could have it both ways? Well, you can't have it like that, Mara, no one can. You have to choose, one thing or the other. Forget the money, it's not money we're talking about here. It's loyalty. Love and loyalty. But those two things mean nothing to you, do they, Mara? You could have had anything you wanted. Anything. Anything you wanted, but that wasn't enough for you."

For a moment he couldn't speak, as if his emotions were choking him. He had always hidden his strongest emotions. His fist uncurled and his hand made a listless motion, a halfhearted wave, as if brushing her away. "The point is, you didn't want me enough."

It was her turn to speak, her turn to say that she did want him. Her chance to plead and bargain and ask him to take her back.

"I did love you, Dan. I'm sorry."

"You better believe you're sorry. You wasted my time, Mara. You wasted my time. What am I supposed to do now? Where do I find someone else to love? You think this is a game, you think I'm still going to take you back. You're shocked that you came back and didn't find me with open arms. I hurt your pride. Do me a favor, Mara; when you change your mind again, leave me out of it."

He grabbed his suitcase. She tried to think of something else to say, some sentence or phrase that might salvage something out of whatever was between them. But he was already out of the alcove and across the lobby. She could see him outside, getting into the backseat of a hired car. The car pulled around the circular drive in front of the hotel and onto the side street. It paused and for a moment she thought Dan had ordered the driver to stop, to back up in the driveway, like a film playing in reverse, so they could start the scene again. But the driver was only waiting for the traffic to clear. The car pulled away, disappearing as it crested the hill at the top of the street.

Fourteen

THE KEY TURNED in the lock and Suzanne came in, tossing her brief-case aside and turning on every light in the apartment. "I can't stand this, Brightfield. Your gloom is starting to permeate my life."

Mara looked up from her place on the couch, shielding her eyes from the bright lights. "What time is it?"

"Dinnertime. Why didn't you answer the phone all day?"

"I was afraid to."

"So you've been sitting here all day again, doing nothing?"

"I've been drinking, or trying to drink." She held up the still full bottle. "I'm not very good at it. I don't like the taste."

"You're pathetic." Suzanne took the bottle away from her and slid it deep into the back of a cupboard. "Are you trying to poison yourself?"

"I don't have to. I feel half dead already."

Suzanne dropped onto the couch beside her. "I can't take much more of this. I'm going to call Guy."

"Don't bother. He won't talk about me."

"Okay." Suzanne sat back, sighing. "If it makes you feel any bet-ter, Lowell is back from Switzerland. Maybe you'd talk to him?"

"What for?" Mara's voice was hollow.

"I don't have much patience for this self-pity act. It's disgusting. How can you stand yourself?"

"I can't. That's the point."

"You always do this when anything goes wrong. You wallow. I wish you'd stop."

"Why should I? I ruined everything. I might as well ruin myself."

"So Dan is gone. Big deal. Good riddance, I say."

"And I agree. I'm glad I didn't go with him. Correction—I'm glad he didn't want me."

"Well, congratulations. That's the bravest, most realistic thing I've heard you say yet."

"It's true, though. I didn't reject him, he rejected me. I'm sad but not sorry. He was right about one thing: it does take time to know someone. But on the way to knowing them you have to believe the evidence of who they are. I know Dan loved me, and I tried to love him, but I kept discounting the evidence. I kept seeing what I wanted to see, not what was really there. Still, he deserves someone. We all deserve that."

"But there's no need to molder over it."

"And I've lost Guy."

"Get him back. He's reasonable. He'll listen if you can explain."

"I've talked enough, he was right about that. I've done too much talking. There's nothing I can do now. I'm too inept to do anything. And the worst part is, I'm bored with myself."

"Then do something. Come on, let's see some action." Suzanne got up. "I'll make coffee."

"None for me."

"You're such a martyr. You were wrong. You made a mistake. So what?"

"It was more than a mistake. A lot more. I got so carried away thinking of Cliff House as mine."

"Guy is angry. Can't you handle a little anger? Eventually he'll forgive you."

"But I don't want his forgiveness. He has no reason to forgive me. It's not just what I did but the way I did it, the way I acted. I was hateful and cruel. I can't take that back."

"Look, you were trying to make an unselfish gesture. You got it wrong, what'd you expect? You're new at this. Enough, already. Enough drama. Take the blame and shut up. This is a form of conceit, don't you see that? You're making yourself the star of a big tragedy."

Mara looked at her in surprise. "That's exactly what Dan said."

"I give him credit for that. He knows you, all right. Look, if you really want to feel better, take some responsibility. Admit you screwed up in a big way."

"It's not enough to admit it. I admitted it to Guy, and all I did was make things worse. If only I could make them right again."

"You can't, cookie. No one could. Learn to move on."

"You're right." Mara glanced at her rumpled clothes. "When's the last time I got dressed?"

"I can't remember."

Mara ran a hand through her hair. "I am disgusting, aren't I?" A peculiar look crossed her face. "You know, Suzanne, it's not true. I could change one thing."

"Uh-oh. Now I'm sorry I started this conversation."

Mara grinned. "Don't worry, I'm not going to do anything. But if I were going to take responsibility, like you said, there's one thing I'd try to fix. One thing that I was responsible for. I might be able to help."

"Hold on, Brightfield. When you try to help, things usually get worse."

"Don't worry, I'm not going to do anything. I'm just talking about it." She stood up. "I think I'll take a shower."

Forty minutes later, bathed and dressed in her white linen, Mara sat beside Suzanne as they negotiated the streets of Presidio Heights, where Julia lived. The residential area was filled with stunning homes in spectacular settings with vistas of the bay and bridge beyond its steeply winding streets. Julia's house was a stucco mansion set on a deep lawn behind an ornate wrought-iron fence. Beyond the fence was a profusion of well-tended greenery, an informal garden leading up to the front door. Brilliantly colored flowers spilled over the black iron window rails and balconies that decorated the house's facade. A cool breeze played gently over the grounds, seeming as if it belonged only to the house and its lawn and garden, as if it were completely self-contained, as if nothing from the outside could disturb the air of calm and reserve.

Mara brushed a hand over her skirt, smoothing any wrinkles, while Suzanne examined the house.

"Well," Suzanne said, "Dan had money, but not this kind of money. It shows, doesn't it? You can tell that Julia's had more of it, and for much longer than Dan ever dreamed."

She pressed a button and announced their names into the intercom. It squawked in reply, and the gate swung slowly open. They drove up to the door. Julia opened the front door herself, beckoning them into a circular entry hall with a white marble floor, stark and hard and cold. She scrutinized them both with quick intensity.

"Oh, yes, I remember you now," she told Mara. "The same dress." She glanced at it dismissively, making Mara feel she should apologize for wearing the same outfit twice within Julia's memory.

"Thank you for seeing us," Mara said awkwardly.

"You said on the phone it was important."

"It is."

Julia waved them into a large room off the hallway, furnished with stiff chairs and small, narrow tables lined against the walls. Mara and Suzanne sat primly on the edge of their seats while Julia sat more comfortably, with an impatient, disinterested air.

"I don't really know how to begin," Mara said.

"Try," Julia said.

"Well, we were hoping it wasn't too late," she began. "That is, too late for you to reinvest in Cliff House. I don't think you should cheat yourself out of a such a wonderful opportunity. The project is going to be finished, and it's going to be magnificent. It's going to make a lot of money. I know Lowell agrees with that. He'll back me up on everything I'm saying. I know you could put your money back in now with very little risk."

"What is this? A pep talk?"

"No. The thing is," Mara said with difficulty, "I really came here to clear up a misunderstanding. I wanted you to know that I'm not part of the picture. I have nothing to do with Cliff House. I was writing an article about the history of the building, but that's all. There's nothing between Guy and me."

A bemused look crossed Julia's face. "Let me tell you about Guy Levin. He has some talent as an architect and builder, but as far as anything personal goes, well, I'd watch my step if I were you."

"What do you mean?"

"I mean, it might have been nice if the marriage lasted longer than it took to finance Marina Bay."

"Now wait a minute," Mara protested. "You made money from that project. Guy didn't take anything from you—just the opposite."

"Don't be melodramatic. I'm not accusing him of marrying me for my money. My money is much too hard to get at. And he doesn't have the patience for that, not Guy. I just mean, make sure you know what he wants from you. When I married Guy,

I thought I knew what he wanted. I thought he wanted to share my life. But he wanted me to share his—and that's not my idea of married bliss."

Suzanne interrupted hastily. "Forget about Guy. Cliff House is still a solid investment. I can't believe you'd throw away that kind of an opportunity."

Julia gazed at Suzanne. "Not that it's any of your business, but I know a good opportunity when I see one. That's why I've invested, and that's why I've recommended my friends do the same."

"But you withdrew your investment," Suzanne said.

Julia looked at her blankly.

"You withdrew your investment and told your friends to do the same," Mara repeated.

"I don't get this. Are you trying to pull some sort of scam?" Julia crossed to the open doorway. "Robert, come here, will you?"

Almost instantly a man appeared in the doorway. He was about Julia's age, swarthy and lithe. He wore velvet house slippers and a white silk shirt that billowed loosely over a pair of voluminously full slacks. He was holding a cup of coffee, and he lifted it invitingly toward Julia. She waved it away.

"These are the ladies who phoned," she told him. She nodded at them brusquely. "Robert French, my fiancé."

"Your fiancé?" Mara gazed from him to Julia.

Suzanne stood abruptly. "Maybe we should go." She took Mara's arm, drawing her toward the door. Robert French stepped aside, an amused look on his face.

"Wait a minute," Mara said. "I don't understand something. Julia, are you saying you've put your money back into Cliff House?"

"I'm saying I never took any money out. I don't know what you're talking about, but if you want me to call Lowell and straighten this out, I certainly will." Besides impatience, there was annoyance in Julia's expression.

"It must be my mistake," Mara said. "I must have misunderstood something. I'm sorry we bothered you."

With Suzanne behind her, Mara hurried to the door. Robert French shut it behind them.

In the car again, Mara turned to Suzanne. "Did you think she was telling the truth?"

"I thought so."

"I did, too. I don't know what's going on."

"Neither do I, but let's get out of her driveway while we think about it."

Suzanne pulled around the drive, and the gate swung open before they had reached it. They drove down through the Presidio and out onto a busy shopping street, where Suzanne parked at the side of the road.

"It doesn't make sense," Mara said. "If Julia never took her money back, why were Guy and Lowell so worried? She must be lying, but why? It doesn't make sense."

Suzanne frowned. "Then we must be asking the wrong questions. If the facts are that Julia didn't withdraw her money, that must mean her money's still there."

"How could it be there? Guy and Lowell think it isn't."

"Then let's try the other facts. Let's say Julia didn't take her money out. But let's say her money isn't there."

"What do you mean, it isn't there?" Mara pressed her fingers against her forehead, trying to concentrate. "Are you saying Julia didn't withdraw her money, but Lowell and Guy think she did? Or are you saying she told them she did but she didn't?"

"No, no, you're making it too complicated. It's probably very simple. Lowell and Guy think the money's gone because it *is* gone. We're asking the wrong questions. The right question to ask is, who took her money?"

"Someone took it?"

"Why not? Suppose Julia is telling the truth. But Lowell and Guy think her money's gone. Ergo, someone took her money but not Lowell or Guy. There's only one suspect I can see—the one person with access to the Cliff House account, and the only one with authority to write checks against it and draw out the cash." She paused for effect. "Carter Berenson."

"Carter!"

"Who else? He controls the escrow account, doesn't he? He could easily divert the funds; it wouldn't be hard at all. You'd have to be devious and slimy to think you could get away with it, and that's Carter—devious and slimy. This is serious stuff, Brightfield, really serious. Carter will be disbarred, and worse. I can't wait to see it. To think that I'll be personally responsible for his downfall . . . what justice."

"Hold it, Suzanne. It couldn't be Carter. What would his motives be?"

"Are you kidding? *Money.* He's a total sleaze. He doesn't need complicated motives."

"Now who's making things up? It couldn't be Carter. Everyone knows he controls the escrow account. It would be too obvious."

"But it can't be Lowell," Suzanne argued, "since he went to Europe to borrow money, and he wouldn't do that if he already had Julia's."

"He might, to cover up the theft."

"I can't believe that," Suzanne said emphatically. "Lowell is no crook."

"Neither is Guy," Mara insisted. "He has no criminal instincts."

"But don't forget, Guy thinks Julia cheated him on Marina Bay; this could be his revenge. There's a simple answer: Guy took the money Julia invested in Cliff House to make up for the money she stole at Marina Bay."

"That's not simple, that's complicated. Guy's the one who sent Lowell to Switzerland for the loan. He wouldn't have done that if he was keeping Julia's money."

"Why not? He's not keeping it for Cliff House, he's keeping it for himself. Don't you see, Brightfield? This way Cliff House still gets built and Guy gets the money Julia owed him, and no one except us knows he's an embezzler."

"Carter would know. And Lowell. They've both seen the books. They'd never let him get away with it. It can't be Guy."

"Well, it has to be someone."

"You're right." Mara reached across the dashboard, turning the ignition key. The motor coughed. "Let's find out who. Drive."

"Where to?"

"To your office. We're going to find out who's guilty. We're going to check Carter's books."

The lobby was bright with overhead lights. It was beginning to get dark out, and the lights reflected off the polished steel elevator doors and mirror-lined walls, making Mara squint as she signed the visitors' log. Suzanne kept her eyes down, also, but out of guilt. She nodded curtly at the security guard as she signed in. Her averted eyes gave her a furtive air, as if she were committing a crime.

"Carter's there, I know it," Suzanne worried as they got into the elevator. "We'll never pull this off. He'll catch us."

"This late at night? He's already gone home."

"You never know. I tried to check the register to see if he'd signed out, but I didn't have enough time. If he catches us . . ." She shuddered.

"Don't be nervous," Mara chided as they entered the elevator. "You work here. You have every right to be in this building."

"This is breaking and entering."

"Hardly," Mara scoffed. "Suzanne, you're allowed to be here anytime you want. You have your own key, don't you?"

"Yes, so I can get into my office, not to rifle someone else's files."

"But this is the firm's business. If Carter's taken that money, the partners will stand in line to thank you."

"And if he hasn't, the line will be a firing squad."

Upstairs, the lights were still on in the law offices. A young woman with frizzy hair was bent over her computer. She seemed glad for company when Mara and Suzanne came in.

"Hi, Melanie," Suzanne greeted her. "Is Carter still here?"

"No, I think he's gone for the day. I was about to leave, too. Are you going to be here long?"

"Not long, no, I don't think so," Suzanne gushed. "But why don't you go ahead and leave? I'll lock up."

"Sure, thanks." Gratefully Melanie shut off her monitor and gathered her belongings, calling good-bye as she left.

Mara followed Suzanne into her office. "Okay," she said, "here's the plan." She grabbed a file folder from Suzanne's desk, holding it upside down and shaking it so that papers spilled over the desk.

"Hey, I need those."

"We'll put them aside for now." Mara shuffled them into a pile. "We need this file as a decoy, to hide Carter's files in. We'll just stick them inside so it will look like you're reviewing your own case."

"I hate when you get like this."

"Relax, Suzanne, you have nothing to worry about. We're just here late doing office work, like you always do."

"Not in Carter's files, I don't. He won't like this. He's the kind who won't let anyone touch his coffee mug. He gets upset if you take one of his pencils by mistake. He fired his last secretary for moving the pictures on his desk."

"We'll take a quick look at the files and be out of there in two minutes. Nothing will happen. Where's Carter's office?"

"This way." Suzanne led her through the main room, turning on every desk lamp along the way.

Carter's office was off to one side. His door was unlocked, and Suzanne opened it wide, as if to prove they had nothing to hide. Inside, the room was compulsively neat. The chairs facing his desk were set at precisely the same angle, an even distance apart. The pillows on the low couch were lined up and carefully plumped. The magazines on the coffee table were arranged in soldier-straight rows, showing equal amounts of headlines at the top.

On Carter's desk a polished marble pen stand was perfectly centered. On one corner were three framed color photographs: a docked sailboat; a rustic cabin surrounded by woods; and a picture of Carter seated on the same sailboat, wearing a white canvas sailor hat with the brim turned up, striped shorts, in bright, nautical colors, and a yellow windbreaker. His mouth was open in a wide smile. The hairs across his balding forehead were unruffled. One hand rested on his knee, and the other was lifted in a stiff, open-fisted wave. In the left corner of the desk a dozen sharpened pencils of equal height filled a leather pencil cup.

"We've got to hurry." Suzanne flung open the file cabinet and pawed through the row of folders. "Here it is."

Mara held out the empty folder while Suzanne pulled a heavy file from the drawer. She spread it open on the desk, glancing quickly through the loose papers. She found a bound ledger and lifted it out, flipping through the pages. She began shaking her head.

"What is it?" Mara demanded. "What did you find?"

Suzanne pulled out Carter's desk chair and sank onto its wide leather seat, pulling the ledger closer.

"What is it?"

Suzanne glanced up with an air of triumph. "The money's gone," she announced.

"Are you sure?"

"Positive. Julia's money and more. Take a look—it's all listed right here. And guess who signed the transferral orders? Carter Berenson."

"Let me see that." Mara grabbed the book, examining the neat entries. "How much is missing?"

"As far as I can tell, almost a million dollars." Suzanne smiled slowly. "I knew it. I knew it wasn't Lowell or Guy. If anyone's a born embezzler, it's Carter."

Mara perched on the edge of the desk, engrossed in the ledger's pages. "That's okay, then—it's going to be okay. It means we can still get the money back to Guy."

"Get it back? How?" Suzanne asked.

"It couldn't be easier. We tell Carter we know everything, and if he doesn't return all the money, we'll turn him in."

"We can't do that," Suzanne said. "That's blackmail. Look, we'll tell the partners about this. They'll take care of it."

"That'll take too long."

"We can't blackmail Carter. I'm not going to jeopardize my whole career when he's the crook."

"It's only blackmail if we demand payment in return, and we're not going to. All we want is for Carter to give back the money. That's not blackmail—that's restitution."

"Forget it. I can't do it, Brightfield."

"You can't *not* do it, Suzanne. It can't be a crime to stop a crime."

"Look, I admit sending Carter up for embezzlement is a nice warm thought. But threatening to turn him in unless he returns the money puts us in the wrong. It's a criminal act. We can't do it. We can only show evidence to get Carter indicted."

"That's not good enough. Even if the court made Carter give the money back to Guy, it'd take too long. We have to do something now. You stay out of it, Suzanne. I'll do it all myself. I volunteer, okay? I'll tell him the jig is up."

"And which jig is that?" Carter stood in the doorway. "What are you doing with those files?"

Mara whipped the ledger behind her back. Suzanne grabbed the decoy file, hastily shoving the papers inside. "It's uh, the Munson brief. Just checking some research."

Carter snatched the folder from her, glancing through it quickly. "This is the Cliff House account. What are you up to?"

"Hold on, Carter," Mara said as Suzanne hesitated. "We're the ones who should be asking the questions. Like, what happened to the money in this account—the money you said Julia Levin withdrew? We just talked to Julia. She never withdrew her money. So where is it, Carter? Where's the money?"

178

Carter stared at her, then drew himself up haughtily. "I don't have time for this."

"You can spare the time. A quick explanation will do."

"She's right, Carter," Suzanne agreed. "You'd better make time, or we'll have to turn you in for embezzlement."

Carter looked at Suzanne condescendingly. "Dear Suzanne," he drawled, "I sincerely hope you're a better lawyer than a detective. Sorry to spoil your fun, but I haven't taken any money. It's all there, in the emergency account."

"What emergency account?" Suzanne asked.

"The account opened to cover unexpected expenses."

Mara shook her head. "What does that mean?"

"It means it is money held out of escrow, allowing Guy or Lowell immediate access to their own funds."

"Are you saying the missing money is in the emergency account?"

"What missing money?" Carter demanded. "Who said any money was missing?"

"Guy and Lowell. They did."

"I don't know what they told you or why, but that account was set up for their convenience. Instead of coming to me for approval of every payment from the escrow account, they can write checks directly, as the need arises. The escrow account was inconvenient. This is a perfectly reasonable arrangement."

"Very reasonable," Suzanne scoffed, "except that it's completely illegal. That defeats the whole purpose of escrow. You're not supposed to give direct access to the principals, Carter. What kind of nice fat payoff did you get to do it?"

"Don't you threaten me." Carter wagged a finger at Suzanne.

"I'll do more than that—I'll let the partners know about this. You won't be so smug then."

"Wait, Suzanne," Mara interrupted. "If that account's illegal, Guy would never have okayed it. Especially not if it involved a payoff." She faced Carter squarely. "I think there isn't an emergency account. I think you're bluffing."

"Do you?" Carter searched through the filing cabinet and pulled out a crumpled folder marked "Miscellaneous." He spread it open on his desk. "See for yourselves. The emergency account—all clearly marked, showing exactly where the funds are."

Suzanne bent over the folder. "It's here." She sounded disappointed. "All the missing money." She ran her finger down the column of entries.

Mara peered over Suzanne's shoulder. "You must have expected some pretty major emergencies."

"I don't know about that," Carter said stiffly. "All I know is that there's been no embezzling."

Suzanne looked up from the ledger. "What's this entry—a hundred and fifty thousand dollars to Lowell, signed with a power of attorney?"

"What's that mean?" Mara asked.

"It means Guy didn't endorse the withdrawal," Suzanne answered. "It means Lowell took that money without Guy knowing."

"You're wrong," Carter said. "Guy didn't know the details, but he knew the intent. That money was for a legitimate business expense. Must I explain everything?"

"Until I understand it," Mara said. "You're saying Lowell knew Julia's money was in the emergency account. But he told Guy it was gone, and then he withdrew some. Why, Carter?"

"I don't know."

"You'd better talk, Carter," Suzanne ordered. "Or I go to the partners."

Carter rolled his eyes impatiently. "You're making a mountain out of a molehill. It's quite simple. Lowell and I opened the account," he admitted, "but it was for Guy's benefit, too. Lowell needed that money, but he didn't want to be accused of bilking anyone, not after Guy's bad experience on Marina Bay. So we agreed to keep it quiet until the deal was completed."

"What deal?" Mara demanded.

Carter sighed. "The foreign loan."

"I'm lost," Mara said. "Guy approved that deal. What were you keeping quiet about?"

"The hundred and fifty thousand that you so rudely accused me of stealing. Lowell needed that money to work the deal. He had to have some collateral to put up to get the loan."

"Wouldn't Cliff House be the collateral?" Mara asked.

Carter gave her a smug look. "The banks aren't interested in Cliff House—only in money. They prefer cash as collateral, if they can get it."

"But if Lowell needed a hundred and fifty thousand dollars as collateral, why didn't he just say so? Why did he pretend that money was missing?"

"I don't know," Carter said. "Can't you just be grateful that Cliff House won't be abandoned? They have more money now than they ever dreamed of. Or they *will* have, as soon as Lowell completes the deal." Carter plucked the ledger book from Mara's fingers and took the file from Suzanne, depositing both of them back in the filing cabinet. "And that, dear ladies, is why no one in this room is a crook."

"I suppose I owe you an apology," Suzanne said grudgingly, "though there's still the matter of the escrow account."

"Carter," Mara asked, "did Guy really approve the foreign loan?"

"Of course. He had to," Carter said. "It's the only thing that makes sense."

"Then why all the secrets, why all the lies? It doesn't sound right to me. Something's still wrong here." She reached for the telephone. "I'm calling Lowell. He'll have to explain it. I want to hear it from him, that everything's okay again."

"Why can't you women take yes for an answer?" Carter sighed. "Cliff House will be finished. What more do you want?"

Ignoring him, Mara punched Lowell's number into the telephone. The speakerphone was on, and the sound of Lowell's ringing phone filled the room. He answered midway through the second ring, barking into the receiver. "Who's there?"

"Lowell, it's Mara. I—"

"Where've you been?" His tone was urgent. "I've been frantic trying to reach you."

"What is it? What's wrong?"

"It's Cliff House. Guy tried to blow it up. You'd better get right over there."

The elevator doors slid open. They burst into the lobby.

"I'll follow in my car," Carter told Suzanne.

"Oh no you don't. You're coming with us," Suzanne ordered. "We're not done with you yet, Carter."

In the front seat of the car, Mara twisted the radio dials, trying to find some mention of the disaster on the local news, but there was no word of it yet. Traffic was light, and they sped across the city to the coastal highway.

"Listen, are those fire sirens?" Mara strained, trying to hear over the street noise. "If only we knew what was happening!"

Suzanne pulled around a double-parked car, barely slowing down. "We'll know soon enough. In the meantime Carter can fill in some of the blanks."

"What blanks? I told you everything I know."

"Not quite everything," Suzanne insisted.

"All right. I'll explain the deal, but you probably won't understand it."

Mara leaned over the front seat. "Try us."

"This project was underfinanced from the start," Carter began. "Lowell had trouble raising money through normal channels. I guess it was because of his scrapes with the IRS."

"What scrapes? I didn't know about that," Suzanne said.

"I'm beginning to think we don't know anything," Mara added.

"Please, let me continue." Carter took a breath. "Lowell is a high roller, well connected, with contacts in all the right places. He decided to finance the project unconventionally, using fallout."

"Fallout?" Suzanne looked startled. "Is he going to drop the A-bomb on a bank?"

"Suzanne"—Carter's voice rose in exasperation—"if you'd just let me speak, I could explain how it works. To put it simply, a Swiss bank agreed to a billion-dollar loan."

"A billion dollars!" Mara exclaimed. "That's enough for ten Cliff Houses."

"Not quite, and you're jumping the gun. He doesn't get a billion dollars. That's not the point. The Swiss bank agrees to the loan. They give Lowell a letter stating that they're willing to lend him one billion dollars. But they want collateral. Lowell doesn't have any, so he goes to his U.S. bank and tells them he's got a billion-dollar loan commitment if he can come up with some collateral. The U.S. bank agrees to sell him the collateral he needs. If you understand that, you'll understand it all."

"I think I get that." Mara looked doubtful.

"It's very simple. The bank agrees to sell Lowell the collateral, for a fee of one hundred and fifty thousand dollars."

"So that's where the money went." Mara frowned. "But it doesn't sound like enough for a billion-dollar loan."

"But it's only a fee," Carter said. "Think of it as a service charge.

For that fee, the bank gives Lowell a promissory bank note—a piece of paper that says the U.S. bank will give the Swiss bank one billion dollars, plus interest, when the note comes due, ten years from now."

"Then the bank made the loan to the other bank," Mara said, "not to Lowell."

"You're catching on," Carter said approvingly. "Lowell isn't actually taking out a loan at all. He's really acting as a conduit for a self-liquidating loan between the two banks. A loan that's going to be paid off."

"You're losing me," Mara said.

"Let me continue. Lowell buys the collateral at a discount. Everyone discounts, Mara. The bank charges him the going rate, which right now happens to be seventy-eight cents on the dollar. On a billion dollars, that comes to seven hundred and eighty million dollars."

"But Lowell doesn't have that kind of money," Suzanne interrupted.

"He doesn't need it, remember?" Carter made an effort to be patient. "He paid a fee for the note. For that fee, the bank gives him the promissory note, worth seven hundred and eighty million dollars. Lowell now has a commitment for a billion-dollar loan from the Swiss, and the collateral he needs from the Americans. Now Lowell takes the next step. He goes to a neutral country, in this case Luxembourg. In Luxembourg he sets up a bank account. The Swiss wire one billion dollars into his account. The Luxembourg bank then wires seven hundred and eighty million of that money back to the U.S. bank, with a promise that the Swiss will pay back the balance of the billion, plus interest, in ten years. Do you understand it now? The Swiss loaned out a billion. Lowell used part of that to pay back the U.S. bank for their collateral."

"Then what happens to the loan?"

Carter looked mystified. "Don't you see? The Swiss bank has the promissory note, the promise that the U.S. bank will pay them the one billion dollars they loaned out, plus interest, when the note comes due in ten years. It's the same as a regular loan."

"Okay, I see that." Mara turned to Suzanne, beside her. "Do you get it?"

"I can't think high finance and drive at the same time."

"Well, explain, anyway, Carter," Mara said. "I see what the Swiss did. They made a loan, and they'll make their money back in ten years."

"Exactly. And in the meantime they get to use that promissory note any way they want, as if it were already cash—to make other deals with—to make money from their money."

"My head is beginning to hurt," Suzanne complained.

Carter ignored her. "Mara, do you understand that?"

"Yes, but what does the U.S. bank get?"

"The loan," Carter said. "They get seven hundred and eighty million dollars. And they have it free for ten years, until the note is due. They're hoping they can use that money to make more than what they'll owe by the time it's due."

"But something doesn't make sense," Mara interrupted. "The Swiss loaned out a billion dollars, but they only paid the Americans seven hundred and eighty million. What happened to the rest? That leaves, what, two hundred and twenty million unaccounted for, left over?"

"Bingo!" Carter grinned triumphantly. "That's the fallout. That's the money Lowell was really after."

Mara stared. "You mean, that's his part of the loan?"

"It's not a loan at all. Like you said, it's leftovers. Free money, there for the taking." Carter let a moment pass while the full impact of what he was saying sank in.

"Two hundred and twenty million dollars left over," Mara repeated.

Carter laughed gleefully. "Beautiful, isn't it? That's the whole point of the deal. Lowell never expected to get a billion dollars; that's just the way this thing is structured. You see, U.S. banks aren't allowed to solicit funds from foreign banks. But foreign banks have money to lend, at very low interest rates. So they use a conduit, to get around the regulations. The foreign bank lends out money and the American bank borrows it, and some lucky dog gets the fallout. In this case it's two hundred and twenty million. For that kind of cash you can put up some first-rate buildings."

"Let me get this straight," Mara said. "Lowell paid a hundred and fifty thousand dollars to buy a bank note that's eventually worth one billion dollars?"

"That's the way it works out. The Swiss get money and the Americans get money and Lowell gets the fallout, and everybody's happy."

Mara shook her head. "It's unbelievable."

"The best things in life are always unbelievable." Carter cackled. "Not a bad return for a plane ticket and a few wires and telephone calls. Not bad at all."

Suzanne had stopped at a red light. She twisted her neck to peer at Carter. "You make it sound so pat. But it's illegal."

"How? How is it illegal?" Carter challenged.

"It's illegal to buy and sell loans."

"It's illegal to solicit funds from a foreign source," Carter quoted. "Lowell didn't do that. He merely bought a promissory note and sold it in Europe, where it's perfectly legal. Oh, here, in the U.S., you're not supposed to buy and sell something that you don't really own— you're not supposed to control large amounts of money with small amounts of money that you don't really have. But how do you think banks made their money? They don't make it off the interest they charge you for a puny little loan on a house or a car. They make deals, big deals. They buy and sell money, as loans or collateral or assets—it doesn't matter which."

"You mean, they do it, anyway," Mara said. "They buy and sell a promise—a promise of money. And that's just what Cliff House is—a promise."

Carter nodded. "The end results are different, but I suppose it is the same thing. Finance and architecture, making promises into something concrete."

Suzanne looked at him sharply. "Coming from you, Carter, that's practically poetry."

Fifteen

THROUGH THE THICK SMOKE the skeleton of the building was only barely visible. A twisted, crippled thing, it seemed to give way without a fight, surrendering to the flames roaring around it. The noise was deafening; sirens screamed as additional fire trucks raced to the scene, and the clatter and bustle of the newly arrived firemen mixed with the din of the shouts and orders of the firemen already on the scene; and those sounds mingled with the shouts and chatter arising from the crowd of excited onlookers, and behind it all swelled the whoosh and boom and crackle of the exploding flames.

The firemen dragged the wooden barricades onto the highway, stopping traffic completely. The crowd, pursued, fell back, spreading into a thin line at the edge of the embankment.

Mara hurried closer, leaving Suzanne and Carter to follow. She spotted Guy's car, abandoned outside the wooden construction fence, and faltered, losing her nerve. Suzanne and Carter caught up to her.

"Can you believe this?" Suzanne marvelled at the destruction.

Mara felt a wave of sickness. She wished she could faint, wished darkness and blackness would overcome her so she wouldn't have to face what he had done. She couldn't face it; the disappointment was too much to bear. She couldn't bear the destruction and the finality of it.

"It's such a waste." Suzanne made a helpless gesture that surprised Mara.

"I know."

"Why did he do it? He cared so much."

"He did it because he cared." Mara's voice was flat as she stared at the flames. "Because he hated compromises and the kind of deals Lowell believes in—that I thought I believed in. He did it because he had to."

A fireman rushed over, yelling at them to get back. He waved them across the street behind the barricades. Mara went reluctantly. Someone called her name, and she saw Epstein waiting on the edge of the crowd.

"Where's Guy?" she demanded, shouting to be heard. "Where is he?"

"Hospital," Epstein yelled back. "He got caught in the explosion and didn't get away in time." His voice dropped. "Or else he didn't try to get away."

"Didn't try . . .?" She shuddered. Had he needed to destroy it all, then, and himself along with it?

Epstein motioned for them to follow him down the highway, away from the site, where they could be heard above the noise.

"Was he badly hurt?" Suzanne asked.

"Don't know, didn't see him. I got here too late—they'd already taken him away. Talk about dumb luck." Epstein scratched his forehead. "I just decided to drive past, check the site. I didn't think anyone would be here. Some motorists saw the explosion and called the police. The ambulance was pulling out. I called Lowell."

"He said he'd do it," Mara murmured. "He said he'd blow it off the face of the earth. He warned us. It wasn't his dream anymore. Everyone tried to take it away from him. Why shouldn't he do it? Why shouldn't he be in despair? He said he'd do it, and nobody listened. Well, he has. He's the only one who could have, the only one who had that right."

"Maybe this place *is* cursed," Suzanne said softly.

"I always knew it was. I think he knew it, too."

Suzanne put an arm around her shoulder. "There's nothing we can do here. Let's go."

Mara seemed not to hear her. "Poor Guy. Poor Cliff House. It's all so hopeless."

Epstein gave her a sympathetic look. "He won't have to take anybody's money now."

"Can't the building be saved?" Suzanne asked. "Won't something be left standing?"

Epstein looked doubtful. "The steel, it won't burn. But structurally it's unsafe now. Nope, it can't be saved. The firemen say it was a sloppy job, explosives set in all the wrong places. That' what started the fire. Otherwise it would've blown clean. Nope, it'll have to be done over—if anyone wants to do it over."

"There's no question he did it, then?" Carter asked.

Mara had forgotten he was there. They all looked at him disdainfully.

"What I mean is," Carter said defensively, "he ruined his chances of an insurance settlement."

"Carter, stop," Suzanne warned.

"That's why he did it, isn't it? To collect the insurance?"

"You don't know a thing about it," Mara said calmly. "That's not why he did it.

"Whatever." Carter shrugged. "There's no doubt he'll be indicted. And if it was a sloppy job, they might even have hard evidence."

Suzanne glared, but Carter pointed at Epstein. "Don't look at me—*he* said so."

The firemen pulled the barricades farther up the road, enlarging the restricted area. The bolder onlookers climbed the side of the embankment, but the bulk of the crowd began to drift away.

"We'd better get back to the car," Suzanne said, "before they close that part of the road, too."

"I can't go," Mara said. "Not yet. I just can't."

"Okay. We'll stay a while longer."

"I'd like to be alone. Do you mind?"

Suzanne hesitated. "I'll wait at the car."

"Thanks." Mara squeezed her hand.

She crossed the highway to the parking lot, near the beach and below the cliffs. Away from the crowds, down below the site, the night was quiet again. Cliff House burning was only a distant curiosity.

On the beach a small crowd had gathered, but the flames on the cliffs above were almost gone, and the excitement of the blaring sirens and the crush of activity had waned. Those remaining milled about aimlessly. In the peculiar half dusk, the sky masked by smoke and dwindling firelight, someone was taking photographs; the flashbulbs popped in startling bursts of brightness. Three teenage boys, grouped around their ten-speed bikes, posed against the smoldering sky, Cliff House merely a backdrop behind them. They smirked and mugged for the camera, showing no respect for the death of the building.

She walked farther up the beach, into the darkness beneath the cliffs. It was probably dangerous to wander there, in range of falling debris, but no one stopped her, and she needed to see the glistening rocks and hear the pounding surf, to be near Cliff House while it slowly disappeared.

Alone there, she had the eerie feeling that the site itself, the craggy cliffs above her, were somehow aware of the building's destruction. As if it were the site, the cliffs themselves, that had inhabited Cliff House and not Cliff House that had inhabited the site. As the flames died above, the last of them licking lamely at the decimated structure, she had a feeling that the power of the curse was dying, too, diminishing along with the building. She felt a profound sadness, as if the cliffs regretted the passing of this building, this manifestation of a dream, as if Guy's Cliff House could have made peace with the site, could have erased the curse and ended it forever.

A wave broke high on the sand, close to her feet. She leapt back to avoid the swirl of water. As she turned again, Lowell was suddenly standing there. A reflection caught in his eyes, a glint of light from the smoldering fire that gave them a look of strange excitement, even satisfaction. She found herself smiling back with sad understanding.

"I guess Guy is purer than the rest of us," she said. "What difference does it make, where the money came from? I wouldn't have minded, but he did."

"You're practical, Mara. You know the way the world works. You told me that once, and you made a lot of sense. More than Guy ever did."

"So he had to take it back from us, all of us who tainted it with our clever games. Guy couldn't play games, could he?"

"That's the pity."

"Tell me something. I don't understand about Julia's money, about you and Carter, telling Guy she'd withdrawn her investment. What was that about?"

"I had to tell him something to make him think we were in dire straits, to set the wheels in motion. If he hadn't thought we were desperate for money, he wouldn't have given me the power of attorney, and I couldn't have made the foreign deal without his signature.

"It was for the fallout, then."

"Of course. It was all a smoke screen, if you'll forgive the pun. You know how Guy is, how he insisted on local funding, local backers. It never would have been enough. But there are great chunks of money out there, Mara, to be had for little effort, if you have the right connections. It's a good game, Mara, but an exclusive one. Not many people know about it."

"Did you have to play games with Cliff House?"

"It happens to be a very good game, Mara. The best I've ever played."

"If you get away with it."

"Get away with what? I've not done anything illegal, Mara. Don't you see that yet? It's perfectly legal."

"It can't be that simple."

"But it is. Simple and neat, clean and legal."

"But you tricked Guy into it. It was all a trick, all an elaborate game."

"Not so elaborate. Simple, in fact. All along I told Guy we were underfinanced. And then it was just a matter of transferring funds into the emergency account, to make it appear we were suffering losses. Carter approved. He knew if the money was taken out of escrow, it would force Guy into the fallout scheme. And any of Carter's misgivings were nicely stilled with a few stray coins. And Guy had no reason to check the balance—every penny of the Cliff House money was accounted for, the money advanced to Epstein, paid for labor or materials. Of course, the figures were adjusted slightly, and I threw in extra invoices whenever I could."

"You made it look like the account was being drained. But no money was actually missing—it was all in the emergency fund."

He gave her a look of appreciation. "I thought you'd catch right on. No extra money was ever spent, not even for Deets's bribe. There never was any bribe, you know. All a bluff. I agreed with you about it completely—in fact, that's when I first began to notice you, once I knew how you were capable of thinking. You're smart. Until then I'd found you charming, but I had no idea how useful you would be. You kept Guy distracted, especially these last few days."

"I was a fool. And I never suspected anything."

"How could you? No one did. And you were perfect. You gave me my best idea, in fact, the real coup—Julia's money. That was a stroke of genius."

"I gave you the idea?"

"At the groundbreaking. I saw the tension between you two, and it was easy to tell Guy that Julia had withdrawn her entire investment and taken others with her. Of course he believed it. He's that impetuous himself. You see, what was really in my favor is a trick human beings have: They expect others to act precisely as they do themselves. It doesn't really work that way. People are quite uniquely loyal to their own peculiar personalities. Julia is hardly the idealist or the dreamer that Guy is, but Guy believed she would do what he would in the same situation—take back her money in a jealous snit. She never would, you know. She's much too practical. That's Julia's flaw—her practicality."

"I thought you said that was my flaw?"

"No, your flaw is a need to make heroes out of ordinary men."

"I'm not sure I like the way you talk about people, Lowell, not about any of us, but mostly not the way you talk about Guy."

"Still making him the hero? How long would it be until you were disillusioned with him and his work? Not long. He's not an innovator, you know—far from it. He's not bringing people anything new. His one good idea is to comfort them with something old. It's not an earthshaking notion, and not a forward-moving one, either. How long would it be until you found that out and recognized his limitations? How long before you started to think less of him for it? There'll be an investigation. People will talk. They'll say Guy was cracking under the strain, that he burned Cliff House in a jealous rage because you left him. They'll come up with a dozen explanations I haven't even thought of. Guilty or not, he'll seem to be guilty, and after that, well, imagine what kind of career he'll have."

"Do you hate him so much?"

"I don't hate him at all."

"At least he had an idea and a dream. I don't have either."

"Most people don't. And you're still more than they are."

"Am I? I've done nothing very special."

"You helped me."

"But I was trying to help Guy. Guy is the one who matters."

"Not Guy. It's too bad, really, that he wouldn't go along with this.

But of course he wants to build his Cliff House. I'm on my way to Luxembourg now, Mara. Come with me."

"I'm not in the mood for a trip."

"You don't understand, do you? I'm not coming back. I wasn't ever going to come back. The money, Mara—that's what I'm interested in, that's all I was ever interested in. Not Cliff House. It was never for Cliff House."

"No! You believed in Cliff House."

"Never. Cliff House was extraneous."

"Then why drag Guy into it at all?"

"I had to. I had to use Cliff House as the bait in the loan scheme. There had to be a property to develop. But I told you—our partnership was very strict. I needed Guy's signature to apply for the loans, so I had to convince him we were so badly underfinanced that we had no choice but to go to a foreign bank. And I needed the fee money. I made a few mistakes with my own funds. I was broke, Mara. I needed the one hundred fifty thousand to set the wheels in motion. But Guy will get that back. It's too small a sum for me to bother with. I don't need to be accused of such petty embezzling. No, I'll send that money back. I don't need it anymore."

"Then it was all a trick, all an elaborate trick."

"Not so elaborate. Simple, in fact. There were no intricate maneuvers, no farfetched schemes. I wasn't trying to commit the perfect crime, you know. That's an amateur's idea, the perfect crime."

She backed away from him. "No, I don't believe you."

"Of course you do. I'm sorry to disappoint you, but I know you'll forgive me, eventually. It's just your pride. We understand each other, Mara. There's no need for excuses between us, no pretense, no standards to live up to. We're well suited. Come away with me, Mara."

"I'm just beginning to understand. Guy must have known—or guessed—and that's why he did this, why he destroyed Cliff House."

"You're priceless." Lowell smiled in amusement. "Cliff House was destroyed for more obvious reasons. The answers are all there, if you look clearly. You have all the information, if you'll only stop to think."

"I don't know what you mean. You frighten me."

"Don't you see? Guy had nothing to do with this. I'm selfish, Mara. And I enjoyed the game. I won't deny that, certainly not to you. But it was different when this all started. Then I had nothing to stay for. Dear Mara. There's no one like you." With one hand he gently stroked the side of her face. "But now the money isn't enough. You surprised me, Mara, surprised me totally. I surprised myself. I never expected this. But there it is, and the only thing standing between us was your obsession with this building, with Cliff House." Lowell laughed at her consternation.

"You blew up Cliff House," she said.

"It seemed the right thing to do—the kind of gesture you'd appreciate. You love drama. And I had to try to implicate Guy, you know. Another smoke screen. Arson is hard to prove. But with Guy threatening to blow up the building and acting like a demented man, yelling disaster when there was no financial disaster and then caught on the site the night it blows up, well, then I thought, people might believe anything, believe that he destroyed his building to collect on the insurance. It doesn't matter what explanations they come up with—greed, desperation, even suicidal depression. I am a little ashamed of myself; it's a messy kind of stunt. I'd rather be on that plane to Luxembourg, but . . . there was you, Mara. I know you're lazy. I know you like to be taken care of. You were willing to take from Dan and even from Guy, so why not from me? Why not, when we're so much alike? You're not really shocked, you only think you should be. We both know, in the right circumstances, you wouldn't hesitate to do the same thing."

"You're wrong."

"Am I?"

For a moment she simply stared at him. "You'll be arrested."

"For what? For borrowing money from a bank? That's no crime."

"But you intended to keep it. You're not putting the money into Cliff House, and that's what you borrowed it for. That must be some kind of fraud, or at least attempted fraud."

Lowell gestured at the cliffs behind them. "How? There is no Cliff House to put the money in."

"It can't be that easy."

"But it is. That's the beauty of it. It is that easy, it is that simple. All that's left now is for me to get on that plane. I should have left by now. I should have been at the airport, establishing an alibi—not that I'll need one. They can't trace this to me."

"I could tell them you confessed."

"A confession isn't proof. There's no proof, I'm sure of that. I like things tidy, Mara." He glanced at the ruined building on the cliffs. "This—coming back for you, planting explosives—this wasn't tidy. Not my usual style." He reached out and caressed her hair. "Oh, I know I didn't have to burn it, but that's my failing, Mara. Sometimes I want things too much. I want you to come with me now. Tonight. You're the part that matters now."

"You're insane."

"That's a feeble excuse. I'm completely sane. What I did made sense. It was logical and easy and legal. How could I resist? Two hundred and twenty million dollars—that's a lot of temptation, Mara. A lot of temptation."

"You're evil."

"Evil? You're drawing fine distinctions now. Look what sins you've committed—small sins of omission, convenient deceptions. Admit it, Mara, you enjoyed the game, enjoyed the contest, bending events to your will. I know you did, don't tell me I'm wrong."

"But I didn't know where it was leading. I did it for different reasons."

"I know you believe that—that's what's wonderful about you. You've already risked more than you know. There's no risk left, only one last step, one plane ride to take. Take it, Mara. You'll be rewarded." He held out his hand. "We are alike; you know I'm right. There's nothing left here for you. Come with me. Think how wonderful it will be."

There was truth in what he said; she couldn't deny that. She had been guilty; she was capable of small treacheries; her definitions of right and wrong had been adjustable, stretching at her convenience to fit her conscience. It was tempting to think she could run away, avoid facing that truth. She was tempted. She knew herself enough to recognize that.

"I see one thing," she said slowly. "I see that you can justify anything."

Lowell smiled. "Possibly."

"Not possibly, definitely. I see that you can twist the definitions, call anything sane or logical or even respectable. But someone has to set the limits. There have to be limits. You say it's all clean and easy, you talk about what's ahead, about your reward. But what about what's behind, what about what we've destroyed, the hope and the dream and the vision?"

"You're still dreaming," Lowell chided. "Give it up."

"No, you give it up, Lowell. Don't go. Stay here. Give it up, give up the idea—a rich exile, that's such a fairy tale. You don't believe in fairy tales. You said it yourself. If there hasn't been any crime, then stay. Use the money for Cliff House. Rebuild it, start over again. This time make the dream come true. Why not?"

"I love my own dream too much." He touched her face tenderly. "Don't be foolish. Two hundred and twenty million, Mara. Think of it. Think of what we could do. Come to the airport, Mara. I'll be there."

From behind them came a bursting sound, as of giant pods popping. She whirled to see great, shooting plumes of flame dashed against the sky. The sky lit with an eerie brightness. A last batch of explosives must have been detonated by a last spark of fire. As the sky lightened, the cliffs glowed in silhouette, and Mara was jolted to see that they resembled the profile of a saddened face.

She turned to find an empty beach before her. Dark waves spilled over the sand, reflecting the light from the flames. The waves took on the tint of the sky, a tint of liquid fire. A footprint remained in the sand, one depression the size and shape of a man's shoe. A wave lapped at its edge and another wave came and that wave swelled over it and when the water receded, the footprint was gone.

The hospital corridor was garish and bright. Their faces looked sickly under the lights, drained of color.

Mara walked reluctantly past the room doors.

"You don't have to see him," Suzanne told her. "But we have to find out how he is."

Mara halted. "You go on. I'll wait here. I couldn't face him, anyway."

"Don't be so hard on yourself. We were all taken in—none of us realized Lowell was capable of this kind of violence, or of the scam. As it turns out, I'm not exactly a brilliant judge of character."

Mara squeezed Suzanne's arm. "Thanks, but I'm the most to blame. I don't know how to live with that yet."

The swinging doors opened at the end of the corridor, and Paddy Manelli darted through, half hidden under an outlandish bouquet of flowers. In the artificial light they matched his hair; flagrantly colored and slightly wild. He squinted at the room numbers, seeming to be lost until he spotted Mara and Suzanne. A smile of relief spread over his face as he hurried toward them.

"I heard everything. Damned shame—terrible thing, really a terrible thing."

Mara stared at him in disbelief. "How can you say that? You fought him every step of the way."

"I had to make a stand. There were principles at stake. But I would have been glad to see that building, especially the public baths. Great for the people of this city, really tremendous."

"But you . . . you attacked me," Mara gasped. "You stopped the trucks and did everything you could—"

"Ah, the grease job," Paddy interrupted, chuckling. "One of my best efforts. A little active resistance always goes a long way."

"Yes, it was very clever," Mara said scornfully. "They lost a day's work to that prank, and a day to the stalled trucks."

"The stalled trucks?" Paddy cocked an eyebrow.

"The day the trucks wouldn't start. What'd you use?" Mara taunted. "Sugar in the gas tanks or maybe watered-down diesel fuel?"

"I don't know anything about that," Paddy said.

"Oh, I suppose it really was the curse," she scoffed.

"I only did the grease job," Paddy swore. "That other day, well, I don't know anything about it. If I were you, I'd take that curse idea more seriously. Meanwhile I want to know about Cliff House. How'd it happen, anyway? An accident?"

"Arson," Suzanne said curtly.

"For the insurance, I suppose."

"Nothing that simple. Guy just got caught in the middle. Lowell was the villain; he used Cliff House as a front, to hustle a ton of money for himself. And it's not even illegal."

"No!" Paddy stared at Suzanne. "Fascinating, isn't it? That whole notion of personal culpability. Is your primary responsibility internal, to yourself; or external, to those around you? Fascinating. I did a whole article on that, you know, for the *Journal of Contemporary Ethics.*"

"I didn't know you wrote."

"Always, when my course load is light."

"You're a teacher?"

"Professor, political theory. Did you happen to see that issue, though? Great piece. Worked really well, I thought."

"It sounds intriguing."

Paddy set the flowers on a molded plastic seat and began to explain his ideas to Suzanne.

Dr. Macy came out of Guy's room and spotted Mara immediately. "Brightfield! Come right over here."

The door to the room was open, and Mara held back, trying to keep out of sight. "How is he?" she asked.

"Not bad, for a fellow who can't seem to keep out of trouble." Dr. Macy laughed at his own joke. "A few scratches, a minor concussion. We'll hold on to him tonight, but he can go home in the morning. Go ahead in. Take a look at him."

"He wouldn't want to see me."

"Go on."

Mara found herself pushed through the doorway. Guy was asleep. One arm, lying outside the covers, showed a small bandage. There were thin, jagged scratches on his face. A bruise was starting on his forehead.

She felt an overwhelming thankfulness; he was going to be all right. Then he stirred in his sleep and she felt a start of fear. What if he woke and didn't want her there? She was afraid of what she might see in his eyes. How could she blame him? She was still a coward. She'd tried to love him, but she'd botched it and made a mess of things. She longed to stay, to be with him, to hold him and comfort him, but she had no right to do that, no right to expect the sweet, easy acceptance of her that had always been there.

"I'm sorry," she whispered. She pushed past Dr. Macy, startling Suzanne as she ran down the corridor. Suzanne's voice echoed behind her.

"Mara, wait! Where are you going?"

Sixteen

THERE WAS NO FENCE left around the site. The wide expanse of bare ground was like a newly cleaned wound. Mounds of dirt, neatly raked, ringed the gaping holes where the foundations had been. Refuse and debris were stacked in huge dumpsters, ready to be hauled away. To one side, away from the highway, was a stack of charred, twisted metal beams.

She walked to the edge of the property, where it overlooked the sea. In the bright sun the surf crashed exuberantly over the rocks below. Guy was there, his back to her, facing the water. Deliberately she kicked at a pile of stones, making a noise to warn him that someone was approaching. She cleared her throat.

"Epstein said I'd find you here." Her voice was unsteady.

Guy turned. The scratches were gone from his face and the bruise on his forehead had faded. For an instant she thought that he was glad to see her, but then his expression changed, becoming guarded and impassive.

"I thought you left town," he said.

"No, I had nowhere to go," she answered awkwardly. "I came by to apologize. I'm pretty much of a coward, but I thought I should do one brave thing and face you long enough for that. You deserve that. And I had to say good-by to Cliff House." She paused. "Don't laugh, but that night, the night of the fire, I felt like the cliffs were sad to see your building go. It was like your Cliff House had made friends with the site. It really would have been something special."

He shrugged. "It still can be. Someone's going to build here. I have enough ego left to think it still should be me. I still think I'd do the best job."

"Then you're not going to give up?"

"No."

"Suzanne says it'd be nearly impossible to prosecute Lowell. You'll never see any of that money."

"I can raise more." He nodded toward the ruins. "The notoriety won't hurt any, not as long as I clear my name. And I think I can."

"I'm glad. I'm glad you're not giving up." She turned so he wouldn't have to look at her face. "I'm sorry for so many things. I'm sorry I ever thought you could blow up your own building. I guess I didn't know what to believe. I thought you had the right to destroy it. We had all disappointed you so badly. Lowell betrayed you, and I . . . well, I thought I was so smart, paying bribes and making threats—what a joke I was. When I found out what Lowell had really done, well, I couldn't bear myself, so I thought it was too much for you to bear."

"I could never have destroyed Cliff House."

"No, of course not. I was so blind about myself, and I was blind about you, too. I should have known you could never have done it."

"Are you sorry you didn't go with Lowell?"

She whirled, giving him a shocked look. "How could you even say that? I thought Lowell was on your side; that's the only reason I ever listened to him. I thought he was really trying to help Cliff House." She gave a self-deprecating laugh. "He knew how easy it was to fool me."

"And what about Dan?" Guy asked. "Why didn't you go back to him?"

"I'd say it was because I came to my senses, but I don't deserve the credit. Dan didn't want me. He had that much sense, at least." She stared down at her hands, speaking with an effort. "I know it won't change anything, but what I said, that I wanted to go with Dan—I never did. I thought I had to, I thought he was all I deserved. I thought it would be best for you."

"I knew that," Guy said.

"You did?" She stared at him and then laughed. "So I hurt you for nothing." She walked away from him, closer to the edge of the

cliff. "I admire you, Guy. After all the disappointments, all the dis-
loyalties, you can still pick up and move on. You know what's important. I wish I had known when I had the chance." She took a deep
breath. "Anyway, I came to apologize, and I haven't yet. I know it's
easy to say 'I'm sorry,' and I know it doesn't mean much, so . . ."
She reached into her shoulder bag. "So I came to give you this."
She handed him a bulky manila envelope.

"What's in here?"

"My article. It's finished."

"Well, good for you." The hint of a smile played at the edge of
his lips. He weighed the envelope in his hand. "Pretty hefty."

"As you said, I always use too many words. I finally did the one
thing I started out to do. I don't have much to be proud of, but I'm
proud of that. It's a beginning, anyway." She gestured shyly at the
ruined site. "I ended the piece with the fire—it made a pretty dramatic ending. I thought you could use it somehow. Maybe for publicity, to help you start raising money again. That is, if you'd want
any help from me. I've been such a fool."

Down below, the waves crashed over the rocks. Guy laid the
envelope carefully on the ground. "We were both fools," he said
quietly.

"Not you. Never you."

"I got conned pretty good."

"You couldn't have known. No one could have." She turned away
again, struggling for the right words. "When I saw you in the hospital room, I felt so helpless. I'd done so many things wrong. The
article was the only thing I could think of, the only way I could
try to make things right."

"You could have stayed with me," Guy said.

"Oh, I wanted to," she cried out. "But I didn't think you'd want
me."

"Why not? You weren't the curse, you know."

"I know that now. But, oh, Guy, I wanted to be so important to
you. I wanted to be as important as Cliff House. I went about it all
wrong, as usual."

"You tried too hard. I can't blame you for that. But you were
important."

"Was I?" She felt a flicker of hope, but Guy turned away.

"What you said, that the land was sorry to see my building go, thanks. That means a lot to me."

"It's true," she said. "There's got to be a Cliff House, and you're right—it should be yours."

"Things are going to be tough this time." His face was turned away from her; he was watching the breaking waves. "This time you'll have to promise me you won't run."

For a moment she thought she had heard wrong. "You mean, you could forgive me? You want me to stay?"

He shrugged. "Why not?"

"But how could you?"

"As far as I can see, your only crime was believing in me too much."

"I still believe in you, Guy."

He grinned. It was the old grin, playful and cocky and wry. "I want you to believe in me. I need that. But this time, will you let me do things my way?"

She wanted to run to him, to fling her arms around him with happiness and relief, but she held back, matching his tone.

"I'll be too busy to help you." She grinned. "You know me—give me too much spare time and I'm bound to get into trouble. No, I'll be working on my next article, whatever it is. I never did finish those walking tours."

"Maybe we'll finish them together," Guy said. He held his arms out to her. "I've missed you, Brightfield." She went to him.

"I've missed you, too."

Down below, the waves broke high over the dark rocks. Bobbing forms appeared under the surface of the water; a pack of seals flapped and struggled onto the slippery surface. Their barking echoed the sound of the waves. In the sun their coats glistened like something smooth and liquid. The seals barked and played, and the waves slapped and danced while the man and the woman stood on the cliffs above, their arms around each other, on the promontory that overlooked the sea.